YOU ARE HOME ALONE AT NIGHT.
SUDDENLY YOU NO LONGER FEEL ALONE.
SOMEONE—OR SOMETHING—
IS IN THE ROOM WITH YOU
PERHA~~~
YOU WANT T~~~
—AND YOU~~~

This award-winni~~~
was chosen by ed~~~
winner of the Neb~~~ ~~~ ~~~osen tales of
terror by:

STEPHEN KING,
author of CARRIE, SALEM'S LOT and THE SHINING

RAMSEY CAMPBELL,
award-winning author of
THE DOLL WHO ATE HIS MOTHER

ROBERT BLOCH,
creator of PSYCHO!

DENNIS ETCHISON,
who novelized that eerie film THE FOG

AVRAM DAVIDSON,
famed short-story teller and author of
''Naples,'' which won its own
individual World Fantasy Award

---

and other renowned authors who are famed for their
expertise in scaring their readers to death.

So settle down in a nice easy chair, open the book to a
particularly nasty story—and turn up the lights.
YOU WOULDN'T WANT TO
CREATE ANY MORE
SHADOWS
THAN ALREADY EXIST.

SHADOWS

EDITED BY
CHARLES L. GRANT

PLAYBOY
PAPERBACKS

SHADOWS

Copyright ©1978 by Charles L. Grant

Cover illustration copyright ©1980 by PEI Books, Inc.

Published simultaneously in the United States and Canada by Playboy Paperbacks, New York, New York. Printed in the United States of America. Library of Congress Catalog Card Number: 80-81628. Reprinted by arrangement with Doubleday & Company, Inc.

Books are available at quantity discounts for promotional and industrial use. For further information, write to Premium Sales, Playboy Paperbacks, 747 Third Avenue, New York, New York 10017.

ISBN: 0-872-16751-8

First Playboy Paperbacks printing October 1980.

CONTENTS

Introduction

It is very nearly impossible to define in absolute terms a horror story; the emotional reaction to those things horrid vary from individual to individual. Yet there must be some lurking common denominator, else this type of story would not be as consistently, continuously popular as it is. The easy answer would point straight to the so-called fear of the unknown, that supposed dark corner in all our souls where we lose sight and grip of comprehension and are faced with that which has no immediate explanation.

But. The modern world is much too sophisticated for that, it says here, and so are we also far too educated to cringe at bumps in the night, creaking doors, ghosts, vampires, werewolves, and the wind that dances with dead leaves in the gutter. That's what it says here, in our collective sophistication manual. If there is to be fear, it must be born in the real world—born of wars and murders, muggings and insidious carcinoma. It is literal nonsense to believe otherwise. The horror/fantasy story is the dark side of Romanticism, and there is no room in the practical world for a Romantic.

It is a pleasant, comforting, encompassing rationalization.

And it's not quite correct.

No matter what scientific (or hope of scientific) terms and definitions are used . . . there is still the unknown; more importantly, however, there is the *anticipation* of the unknown. Despite the indisputable facts of our education, sophistication, science, and technology, there is still the ghost of the savage. We don't like to think about that. We pretend he does not exist, that he has been destroyed, that we have even (perhaps, if we're lucky) been born full-blown and Minerva-like within the confines of a blossoming civilization. And we tell ourselves that so often, have done so for so long, that we almost, *almost* have come to believe it.

What we have done, however, is simply locked away the savage beneath a platform constructed of our progress from fire to fission. He's been hidden away so that we need not be reminded, frightfully, of our origins quite so emphatically, nor that we be reminded that he still exists, somewhere . . . waiting. We carry on, then, and, and make more elaborate additions and connections and, above all, do not look down. Every so often, however, the platform becomes warped and a crack appears, and the savage peeks out. What he sees he cannot understand, and what he cannot understand . . . he fears.

And when the savage fears, we *are* reminded.

That is what *Shadows* is all about.

It is not what the current spate of horror films and novels are about, however. They, most of them, deal primarily with *shock,* not true horror. For all the learned pamphlets and discussions on the religious foundations of *The Exorcist, The Omen, Audrey Rose,* and dozens of lesser-budgeted films, what they have failed to grasp is the possibility of satanic possession, reincarnation, or conjuring of gods/demons from arcane mythologies— we are, rather, *shocked* because of the blood, the vomit, the decapitations, the mutilations, and the transformations in vivid crimson color.

This is not fear. It's revulsion.

What really frightens us, for the most part, is not all that we (and the savage) do not completely understand, but all that we do not *see,* even though we know it is there. The classic case in the media? The film *The Haunting,* and in it the scene in the house library when the extraordinary wind sweeps thunderously down the hallway, the echoing pounding on the heavy oaken doors begins . . . and the wood *bends inward* as whatever is out there tries to get in. That we do not see what is there (and never do), frightens us. And the anticipation of *seeing* it unnerves us even more.

The savage, scuttling away from the platform crack into the more comfortable darkness.

And so it is with a good horror story—without the reliance on blood and gore, mayhem, ghosts, and the usual stable of monsters, both mythological and psychological. These elements may, in fact, appear, but they are merely parts of the whole and not the point; they are segments only of a larger nightmare.

Shadows, then, deals with what that title suggests . . . those shadows over there in the corner that do not quite resolve themselves into objects familiar, the shadow formed by a coat over the back of a chair at the foot of your bed, the shadow that presses across an empty autumn street . . . the shadow that has no light to give it birth. Despite some of the thunder, it's a quiet sort of horror we're dealing with here, and a quiet way to scream.

And thus must I now succumb to an aged, even clichéd admonition: For the sake of the authors, and for the sake of your enjoyment, do not read this book from cover to cover at a single sitting (even horror dissipates itself in surfeit). Take one, two, perhaps three at the most, and lose yourself in their creations. Some of them will get to you immediately you read the last line; others depend on a moment or two, or a minute or two afterward before the effect of the material sinks in and draws blood. Some will downright frighten; others will linger and work on the back of your neck when you least expect it.

Quietly.

Gently.

And in an age that seems to demand speed even in reading, I would ask that you take your time, as you would with a fine brandy.

Ideally, use the evening.

Practically, use whatever place you can find where you can sit undisturbed and read and enjoy.

Only . . . watch for the shadows. Be sure, somehow, there's a light there to make them.

CHARLES L. GRANT
Randolph, NJ, May 1977

Avram Davidson is not an ordinary writer, nor is he an ordinary man. He demands more from his readers than most, and when the contract is made there are no losers.

In a story as short as "Naples," not a phrase, not a word, can be wasted. Some writers build worlds; Avram Davidson builds sets in which he places the reader carefully, prop by prop, stroke by stroke, not revealing his intent until everything from sight to scent has been firmly established.

Then, and only then, does he turn out the lights.

NAPLES

by Avram Davidson

It is a curious thing, the reason of it being not certainly known to me—though I conjecture it might be poverty—why, when all the other monarchs of Europe were still building palaces in marble and granite, the kings of that anomalous and ill-fated kingdom called Of Naples and the Two Sicilies chose to build theirs in red brick. However, choose it they did: These last of the Italian Bourbons have long since lost their last thrones, no *castrato* singers sing for them from behind screens to lighten their well-deserved melancholy anymore, and their descendants now earn their livings in such occupations as gentlemen-salesclerks in fashionable jewelry stores—not, perhaps, entirely removed from all memory of the glory that once (such as it was) was theirs. But the red-brick *palazzi* are still there, they still line

11

a part of the waterfront of Naples, and—some of them, at least—are still doing duty as seats of governance. (Elsewhere, for reasons equally a mystery to me, unless there is indeed some connection between red bricks and poverty, buildings in the same style and of the same material usually indicate that within them the Little Sisters of the Poor, or some similar religious group, perform their selfless duties on behalf of the sick, the aged, and the otherwise bereft and afflicted; and which is the nobler function and whose the greater reward are questions that will not long detain us.)

Some twenty years ago or so, a man neither young nor old nor ugly nor comely, neither obviously rich nor equally poor, made his way from the docks past the red-brick *palazzi* and into the lower town of ancient and teeming Naples. He observed incuriously that the streets, instead of swarming with the short and swarthy, as foreign legend implies, swarmed instead with the tall and pale. But the expectations of tradition were served in other ways: by multitudes of donkey carts, by women dressed and draped in black, by many many beggars, and by other signs of deep and evident poverty. Almost at once a young man approached him with a murmured offer of service; the young man clutched the upturned collar of his jacket round about his throat, and, as the day was not even cool, let alone cold, it might have been assumed that the reason for the young man's gesture was that he did not wish to reveal the absence of a shirt. It was not altogether certain that the young man had no shirt at all, probably he had a shirt and probably this was its day to be washed and probably it was even now hanging from a line stretched across an alley where the sun did not enter in sufficient strength to dry it quickly.

There were many such alleys and many such lines, and, it is to be feared, many such shirts. There were also many such men, not all of them young; and if a count had been made, it might have been found that there were not enough shirts to go around.

Naples.

The traveler continued, with frequent pauses and considerings, to make his way slowly from the port area and slowly up the steep hill. Now and then he frowned slightly and now and then he slightly smiled. Long ago some humble hero or heroine discovered that if the hard wheat of the peninsula, subject to mold and rust and rot if stored in the ear, be ground into flour and mixed with water into a paste and extruded under pressure in the form of long strips, and dried, it would never rot at all and would keep as near forever as the hunger of the people would allow it. And when boiled it formed a food nutritious as bread and far more durable, and, when combined with such elements as oil or tomato or meat or cheese and perhaps the leaves of the bay and the basil, be good food indeed. However, the passage of time failed to bring these added ingredients within the means and reach of all. So, to vary in some measure at least the monotony of the plain pasta, it was made in the widest conceivable variety of shapes: thin strips and thick strips, ribbons broad and narrow, hollow tubes long and hollow tubes bent like elbows, bows and shells and stars and wheels and rosettes and what-have-you. And, if you have nothing, it is anyway some relief to eat your plain pasta in a different design . . . when you have, of course, pasta to eat.

At least every other doorway in the narrow streets and the narrower alleys kept a shop, and many of the shops sold pasta: for the further sake of variety the pasta was not merely stacked up in packages, it was also—the straight kinds—splayed about as though the stalks held flowers at their upper ends. And when the traveler saw these he faintly smiled. The young man who paced him step for step also looked at these modest displays. But he never smiled at them. In fact, although he continued his soft murmurs, he never smiled at all.

Most of these ways seemed hardly wide enough for outside displays, but such there were; there were second-hand clothes and fewer by far displays of some new clothes; there were whole cheeses, although none hereabouts were seen to buy them whole, and perhaps not very many very often bought them by the slice or crumbling piece. And there were small fish, alive, alive-o, and larger fish in dim slabs that had not been alive in a long time, dry and hard and strong-smelling and salty, redolent of distant and storm-tossed seas. Tomatoes and peppers lay about in baskets. Oil was poured in careful drops into tiny bottles. There were also olives in many colors. Pictures of saints were sold, and the same shops sold, too, odd little emblematic images in coral and silver and—this was surely strange in such a scene of poverty—even gold: behind the narrow windows of narrow shops, crosses, too, yes, and beads: the universal signia of that religion. . . . But what were these horns? What were these tiny hands, fingers tucked into a fist with the thumb protruding between first and second fingers?

Best not to ask, you would empty the street in a trice. Everybody in Naples knows, no one in Naples would speak of it above a whisper . . . to a stranger, not at all. Speak not the word, lest it come to pass. Look not overlong at anyone in these streets, particularly not at the children they produce in such numbers of abundance. Who knows if your eye be not evil?

The eye of the traveler passed over the swarming and ragged *bambini* without stopping, and in the same manner he glanced at the scrannel cats and the charcoal braziers fanned by the toiling housewives: When one's home is but one room, one may well prefer the street as a kitchen.

When one has that which to cook, and fuel with which to cook it.

At length the passageway widened into a sort of a *piazza*. At one end was a church, on either side were the blank walls of some *palazzio* a good deal more antique than the brick ones down below: perhaps from the days of Spanish viceroys, perhaps from the days of King Robert. Who knows. There were anyway no more shops, no stalls, no wide-open-to-the-street one-room "houses" . . . and, for once, no masses of people . . . no beggars, even . . . there was even a sort of alley that seemingly went nowhere and that, surprisingly, held no one. And the traveler, who had so far only from time to time looked out from the corners of his eyes at the young man cleaving close to him as a shadow does, and who had made no reply at all to the soft murmurs with which the young man (ever clutching his jacket round about his naked throat) continually offered his services as "guide"; now for the first time, the traveler stopped, gave a direct look fleeting-swift, jerked his head toward the tiny passageway, and stepped inside.

The shirtless one's head went up and he looked at the heavens; his head went down and he looked at the filthy worn stones beneath. His shoulders moved in something too slight for a shrug and his unclothed throat uttered something too soft for a sigh.

He followed.

The traveler turned, without looking into the other's eyes, whispered a few short words into the other's ears.

The face of the young man, which had been stiff, expressionless, now went limp. Surprise showed most briefly. His brows moved once or twice.

—But yes—he said. —Surely—he said.

And he said, with a half bow and a small movement of his arm—I pray, follow. Very near—he said.

Neither one paused at the church.

And now the streets became, all of them, alleys. The alleys became mere slits. The shops grew infrequent, their store ever more meager. The lines of clothes dripping and drying overhead seemed to bear little relation to what human beings wore. What actually dangled and flapped in the occasional gusts of flat, warm, and stinking air may once have been clothing. Might once more, with infinite diligence and infinite skill, with scissors and needle and thread, be reconstituted into clothing once again. But for the present, one must either deny the rags that name, or else assume that behind the walls, the scabby walls, peeling walls, broken walls, filthy damp and dripping-ichorous walls, there dwelled some race of goblins whose limbs required garb of different drape.

The traveler began to lag somewhat behind.

How often, now, how carefully, almost how fearfully, the youngman guide turned his head to make sure that the other was still with him. Had not stepped upon some ancient obscenely greasy flagstone fixed upon a pivot and gone silently screaming down into God knows what. Had not been slip-noosed, perhaps, as some giant hare, hoisted swiftly up above the flapping rags ... Rags? Signal flags? What strange fleet might have its brass-bound spyglasses focused hither? Or perhaps it was fear and caution lest the other's fear and caution might simply cause him to turn and flee. In which case the youngman guide would flee after him, though from no greater fear than loss of the fee.

When one has no shirt, what greater fear?

Turned and into a courtyard entered through a worm-eaten door whose worms had last dined centuries ago, perhaps, and left the rest of the wood as inedible. A court-yard as dim, as dank as the antechamber to an Etruscan Hell. Courtyard as it might be the outer lobby of some tumulus, some tomb, not yet quite filled although long awaiting its last occupant. Shadow. Stench. The tatters hung up here could never be clothing again, should they in this foul damp ever indeed dry. At best they might serve to mop some ugly doorstep, did anyone within the yard have yet pride enough for such. And yet, if not, why were they hanging, wet from washing? Perhaps some last un-stifled gesture of respectability. Who knows.

Naples.

Around a corner in the courtyard a door, and through the door a passageway and at the end of that a flight of stairs and the end of the flight of stairs a doorway that no longer framed a door. A thing, something that was less than a blanket, was hung. The young man paused and rapped and murmured. Something made a sound within. Something dragged itself across the floor within. Some-thing seemed simultaneously to pull the hanging aside and to wrap itself behind the hanging.

At the opposite side to the door a man sat upon a bed. The man would seemingly have been the better for having been in the bed and not merely on it. On the cracked and riven and flaking, sodden walls some pictures, cut from magazines. Two American Presidents. Two Popes. And one Russian leader. And two saints. Comparisons are odious. Of those whose likenesses were on that filthy fearful wall it might be said they had in common anyway that all were dead.

—Good day—the youngman guide said.

—Good day—the man on the bed said. After a moment. He might, though, have been excused for not having said it at all.

—This gentleman is a foreigner—

The man on the bed said nothing. His sunken eyes merely looked.

—And he would like, ahem, ha, he would like to buy—

—But I have nothing to sell—

How dry, how faint, his voice.

—Some little something. Some certain article. An item—

—But nothing. I have nothing. We have nothing here—

His hand made a brief gesture, fell still.

A very small degree of impatience seemed to come over the face of the older visitor. The younger visitor, observing this, as he observed everything, took another step closer to the bed. —The gentleman is a foreigner—he repeated, as one who speaks to a rather stupid child.

The man on the bed looked around. His stooped shoulders, all dirty bones, shrugged, stooped more. —He may be a foreigner twice over, and what is it to me—he said, low-voiced, seemingly indifferent.

—He is a foreigner. He has, fool, son of a jackal, son of a strumpet, he has money—the young man turned, abruptly, to the traveler. Said—Show him—

The traveler hesitated, looked all about. His mouth moved. So, too, his nose. His hands, no.

—You will have to show, you know. Can you pay without showing—

The traveler suddenly took a wallet from an inner pocket of his coat, abruptly opened it, and abruptly thrust it in again, placed his back not quite against the noisome wall, crossed his arms over his chest.

Slowly, slowly, the man on the bed slid his feet to the floor.

—Wait outside—he said. —Halfway down—he added.

On the half landing they waited. Listened. Heard.

Dragging, dragging footsteps. A voice they had not

heard before. —*No*NO— A voice as it might be from behind the curtain or the blanket or the what-was-it in place of the door. The faint sounds of some faint and grisly struggle. Voices but no further words. Gasps, only.

Something began to wail, in a horrid broken voice. Then, outside the doorframe, at the head of the stairs, the man, tottering against the wall. Extending toward them his hands, together, as though enclosing something within.

—Be quick—he said. Panting.

And, all the while, the dreadful wail went on from behind him.

The young man sprang to the top of the stairs, his left hand reaching forward. Behind his back, his right hand formed a fist with its thumb thrust out between first and second fingers; then both his hands swept up and met both hands of the other. The young man, face twisted, twisting, darted down the steps to the half landing.

—The money—

Again, hands met. The traveler thrust deep into his bosom, kept one there, withdrew the other. Withdrew his wallet, fumbled.

—Not here, not here, you know—the young man warned. —The police, you know—

One look the older man flung about him. —Oh no. Oh God, not here—he said. —On the ship—

The young man nodded. Roughly divided the money, tossed half of it up and behind without looking back. He did not come close to the older man as they hurried down the stairs.

Above, the wailing ceased. That other voice spoke, in a manner not to be described, voice changing register on every other word, almost.

—Curse the day my daughter's daughter gave you birth. May you burn, son of a strega and son of a strumpet, burn one hundred thousand years in Purgatory without remission—

The voice broke, crocked wordlessly a moment. Resumed.

—One dozen times I have been ready to die, and you, witch's bastard, you have stolen my death away and you have sold my death to strangers, may you burst, may you burn—

Again, the voice broke, again began to wail.

The two men reached the bottom of the stained stairs, and parted, the younger one outdistancing the other and this time never looking back.

Above, faintly, in a tone very faintly surprised, the man who had been on the bed spoke.

—Die? Why should you die when I must eat?—

Naples.

Ramsey Campbell is a more evocative writer than most, and well suited for the parameters of Shadows. *Short-story writer, novelist* (The Doll Who Ate His Mother) *editor* (Superhorror), *he acknowledges his debt to Lovecraft and such, yet does what is considered to be his best work when he deals with the contemporary that is not exactly what we think it is.*

Writers are, as a lot, loners . . . and sometimes lonely. It is no surprise, then, that many fantasy horror tales deal with just such people, those who have, by choice of design, been relegated to a life split into two not necessarily equal parts: the professional or workaday life where there are acquaintances but not friends, and the life that takes up most of one's time—at home, alone. One need not be lonely, of course . . . only alone. But by being alone . . .

THE LITTLE VOICE

by Ramsey Campbell

When Edith Locketty went downstairs the old man was already staring. She couldn't draw the curtains; during the night her curtain rail had collapsed again. On the wall that divided the yards, weeds nodded helplessly beneath rain. Beyond them, through his window that was the twin of hers, the old man stared at her.

He was smiling. She pursed her lips, frowning at his baggy face and veined dome, patched with gray hair and discolored skin as if abandoned to dust and spiders. His eyes were wide, but were they innocent? His smile looked sleepy, sated, reminiscent; reminiscent of . . .

She remembered her dream. Her face became a cold disgusted mask. Filthy old creature, it was written on his face what he was. But he couldn't know what she had dreamed. No doubt his mind referred to something equally disgusting. She cracked her egg viciously, as though it were a tiny cranium.

He turned away. Good of him to let her eat in peace! Bars of rain struggled down the window; beyond them, at the edge of her vision, he was a dim feeble shifting that felt like an irritation in her eye. The downpour hissed in the back yard and the alley beyond, prattled in the gutters. Gradually, through the liquid clamor, she made out another sound. In the old man's house the child was chattering.

She glanced reluctantly across. She knew neither its sex nor its age. Again she wondered whether he kept the child out of sight deliberately because he knew she was a teacher. Did it ever go to school? If it wasn't old enough, what possessed him to keep it awake at all hours?

Perhaps the child was beyond his control, and kept him awake. His smile might have been weary rather than sleepy, and meant for the child rather than for her. He sat at the dim bare table, gazing into the underwater room, at the muffled childish piping.

She dropped the crushed shell into the pedal bin, glad to be ready to leave. There was something nasty about him, she'd seen it skulking in his eyes. And he couldn't be helping the child to develop. She'd never heard the thin incessant voice pronounce a recognizable word.

The pavements glittered, bejeweled with rain and snatches of sun. The clouds had almost drained, the last shafts of rain hurried away on the wind; puddles puckered vanishing mouths. To think of leaving a child alone with him! If she had ever had a child—she halted her thoughts firmly. That was long past.

Nearing the school, she became her role: Miss Locketty the teacher. The children knew where they were with her, as they needed to. But the old man was troubling her: his stare, his sly pleasure, her recurring dream of his dry piebald flesh groping over her in bed.

She shook off the memory, squirming. How could anyone allow him near? His housekeeper might have, if that was what she was; perhaps the child was theirs. To think of his flesh jerking spasmodically like an old machine! One man had been enough to disgust her for life. She strode furiously into the schoolyard.

Mr. Prince was on yard duty. His hair was longer than most of the girls'. It was his last day at this school, and he seemed not to care what the children did—although, in her opinion, he never had cared. Children sat on their wet raincoats. "Hang those up, please," she said, and they did so at once. Others were kicking puddles at each other, but ceased when she said, "You're too old for that." Already she felt calmer, more sure.

After assembly she led her class to their room. "You may play games quietly." They fought pen-and-paper battles, but noise came blundering through the wall from Mr. Prince's class. On the other side, the murmur of Sue Thackeray's children was hardly audible. At least it was Prince's last day.

Drat it, she'd forgotten to bring the Enid Blyton book to read to her class, their end-of-term treat. At lunchtime she made for the gates. A woman was reaching through the railings, as though the street were a cage. Her hand was bones gloved in skin, groping for the children, beckoning. In her pocket a bottle dribbled wine around its rakish stopper. "Come away from there, please," the teacher told the children. Poor woman; probably beyond help. As she turned away, the woman's eyes puckered wistfully.

The teacher strode home. More rain loomed overhead; the glum sky doled out light. The book lay on the kitchen table, where she'd left it to remind her. The old man sat at his table, reaching for, and talking to, the obscure gloom. His hands were playing some complicated game.

When he turned to stare at her, his smile looked gloating. Somewhere near him the voice clamored thinly for attention. "Yes, I can see you, you dirty old swine," she said loudly without thinking. "Just you watch yourself." She hurried away, for she thought he'd begun to tremble—

though surely he couldn't have heard her words. His staring face looked frail as shadow.

She read her book to her class, and watched their faces dull. Ranks of uniformed waxworks stared at her, drooping a little. Did they think they were too old for the story, or that she was out of date? She saw the old man trembling. Noise from next door floundered about her room, like a clumsy intruder. If she didn't act she would lose control of herself. "Talk quietly until I come back," she said.

When Mr. Prince deigned to answer his door, she said, "Will you control your class, please? You're making it impossible for me to read."

Sandwiched in her book, her finger pointed at him. He glanced at the cover with a motion like spitting. His mouth quirked, meaning: Jesus, that's just what you'd expect of her. "Never mind what you think of it," she blurted. "Just do as you're told. I could teach you a few of the basics of teaching."

He stared incredulously at her. "Oh piss off and leave us alone."

The head listened to her tale, sucking his pipe loudly; she could tell he'd been looking forward to a quiet smoke. "I'd have smacked a child for saying it," she said.

"I hope you'd do nothing of the kind." As she stared, feeling betrayed, he added more gently, "Besides, it's his last day. No point in unpleasantness. We all need a rest," he said, as though to excuse her. "It's time we all went home."

From her window she watched her class crossing the schoolyard, eager for freedom. "Have a good Easter," one had said, but had that been sarcasm? She could feel only the burning knot of anger in her guts. And she was faced with two weeks of the old man's stare.

But the house next to hers was silent. Only the dark, uncurtained window gaped at her, vaguely framed by twilit brick. She immersed herself in peace. Her anger dulled and went out, or at least became a vague shadow in her mind.

She served herself dinner on the Wedgwood service, which her parents had kept for best. The window opposite reminded her of an empty aquarium, grimy with neglect; it made her kitchen feel more comfortable. Tomorrow she'd put up the curtain rail. She read Georgette Heyer until exhaustion began to disintegrate the phrases.

She was sitting at a table, gazing across it at darkness. Very gradually a shape began to accumulate twilight, scarcely more distinct than the dark: a developing fetus? It must be too dark for her eyes to function properly, for surely no fetus ever took shape, or moved so swiftly around a table. When she woke, the silence seemed shrill and very large, alive with memories. She had to urge herself to climb the stairs to bed.

Someone was knocking, but not at her door; she turned comfortably within her own warmth, and slept again. It was the sounds of the crowd, of footsteps booming muffled through the house, that woke her.

They were next door, she realized, as she blinked herself aware of the midday sunshine. She peered between the curtains, annoyed that she felt guiltily furtive. A policeman was emerging from the old man's house; a police car squatted outside.

At last she let go of the curtains. She rushed herself to the bathroom and slapped her face with water, scrubbed her armpits. What she'd said had served the old man right. Surely he hadn't—in the mirror her face deplored her faltering. She must find out what had happened.

Her body fumbled as though to hinder her dressing. As she strode down the path, trailing grasses clung to her ankles. Her stomach clenched—but she couldn't retreat, for the housekeeper had seen her. "What's wrong?" the teacher called, and felt forced to hold her breath.

The woman dragged her coat tighter, shivering in the April wind that fought for the parcel in her hands. "Mr. Wajda has died," she said.

He'd been a foreigner? Questions struggled half formed behind the teacher's lips: How did he? Why did he? It seemed safest to ask, "Who found him?"

"The postman. He was trying to deliver this." The woman held out the parcel; her small eyes looked careful, limited, determined not to speculate. "He saw Mr. Wajda at the bottom of the stairs."

"He fell downstairs?" The teacher tried not to sound as hopeful as she felt.

"They think there was a loose stair rod. Of course, he couldn't see it."

She managed to keep her relief from her face. But "Of course?" she repeated, puzzled.

"Yes, of course. He was blind."

"I see," she lied, and retreated mumbling, "If there's anything I can do." The housekeeper looked as bewildered as the teacher felt, and was staring at the opened parcel, which contained a skipping rope.

So the old man had been staring only at her sounds. His wide eyes hadn't meant to pretend innocence. No doubt his hearing had been acute; he must have heard her words. Still, blindness didn't make him innocent; indeed, it explained the way he had fumbled over her in her dreams. Enough of that. His death had been nothing to do with her, he would have fallen anyway, of course he would. She could forget him.

But she could not. He must be lying still in the dark house. His gloomy window looked ominous, as though threatening to stage an unpleasant surprise. It unnerved her for climbing up to replace her curtain rail. Instead she cleaned her house before it annoyed her further. Somewhere a child was either sobbing or laughing.

Next day the hearse arrived. Quick work: Perhaps he'd had friends in the business. Now the house next door felt simply empty. She smiled at the flat blank window. No hurry now to put up the rail.

A child sang tunelessly: *la, la, la.* The teacher went shopping beneath a thick gray sky, and told children to leave the old man's garden. The news must have spread that his house was no-man's-land. Returning, she had to chase the children again. "Do you want the police?" she demanded, and watched while they fled.

La, la, la. She unpacked her purchases. *La, la, la.* The sound was above her. In the adjoining house. The childless black couple must have a visitor, and she wished they'd keep it quiet. Just a fortnight without children, that was all she wanted.

In her bedroom it was closer. *La, la, la.* She pressed her ear to the wall; a faint blurred thudding of reggae filtered through. Jungle drums, she thought automatically, and then her thoughts froze. The child's voice was beyond the far wall, in the old man's house.

It sounded alone and preoccupied. Perhaps it had been with the children she'd chased. If it had heard her threat of the police it mightn't dare to venture out. Suppose the stair rod were still loose?

The sky was sinking beneath its burden of unshed rain. Thick fringes of grass flopped over the old man's path. Her own garden was untidy as the blind man's; she must take it in hand. His windows were curtained with grime. The actual curtains, drooping within, looked like fat ropes of dust.

About to knock, she halted. A stair rod wedged the front door, too timidly ajar to be noticeable from the pavement. Perhaps this was the lethal stair rod—but it meant the child was a meddler, dangerous to itself. She pushed the door wide.

A dim staircase rose from the hall, which might have been a mirror's version of her own—except that she hoped that hers was infinitely cleaner. The woman could have done nothing but his shopping. Above the stairs, festoons of dust transformed a lampshade into a chandelier.

"Come here, please. Before you hurt yourself." Muffled as dust, the house dulled her voice, as though she were shouting into blankets. No answer came. Perhaps the child was downstairs now. She strode toward the kitchen, unwilling to climb toward the box of secret darkness.

The house smelled of dank wallpaper. The sky's lid allowed scant light into the kitchen. When she switched on the bulb, as gray as an old pear, the light felt thick as oil. The room was empty—perhaps too empty: there was no chair opposite the old man's at the table. Nothing else in the long cluttered room seemed worth noting, except a spillage of cans of baby food surrounding a bin beneath the sink. Beyond the window, her own kitchen looked darkly unfamiliar, hardly hers at all.

Enough dawdling. She hurried back toward the stairs; her echoes seemed indefinably wrong. She halted. Had there been a high sound, perhaps an inadvertent snatch of song, among her last echoes? "Come down here, please. I'm not going to hurt you."

The dark above her swallowed her call, and kept its secret. It stood blocking the top of the stairs. Good God, was she going to let her nervousness in an empty house prevent her from saving a child? She tramped upstairs. "Come here to me," she called.

At once there was movement in the dark. Someone came running toward her, down what sounded like an impossibly long hall. Above her the dark seemed crowded with sound, and about to hurl the source of that sound at her. The child was going to play a trick, to leap at her as she stood vulnerable on the stairs.

Her loss of dignity angered her, but she ran. Once she reached the hall she'd give the child a piece of her mind. The noise raced toward her, sounding thin, hollow, dry, and far too large—deformed by dust and echoes, of course. It was close behind her. Her clutching hand scraped a wad of dust from the banister.

The noise had halted. She gripped the banister tight as a weapon as she turned, for fear of an unbalancing prank. But the stairs were deserted.

Outside, the muddy sky gave her less light than she'd hoped. Of course, all the sounds must have come from the house beyond the old man's. The threat of rain filled her mind, like fog. She had almost reached her front door when it slammed in her face. She fumbled irritably for her key. Enough tricks for today.

La, la, la. Determined to ignore the sound, which seemed to have moved above her, she dined at the nearby Chinese restaurant. Mellowed by Riesling, she ambled home through streets polished by rain. Shops displayed beds, bright and deserted. Her house displayed darkness. As she climbed the stairs her echoes sounded more numerous than she thought they should, as though someone were imitating her. Of course, that was what had sounded wrong in the old man's house. She smiled vaguely and went to bed.

*

Pale quick movement woke her. For a moment it hovered; it had opened the ceiling to peer down at her. She was still trying to prop her eyes open when it slid away, gliding down the wall to the floor. It must have been the stray light of a car.

Her eyelids settled shut, then her brow tautened. She must be half engulfed in a dream, for she thought she remembered the pale oval crossing the floor and hiding beneath her bed. No car's beam could have reached so far. Determinedly, she relaxed. Her brow was beginning to squeeze forth a headache.

She dozed amid distractions. The tick of her clock was shouting, like an ignored child; a drip in the kitchen seemed eager to remind her how largely empty the house was. Something—a fly, it must have been—kept touching her face lightly, silently. Grumbling, she withdrew beneath the blankets. Somewhere in a dream she could still feel the timid touch.

She must have dreamed that it managed to pluck the blankets away and crawl in beside her face. Daylight showed her a deserted room. Perhaps the fly had fallen under the bed to die; she wasn't looking. She ate breakfast and stared at the weeds on the yard wall; lingering rain-drops made their leaves crystalline. The weeds wept on her fingers as she uprooted them triumphantly. She'd left them growing to avoid arguments with the old man—and of course he wouldn't have noticed.

She read the Heyer. The street sounded like a school-yard; footballs beat like irregular hearts. Later, the library was quiet, until children came in for a chase. She couldn't escape them at all, it seemed. She smiled wryly at the harassed librarian.

La, la, la. Couldn't they teach the child a few more notes, or at least to stay firmly on the one? She added her coat to the load on the hall stand, straining her ears to determine the location of the sound. It was above her, on the old man's side. It moved slowly to the other side. But it couldn't do that unless it was in her house.

She ran upstairs. Her footsteps filled the house, but there was no need for stealth; the child was in her bedroom, trapped. It sang on, indifferent to her. She'd smack its bottom for that as well. She flung open the bedroom door.

The bed was spread with sunlight, the room blazed. The singing persisted ahead of her, tantalizingly, as she forced her eyes not to blink; then it moved through the wall into the spare bedroom. Just an acoustic trick. She was disconcertingly unsure what she felt now she'd been robbed of the naughty child. The house walls were too thin, that was for sure. She sat downstairs, riffling through her new books. When the singing recommenced she pursed her lips. She'd been tricked once.

She woke. She was sitting in the chair, an open book roofed her knee. For a moment she forgot that it was the next day, that she'd been to bed meanwhile. Some perversity of her metabolism always exhausted her after the end of term.

No doubt the tapping of rain had wakened her; the panes looked cracked by water, the room crowded with dim giant amoebae. But the movement, or the version of it that her sleep had admitted, had sounded heavier. Though she quashed the memory at once, she thought of the departed footsteps of her parents. The sound came again, rumbling in the cupboard in the corner of the room.

Reluctantly she tiptoed closer. Dry waves of rain flooded down the cupboard door. With one hand she switched on the standard lamp, with the other she snatched open the door. The gas meter peered up at her, twitching its indicator. There was nothing else, not even a mouse hole. It must have been the black couple, being far too noisy.

In the kitchen all the cupboards were open. Their interiors looked very dark, and more full than they should have, especially where they were darkest. Wake up! She slapped her face, none too gently. What was her mind playing, hide and seek? She slammed the doors, refusing to peer within.

Her mind tried slyly to persuade her to dine out. Nonsense, she couldn't afford that every night. After dinner she wrote to Sue, suggesting a restaurant, then tried to read. Didn't they ever put that child to bed? It was such a dismal sound, it made her house seem so empty.

Next day she lost patience. Never mind sitting about, moping. Who was going to put up the curtain rail, her father? This time she'd do it properly. She replenished the sockets in the plaster with filler, though replacing the screws was more tiring than she'd thought, and halfway through she was prickly with sweat. "Shut up with your la, la, la," she snarled. She'd complain, if she only knew where. Grasping triumphantly, then, she tightened the last screw and stood gazing at her handiwork, ignoring the blisters on her palms.

The singing insinuated itself among the words of her books, it began to pick apart her thoughts. What annoyed her most was its stupidity. It sounded mindless as a dripping tap.

On Good Friday she rode a bus into unexpected sunshine, but there seemed to be an indefinable thin barrier between her and her enjoyment. Among the children who crowded the fields and the woods a tuneless song kept appearing. She returned home before she'd planned to, toward slabs of cloud.

She lay listening furiously. *La, la, la.* It was hours past midnight, hours since she'd tried to sleep. Tomorrow she would track down the child's parents—except that deep in her mind she dreaded that nobody would know what she was talking about. She knew none of her neighbors well enough for a calculated chat.

On Easter Sunday she went to church, in search of peace, though she hadn't been for years. Above the altar Christ rose up, pure, perfected. She gazed in admiration, surprised how much she'd forgotten. There was a real man, probably the only one. She'd never met one like him.

The choir sang. Boyish trebles pierced the hymn: *La, la, la,* one sang tunelessly. Her shoulders writhed and shuddered, but she managed to stay kneeling. She'd had hallucinations with insomnia before: bushes that smiled, trees that raised their heads from grazing. The choir was in tune now. She sat back gratefully. But when the sermon mentioned spirits—ghosts—she found she was trying not to hear.

She strode into her home. Now, no more nonsense. She hooked her coat onto the stand, and at once heard it fall behind her. The fall sounded far too heavy for a coat. On the floor, whose shadows seemed thickened rather than diluted by the light that leaked beneath the door, all the coats lay in a mound—her parents' too, which she kept meaning to give away. The mound looked as if a lumpy shape were hiding underneath.

They were coats. Nothing but coats. Good God, it wasn't as if they were moving. But if the lurker were holding itself still, waiting to be uncovered . . . She stumbled forward and snatched away the coats. She stood glaring defiantly at the bare floor. The coats didn't seem bulky enough to have composed so large a mound.

She felt strange, handling her parents' clothes so roughly. Had she left them on the stand because she hadn't known how to touch them? That afternoon she took them to the presbytery for the jumble sale.

Her house seemed very empty; the restless prattling made it more so. All she needed was sleep. After midnight she slept fitfully, when the voice allowed her. Surely she wouldn't need a doctor. Sometimes, when her self-control was barely equal to her job, she'd dreaded that. *La, la, la.*

On Monday Sue Thackeray came visiting. They returned from the Chinese restaurant companioned by a bottle of gin. Edith was glad of Sue, whose throaty laugh gave the echoes no chance to sound hollow.

Sue's armchair wheezed as she sat back bulging, tenderly cradling her refilled glass. Her arms were almost as thick as the stuffed chair's. Memories of her parents, whom she had recently lost, floated up on the gin. "At least you lived here with yours," she said. "I didn't see mine for months."

"But the house seems so empty now."

"Well, it will. I thought you looked a bit peaky, love." She stared hard and blearily at Edith. "You want to get away."

"I'm going to Minorca this summer. I can't afford to go anywhere else as well."

They fell silent. The silence rustled with the approach of rain. "Anyway," Sue said, slapping her knee, beginning to grin. Edith hushed her. "Can you hear that?" she blurted.

La, la, la. "Rain," Sue said.

"No, I don't mean that." It was so difficult to force the words past her confusion that surely the effort must be worthwhile. "Can't you hear the child?" she demanded, almost pleading.

Sue gazed at her rather sadly before saying, "No." She thought it was Edith's imagination, did she? She thought Edith had wished a child into her mind, did she?

"Did you ever want to adopt a child?"

"No," Edith declared angrily, "I never did, and I don't want one now. I have enough of them at school. I like my freedom, thank you." Why was she shouting, with only Sue to hear?

"All right, all right," Sue said grumpily. "I didn't mean—"

The crash turned her next word into a gape. Edith was already running to the door. But it had warped somehow, and refused to budge. She mustn't lose her temper, things were like children sometimes. But she must get out to see what had happened! At the third wrench the door set her free.

The fallen rail lay tangled in its curtains, scattered with plaster. Above it, her filled sockets had been gouged. "Look at that," she said incredulously. "It's been torn down."

"Don't be silly," Sue rebuked her. "It's just fallen."

When Sue left, hurrying bowed beneath rain, Edith stood staring at the dull street. The air was latticed with transparent slashes. Just fallen, indeed! How could the woman be so smug about her blindness? At least her smugness had convinced Edith that the child must exist objectively outside her own mind, however unnaturally. The gin allowed her thoughts to be comfortably vague. Whatever it was, it wouldn't drive her out of her own house. "You'll go first," she shouted to her echoes.

A child was laughing. The sound seemed peaceful. Perhaps she might enjoy having a child in the house. She woke to the touch of cold rubber on her feet; the hot-water bottle felt dead. No, she didn't want a child. The hard hot poking that preceded it had been bad enough: that, and the doctor's groping to get rid of it, and the sight of it—it hadn't looked at all human, it had never had the chance. She had had it murdered. She could never have had a child after that, even if she had wanted to.

"I want no child," she snarled at the dark. Then she froze, remembering what she'd felt as she had awakened.

Of course it had been a dream: the face nuzzling hers eagerly, the hand reaching playfully to touch her feet and the bottle. Only in dreams was such a reach possible. But she lay stiffly, trying to hush her breath, willing the bed to be empty, willing the dark not to nuzzle her face. Perhaps she lay thus for hours before, inadvertently, she fell asleep.

In the kitchen, a dim face was staring at her from the empty house. Has it gone back? she thought, immediately anxious not to understand what she meant. But it was the housekeeper, who hadn't kept house. Impulsively Edith ran to the yard wall. "Excuse me," she called. "Excuse me."

Eventually the door opened to let out the reluctant face. Edith felt drained of words, tricked by her own impulse. "When Mr., er, died," she said, still unwilling to think what she meant. "Was the child there?"

The woman's eyes narrowed, though they hadn't much scope to do so. "What child?"

"The one who lived with him." Perhaps she could shock the woman into truth. "It was your child, wasn't it?"

"It certainly was not," the woman said, turning away.

"But he had a child," Edith pleaded.

"I don't know who's been talking. He never had one that lived," the woman muttered resentfully. "It killed my aunt before she could bear it."

Perhaps her aunt had been married to him. Or perhaps not. Dirty old man. Irrelevant, Edith thought impatiently. She pointed behind the woman. "Surely there must have been a child. What about all that baby food?"

"He had no teeth," the woman said smugly. Her eyes reminded Edith of a pig's: small, dull, penned in. She was closing the door. "But the skipping rope." Edith protested.

"Listen," the woman said, "whatever he may have done, he's dead now. I won't discuss it. And you better hadn't, either."

The door snapped shut, like disapproving lips. Perhaps he'd lured children to his house for sexual purposes; no doubt most men would, given the chance; but that wasn't the point. That wasn't what the woman, too stupid to realize she had done so, had confirmed. Her very stupidity, her refusal to think, had confirmed it. There *had* been a child in that house, but nobody had seen it—because it couldn't be seen.

Now it had come into Edith's house. Today she found the thought of its objective existence less comforting. But at least it meant there was nothing wrong with her. "Yes, la, la, la," she said loudly; it was distant and muffled. "Go on, keep it up as long as you like."

Sometimes she managed to switch off her awareness, as she often did with her class. Whenever she heard the sound again she laughed pityingly. It was no worse than the cries of children outside, though they had become aggressively distracting. She tried to doze. The library might be more restful, but she wouldn't be driven out of her own house. When the song became more insistent, frustrated by being ignored, she laughed louder.

A bath might relax her. She turned on the taps, and the steam expurgated her reflection, diluted her colors, softened her swollen curves; she no longer looked heavily fleshy—almost attractive, she thought. Steam surrounded her reflected face with a vignette's oval that shrank like an iris in an old film.

She sank into the water, wallowing, yet she couldn't relax. As her muscles loosened they seemed to liquefy, and her mind felt helplessly afloat and vulnerable. The walls looked insubstantial, as though infiltrated by a fog that muffled the room, deafening her to anything approaching the door.

She felt she was being watched. She washed quickly and rose sloshing. She rubbed herself roughly with the towel. Was something playfully touching her? She whirled, and glimpsed a face.

It had been spying on her from the mirror, through the peeling steam. Her own face, of course, and she wiped the mirror clear. But as the steam re-formed she seemed to glimpse beyond it a dim movement, with eyes. Instinctively, infuriatingly, she covered herself with the towel. She wrenched at the door, which had warped shut. She closed her eyes, trapping her cry behind her lips, and tugged until the door pulled free.

As she dressed she grew coldly furious. It wouldn't get the better of her again. She read, determined not to hear the tuneless babbling. She slept a little, despite the almost insubstantial groping at her face in the dark.

A pile of cans was waiting to fall on her when she opened a cupboard door. How stupid and infantile. She pushed them back and checked the other cupboards, which were innocent. She smiled grimly—oh no, it wouldn't play that trick on her—and climbed the stairs slowly, examining the stair rods.

All of its tricks were moronic, and some were disgusting, but none was worth her notice. Amid the clamor in the street a voice prattled, distant or muffled. She refused to hear its words. It might only be her lack of sleep that made it rush toward her.

She dreamed that she had died and that the house was full of laughter. The dream shifted: Something was kissing or licking her cheek. When she struggled awake it was there on her pillow—a fat encrusted earthworm. Stupid, disgusting. She hurried downstairs to throw it out, but not too fast to check the stair rods.

Hadn't she read this page before, more than once? The window cleaner gazed at her, making her feel caged, on show. His sluggish progress round the house, his dull dabbing at the panes, unnerved her. Nor did he seem to have lightened the rooms. She had never realized how many dark corners the house contained. Many of them had begun to acquire objects, some of which moved, none of which were there when she strode close.

Once, when the cries of children outside seemed especially violent and threatening, she heard an object being dragged upstairs. She ran into the hall, and seemed to glimpse a dim movement as it climbed onto the landing. It seemed dreadfully large, or shaped like a nightmare, or both.

Whatever it was, she wasn't having it in her house. She climbed, scrutinizing the stair rods. She heard her bedroom door open, and the fall of something moist and fat within. Had it been dragging a burden that it had now dropped? Was that why it had looked so grotesque? Her hand clenched on the doorknob when she heard the giggling within; it took her minutes to open the door. But the room was mockingly bare. She went downstairs white-faced . . . checking the rods.

She had to sit down, to calm her heart. Her tormentor had almost reached her. To have let such stupidity touch her! She wouldn't again. She found herself looking forward to next term: School would make her sure of herself again. Only three more days. In the corners, objects kept her company. She slept, when she managed to sleep, with the light on. Only two days. *La, la, la.* Only one.

The sight of the fallen rail depressed her. If she replaced the rail it would only be torn down again. No point in moping. Less than one more day. To cheer herself up, she ate dinner using the Wedgwood service.

She must go to bed early and try to sleep, but not just yet. She wouldn't be trapped any more than she would be driven out. She washed up swiftly and left the plates on the table.

A few children ran among the tables, for a last chase. "We'll be glad to give them back to you," the librarian said wryly. There were no books that appealed to Edith, except ones she'd read. Impulsively she chose some new children's books, to find out what they read these days. Maybe she'd read them to her children.

It had begun to rain. Buds of water grew on the hedges, gleaming orange with sodium light. The lampposts

were rooted in shallow, glaring pools. Rain pecked at her;
houses streamed, their windows tight and snug.

Her own house looked bedraggled; its windows
drooled. The unkempt lawn struggled to stand beneath the
rain. Water snatched at her as she slammed the door
behind her. The slam resounded through the house, as
though all the doors were mocking her.

The darkness became still, preparing its next trick. She
wouldn't give it the chance. Clutching her books, she switched
on the hall light. The hall stand appeared beside her, it's
head swollen with coats. With the adjacent switch she drove
back the dark on the landing, then she hurried into the front
room. The house hemmed her in with echoes. Only echoes.

The window was frosted with rain; watery shapes
crawled about the room. Would her groping hand meet the
light switch, or something soft and tongued? Of course it
was the switch, and the light destroyed the shapes. She
drew the curtains, trying to make the room cozier.

As she did so, what had been hiding behind a chair
rose up, to scare her. She refused to look, although the
grinning object seemed too large, and grotesquely lacking.
She couldn't have glimpsed so much from the corner of her
eye, but hadn't the object been held up by a hand rather
than a neck, even though it had rolled its eyes? Rubbish.
She clashed the curtains together as if cutting off a play,
and turned to confront the empty room.

She stalked to the kitchen, ignoring the crowd of her
sounds. The Wedgwood was arrayed on the table. The
sight of the empty window deformed by rain troubled her;
as she moved, the window twitched like a nervous blind
eye. She gazed out into the hectic night. Tomorrow she'd
put up the rail. This time she'd make sure it stayed up.

Something in her room was very wrong.

She stood trapped, trying to recall what she'd seen,
afraid to turn until she knew. The night was vicious with
glittering. Suddenly she turned; of course, she'd used only
a part of the Wedgwood, yet the entire service was laid out.
How stupid—hardly even a trick.

She reached for a plate. But her hand faltered and
hung slackly as she moaned, unable to accept what she was

seeing. She had to pick miserably at a plate before she was convinced. Although they had been reassembled with terrible minuteness, every item of the service was shattered into fragments.

Her panic threw her stumbling toward the hall. The hollow desertion of the house overwhelmed her. But she was not entirely alone, for although the switch stayed on, something was clapped over the light, trapping her in darkness.

The room whirled as she did. The blind window gazed across, streaming grimily. She wrenched at the door, which had warped shut more stubbornly than the others. She stumbled across the flowing room toward the door to the yard, groping feverishly for her keys.

She halted, squeezing her eyes tight in terror and rage. Whatever it did, she was determined not to see it. She could hear it running toward her, large and unbalanced, as though crippled. It was about to leap on her. Let it do its worst.

The light blazed again through her eyelids. Her tormentor was standing before her, waiting to be seen. Her forehead felt as though her skull were shrinking, squeezing out needles of sweat. She clenched her eyelids desperately.

It touched her. Its large, loose face crawled moistly over hers. Its hands plucked at her. They felt unformed, and terribly far apart. Its face returned and clung to hers, snuffling. Nothing could have forced her to open her eyes.

Her whole body squirmed with a revulsion beyond nausea. She was terrified to move: What might she touch blindly? Suddenly, in utter desperation, her mouth opened. Words came uncontrollably as retching, but slowly, deliberately: "Get away from me, you filthy thing."

She felt it leave her, and stood frozen. Was the stillness a trick? At last she had to open her eyes, for the aching void made her giddy. The room felt as empty as it looked, and she sat down before she could fall. Eventually she swept the Wedgwood into the bin. She switched on all the lights, then opened the front-room curtains and sat with her back to the window. Before her, her faint outline trembled incessantly with rain.

Dawn seeped into the room. Her eyes felt hot and bloated. When she switched off the lights the room turned ashen. She sipped boiling tea, trying to taste it; her stomach writhed. The colors of the house struggled with the gray.

She trudged through the soaked streets. She'd forgotten to bring the library books. No time now. She wouldn't have been reading them today, she must make herself sure of her children again. They needed to be sure of one another, she and the children. She felt uneasy, unwilling to face them. As she trudged she grew tense. Her legs were aching, and her mind.

Through the bars she could see some of her class. Thank God, they weren't looking at her; she hadn't decided how to approach them. Their cries sounded alarmingly jagged, menacing. She was still trying to decide as her automatic trudging took her into the schoolyard.

At once the crying began.

How could the other children ignore it, that inconsolable, atrociously miserable cry? But she knew what it was. She strode glaring toward the school. Once she was inside and away from the sound she'd be all right.

But the cry wrenched at her. It was so thin and feeble, yet so penetrating; so helpless and desolate, beyond any hope of being comforted. She couldn't bear it. As she strode toward the children she could hear it coming closer. They gaped at her as she hurried among them, pulling them aside to peer for the abandoned wailing.

She faltered, and gazed at them. The plight of the crying victim could be no worse than theirs, with their home lives, their stupidity, their inability to find themselves. Wasn't there a plea deep in their dull eyes? She couldn't reach the crying, but at least she could touch these children; that must be worth something.

Her eyes spilled her grief. "I'm sorry," she said to the gaping children. "It's all right," she said, reaching out, trying to embrace them as they began to back away. "Come here, I won't hurt you. I'm sorry. I'm sorry." Surely her cries must drain some of the enormous guilt that bowed her down.

At last, when the schoolyard was empty of children, and Sue and her colleagues had ceased trying to coax her into the school, she stumbled away. The crying accompanied her home, and everywhere she went. Sometimes, as they emerged from school, her children saw her. They fled, leaving her pleading with the air, trying to embrace it. Surely the crying must stop eventually, surely the voice must grow happy again. "La, la, la," she pleaded. "La, la, la."

*William Jon Watkins is a poet, a novelist, a short-story
writer, a college instructor. He looks like a nineteenth-
century mountain man who somehow took the wrong turn
at the Colorado River. His novels include* The Litany of
Sh'Reev *(with Gene Snyder) and* Clickwhistle, *and his
stories have appeared in such diverse publications as*
Cosmopolitan *and* Isaac Asimov's Science Fiction *magazine.*

*"Butcher's Thumb" is not quiet, nor is it gentle; yet
beneath the surface there is a remarkably deceptive calm
that belies the thunder of what is happening above—belies
it, and is much more frightening.*

BUTCHER'S THUMB

by William Jon Watkins

"The right brain has a will of its own. The left hand is its
servant."

Peter Kessler nodded, but he understood none of it.
Dr. Bryant smiled as if it made him feel good to know that
Peter couldn't understand something he himself found so
easy to explain. The left hand curled itself into a fist the size
of a small cleaver. Cutting meat for twenty-five years had
made the hand thick and strong. People joked that they
could not afford a butcher with such big thumbs, but they
were only teasing him. Peter gave good weight and his
customers knew it. Some of them had been with him fifteen
years or more.

He wondered how his wife was handling things. Paul, his assistant, could do most of the heavy lifting, but there was more than enough cutting for two men, and Katrine was not made for heavy work. The greatest sorrow of his illness was that he had had to put so much of the burden on Katrine. He chafed to go back to work. But the doctor still said he needed more retraining and Katrine would not hear of his going into the shop without it. And she was right. The one time he had tried to work, he had barely missed cutting off his left hand with the big cleaver. He did not tell Katrine about it, she would only have worried. Still, there was something odd, almost deliberate, about the accident that had made him uneasy enough to come back to Dr. Bryant.

"Maybe that's too poetic," Dr. Bryant said. "Let me put it another way." There were so *many* other ways he could put it. It made Peter ashamed of his own difficulties with the language. "Now, the brain has two halves called lobes. Each lobe carries different abilities. Speech in the left, along with rational thought. On the right, emotion, art, imagination, who knows what else. Most people use their left brain more than their right." He held his right palm up and wiggled it as if he thought that Peter could at least follow *that* much of the explanation.

"All depends on what *handed* you are. The right hand develops the left half of the brain. The left hand develops the right side of the brain."

Peter cocked his head. Sometimes *right* and *left, up* and *down, in* and *out* got confused in his speech. The words were different enough, but he could never remember which one was which. Peter raised his left hand and touched the right side of his head. "The left hand goes to the *right* side of the mind?"

"Brain," the doctor corrected. "But yes, left hand, right brain. The nerves get sort of twisted here at the base of the skull where they enter the *foramen magnum*." Peter nodded sullenly.

"Normally," the doctor smiled, "the two lobes of the brain are connected by a tiny little bridge called the *corpus callosum*." He pressed his middle finger against the center of his forehead. "We had to cut that little bridge to keep your seizures from killing you." He smiled benignly as if he had returned Peter from the dead.

Something moved Peter's eyes to the right, looking for a weapon.

The doctor shrugged. "Unfortunately, as a side effect, the two halves of your brain can't communicate anymore." He looked at Peter as though he were a laboratory animal. "There's a great deal we can learn about the brain from a condition like yours, Peter. Your particular operation shows some interesting side effects. Will you co-operate with me?"

The questions were irrelevant, crazy. Peter was interested only in putting his life back together. "It will help me to go back to work?"

The doctor grimaced. "Well . . . not immediately. But everything we learn from you will bring us that much closer to finding a way to compensate for your disability."

It sounded like yes, but Peter was not sure. He was sure only that he had no other hope. "I will . . . " The word eluded him.

"Co-operate?" Dr. Bryant suggested. Peter nodded. "Good. Let's get on with it then. Close your eyes if you would, please."

Peter closed his eyes, but not before something located a scalpel on a silver tray at the far end of the room. Dr. Bryant bustled in Peter's darkness, fastening the blindfold. Finally he put something in Peter's left hand. The hand squeezed around it like a knife.

"I've put something in your left hand. I want you to tell me what it is."

Peter shrugged helplessly. "My hand doesn't work since the operation. It's . . . no feeling . . . numb. It is numb. I feel nothing."

"But you can move it?"

Peter nodded. Always when the doctor spoke to him, part of him wanted to jump up and shout, "I am a butcher! I am a foreigner to your country. A butcher is not an idiot! A man does not have to be born speaking your language to have a brain in his head." But he never did. Most of him was kind and good-natured and made allowances for the shortcomings of others. Most of him believed Dr. Bryant was truly sincere in his desire to help. But there was something else, something not really a part of him. The something else thought otherwise.

"I want you to try a series of experiments with me." Dr. Bryant moved around Peter adjusting the blindfold. "I'm going to take the object out of your left hand." The left hand gave it up reluctantly. Peter did not even feel it begin to move. "Now I want you to feel around on this tray of objects." Dr. Bryant pressed Peter's left hand down onto the tray. "And I want you to select the object you just held in your left hand."

"Doctor . . . " The voice was pained, frustrated. "I cannot *feel* with that hand. It is numb. He prodded with his finger as if to stir up the doctor's understanding. "Since the operation."

Dr. Bryant smiled, a patient father watching the obstinance of a child. "That's all right. Just feel around on the tray until you find an object that seems right."

Peter hung his head. Obviously the words had been wrong. There was no understanding. "My hand does not *KNOW!*" The word was a guess. It failed utterly.

Dr. Bryant patted his shoulder. "It's all right, Peter. Think of it as a game. If you're wrong, you're wrong, that's all."

Peter sighed. "I would have to . . . " The word hid from him. "When you don't know a thing but have to answer . . . " His right hand filled the air with gestures. The left lay sullenly in his lap, waiting. "I would have to . . . guess," he said.

"Don't worry about that, Peter. There are twenty objects on the tray. Guessing wouldn't make you right more than one time in twenty even if you knew what the objects were."

Peter scowled. It all seemed so senseless. Something wanted to overturn the tray and storm out. The left hand tightened into a fist again. Peter knew it had moved but without being able to see it, he could not even guess what shape it had assumed. He leaned his head back trying to look out under the blindfold at the hand. It had to be watched night and day. Even in his sleep it wandered about, picked up things, dropped them, pulled at the covers. Other things too. He did not want to think about that.

"Have a little patience, Peter. It will all be clear to you in a moment. That's right. Just move your hand around on the tray."

Peter's left hand scrambled across the tray looking for the scalpel. It found only the comb. "Good!" Dr. Bryant said. "Now we're going to do a few more of those objects doing exactly the same thing. I'll give you an object in your left hand; you feel it, then pick it out from the other objects when I put it back on the tray. All right?"

"The hand does not feel," Peter insisted. "It moves . . ." He wanted to say that it moved by itself, but Dr. Bryant would probably think him crazy and he was not sure of the words.

Dr. Bryant put the second object in his hand as if whatever Peter said meant nothing. The left hand took it, hoping it was the scalpel, gave it back, and searched the tray. No scalpel there either. It selected the rubber ball. Twenty objects later, Dr. Bryant put something in his right hand. "Feel it," he said, "and tell me what it is."

"It's a comb," Peter said. His voice was sharper than he meant it to be. Frustration ran through it like a snarl. Dr. Bryant had been his only hope for so long. Four other doctors had said so, and all of them agreed that nobody could do the operation better than Dr. Bryant. And they had been partly right. He no longer had the seizures, the convulsions, the dangerous paroxysms in which the cleaver flailed out of control. Only a miracle had kept him from cutting off a hand or killing someone. But the miracle was a mixed blessing. He couldn't feel anything on his left side anymore, and the left hand had been doing things on its own since the beginning—cruel, vindictive, alien things. All Dr. Bryant could offer him now were games, tests, words.

Katrine helped him from the hospital bed. He stood stiffly, fumbling with the belt of his robe. Only his right hand moved over it, shaping it slowly into the parody of a knot. He looked at it and grinned awkwardly. The relearning came so slowly. Katrine looked as if she were going to cry despite her promise. The right hand moved to stroke her cheek.

The left hand jerked at the long tongue of the belt, and the knot evaporated. Katrine reached to tie it for him. The left hand slapped at her hand and pushed it away. It brought the tears down her cheeks. He tried to apologize, but the left hand kept fending her off, making little jabs at her as if it weren't quite strong enough yet to drive her away. She cringed back as if it were alive. When he tried to stroke her cheek again, she jerked back involuntarily.

At home it had been worse. The left hand spilled hot coffee on her. Crumpled up the mail addressed to her. Locked onto her wrist when she tried to feed him, and twisted feebly. She began to stay on his right side, all the time looking at the left hand as if it were some sinister animal waiting to pounce. She had begged him to go back to see Dr. Bryant. But he had refused to listen.

And then the left hand had mauled her. The look of pain and outrage on her face as she fought her way out of the bed and stood screaming at him made him want to cut the hand off and fling it away. The next morning, he had called Dr. Bryant.

Dr. Bryant took the comb out of his hand. "Now I want you to find the comb on the tray with your left hand."

"I can't do it," Peter said flatly. The left hand moved awkwardly across the tray and picked up the door key, sliding it clumsily between its fingers like a punching spike. Dr. Bryant plucked it deftly from between the fingers and scratched on the clipboard.

"Now another." He pressed a small rubber ball into Peter's right hand. "What is it?"

"A little rubber round . . . rubber *ball.*" Peter scowled. The words were beyond his recall more and more every day, like a paralysis creeping across from the left side. Dr. Bryant took the ball away.

"Now find it with your left hand."

"I *can't!*" The left hand slammed down on the tray. Objects bounced off onto the floor. Dr. Bryant's voice was soothing.

He patted Peter's right hand like an ally. "Just try a few more. I'll explain when we've finished."

Peter waited for the left hand to pound on the tray again. He waited for it to go off on its own again, just waving or punching the air, like a fighter getting stronger with each day. Whatever it did, he couldn't stop it until it had tired itself out. At first, he had been able to fight it, control it, but his power over it had slipped away gradually, a day at a time, like his words. He had not even been able to stop it when it had started in on Katrine. He apologized. Dr. Bryant was understanding. They did the other nineteen objects without incident.

Dr. Bryant snipped the strings of the blindfold and stuck the scissors back in his lapel pocket. Peter rubbed his eyes and blinked. Something zeroed his eyes in on the scissors. Slowly, the left hand began to move. Dr. Bryant flipped the clipboard around and pointed at the columns. "Here's the object I put in your left hand each time. Here's the object your left hand selected from the tray."

Peter stared at the columns in disbelief. "It cannot *be!*" The lists were identical.

Dr. Bryant gave an amused smile. "It's what I've been trying to tell you. The right brain knows what the left hand holds, and the left brain knows what the right hand holds. But neither half of the brain knows what the opposite hand holds, not since we cut that little bridge of tissue."

Peter shook his head. "How could it not know?" There was a tinge of fear in his voice disguised as anger. "How can a man have two brains?"

Dr. Bryant tapped the clipboard. "Look at the results. When I put an object in your right hand, you could identify it easily. *But your left hand couldn't find it on the tray!*" Dr. Bryant smiled as if he had solved everything. "There's no escaping it, Peter. The left half of your brain doesn't know what's in your right hand, and the right half of your brain doesn't know what's in your left."

Peter scowled at the words. Surely they meant something else. "I have two minds?"

Dr. Bryant gave an equivocating shrug. "Functionally, you have two brains. Separate and independent."

Peter wanted to deny it, but he knew it was true. The something that moved his left hand was not him, and he knew it. Dr. Bryant smiled. "We all have two brains, Peter. One talkative, rational, pragmatic, and the other a dark, left-handed alien who lives in us like a mute stranger full of passions the talking part of our brain can't even begin to guess at."

The truth was terrible, but it allowed him to at least talk about it. "The left hand is . . . it does what it wants." His eyes begged for understanding. The English words for it were so slippery. "Not what *I* want, you understand, *not what I want!*" A high, tinny whine of panic threaded through the low rumble of his voice. "It does . . . terrible things, terrible." He thought of the anguish in Katrine's eyes, the way she wiped at her body with the sheet as if the hand had defiled her. He could not go on. "It is a monster! A demon!"

Dr. Bryant nodded solemnly. "Yes," he said, "some people who have had the operation have said that the speechless self that lurks in there is a demon. But they make the adjustment in time. The right brain takes over again after a while." He shrugged. "We're not quite sure how. Some researchers in Illinois have said that the two halves of the brain are not only polar opposites but also mortal enemies. They say the only thing that keeps them from trying to destroy each other is that little bridge of tissue that we cut to save your life." He smiled confidently at Peter. "That's all speculation, of course." Peter's left hand moved slowly toward the point of the scissors.

Dr. Bryant's face was sad, almost guilty. "I don't know a better way to say this, Peter, but your two brains can't co-operate any more, so they're fighting it out for dominance." He leaned forward and put a hand on Peter's shoulder. "I'm sure the rational half of your brain will eventually get control again, but I'm afraid you're in for some pretty harrowing experiences in the meantime."

The left hand leaped like an animal. His right hand grabbed for it, but it was too late. He was standing. The doctor had pulled back in surprise. The scissors flashed up with speechless strength and plunged down with a butcher's infallible knowledge of anatomy. Peter recoiled within himself. The left hand struck twice more, but there was no need. There was blood everywhere. Peter watched like a witness. The left hand threw the scissors on the tray. When his body jerked toward the door, Peter had no will to stop it. Even when he realized that the car was headed for the shop and Katrine, he could do nothing.

All the way downtown, he prayed that there would be no customers. If there had to be people, he prayed that Katrine would not be one of them. When the car jerked to a stop in front of the shop, Peter counted the customers through the front window. There were four of them. Paul made a fifth standing behind the cutting block in his white apron that never seemed to get blood on it, no matter how much he cut.

At least, he told himself, Katrine was not there. He prayed that she had gone to the bank early with the day's receipts. But he knew he was kidding himself. She was in the back, and the screams would bring her running before the left hand was finished with its work. The whole scene unfolded before him like a movie sent as a message from his left hand:

Dr. Bryant had been quick and quiet. The shop would be a chaos of blood and screaming. He would erupt out of a cloud of good wishes about his health with a cleaver wrenched from Paul. Spinning toward them like a pinwheel of blades, separating bone from bone through the thin tissue of the joint, severing the main arteries of the throat to drain off the blood, splitting the skull with the blunt end of the cleaver like the flat end of an ax.

The shrieking faces would fly and fall before him. The floor would be slippery with blood. Mrs. Cherninski would go down in a puddle of it trying to flee, and he would cleave her braincase with a passing downstroke on his way to annihilate Paul. Mrs. Cherninski's three-year-old son would crawl under the cutting block and hide there watching in indelible horror as Peter hacked and notched and split, until there was nothing left but carcasses.

Then the left hand would hear the whimpering and turn him toward the chopping block and the child beneath it. Halfway to the whimpering, the left hand would stop and wheel toward the back of the shop and Katrine. He would try to yell to her to run, but the voiceless brain would smother his warning into a strangle of rage. She would stand there helpless as he swung toward her, and he would cut her down, crying silently in great sobs that would come out like grunts of pleasure.

The left hand jerked him out of the car. The right hand grabbed the door and clung. The left hand wrenched at it. Taken off guard, the left hand might be overpowered, but it had the momentum and it could not be stopped. The fingers of the right hand uncurled slowly and the doorframe slipped from his grasp. He staggered toward the shop like a man paralyzed down his right side. The left side dragged the rest of him forward and banged open the glass door.

Mrs. Cherninski waddled toward him. Old Mr. Thayer raised a shaky hand to pat his shoulder and wish him well. Young Carolyn Howard grinned a stewardess's welcome at him while Stashu Cherninski hid behind his mother's leg and began to cry. They crowded around him, their faces waiting to be splashed with blood.

His snarl shocked them into silence. They melted away from him. At the chopping block, Paul backed away from him, smiling uncertainly. Tears ran down Peter's face. The left hand reached for the cleaver. The right hand knocked it down onto the chopping block and pounded it with an enormous fist. The left hand crawled steadily across the wood. The fist came down again and again like a blacksmith's hammer. But the left hand did not stop. It was less than a fingerlength from the big cleaver when Katrine shrieked his name from the doorway.

Peter's face turned toward her, twisted with agony. She looked so young suddenly, so helplessly young and beautiful. When he cried out her name, the left hand twisted it beyond human recognition. Katrine ran crying toward him. The swish of the cleaver cut through his mind toward her. There was nothing left to do.

The left hand jerked forward. The right hand grabbed the handle and swung it all in the same motion. The blade bit through bone like a final solution. Beyond the cleaver's blade, the left hand twitched, pumping its power out onto the wood.

He screamed, *it screamed,* and his knees buckled as Paul raced around the block to grab at his waist. Katrine screamed . . . *it screamed* . . . for the others to get out of the shop, then she knelt beside him, weeping, fumbling as she applied a hasty, makeshift tourniquet. But she would not touch the hand. Nor would Paul. Through his moaning and the haze that veiled his vision, Peter could see them struggling to keep their eyes away. Moments later, the men from the ambulance squad packed it in ice, but even they shuddered as they dropped it into a sealed metal case.

Only the doctors at the hospital treated it as just another piece of meat. They told Katrine her husband was lucky, patted her shoulder, and assured her that when the graft healed, the hand would be as strong as ever.

*Thomas F. Monteleone, in the space of less than a decade,
is the author of more than two dozen short stories and
novelettes, four novels, and is the editor of an illustrated
anthology,* The Arts and Beyond. *He is currently the
Secretary of the Science Fiction Writers of America, and
has been a finalist for both the Nebula and John W.
Campbell awards.*

*All of this, it should be noted, is in the field of science
fiction.*

*With "Where All the Songs Are Sad," however, he
turns for the first time to fantasy. He has traded in his cus-
tomary lean prose and rapid pacing for a cat-stalking, de-
ceptively innocent examination of an island more noted in
the popular mind for its stubborn resistance to conquest
and Mafioso clans than for its placement in a century that is
not quite ours. Sicily places a heavy claim on her descendants (Lord help the Sicilian who calls himself an Italian),
not the least of which is a call to a time when the shadows
of Etna held more than just a simple physical threat.*

WHERE ALL THE SONGS ARE SAD

by Thomas F. Monteleone

When Vincent Manzara stepped off the plane at Palermo's
International Airport, the first thing he saw was an angry,
swirling sky that stained the low-slung clouds beyond the
runways. It was a moody sky, he thought, and captured
the essence of Sicily almost preternaturally.

As he crossed the tarmac and entered the terminal, he studied those swarthy, handsome people of the ancient island that he could see, and could not help but notice the intensity of their faces—dark eyes like polished onyx, rippling shocks of black hair, complexions like sunburned almonds, strong jaws, and eternally expressive mouths. From such people as these had he descended, and he instantly thought of his grandfather, Francesco, who had emigrated alone from Palermo at fifteen; he had arrived at an 1890s New York that teemed with foreign-speaking laborers and dirty, congested, ethnic neighborhoods.

He often thought of his grandfather, imagining that he must have been a fierce, energetic man—especially since he had, within five years of his arrival, worked and saved enough to bring over most of the rest of his family. Within a decade, the man had owned two Italian bakeries in Brooklyn, and lived in a marble-terraced home on East Twenty-fourth Street, where he raised a large family. But Vincent's memories of the old man were faint and cloudy, like old tintype photographs; what he remembered most were the endless stories the relatives told about the patriarch; and as a result, Vincent felt close to him because he admired him, and because those same relatives always remarked that they looked and acted so much alike.

It was this closeness, in fact, that caused him to spend one afternoon in his parents' attic, sifting through a chest of Francesco's papers. It was there that he discovered a letter from a sister, Margarita, in Sicily, dated August 15, 1931. The back pages were missing, but the first mentioned something about a missing child. When he questioned his family about it, he found it curious that no one would confess knowing anything, either about the sister or the lost child. He wondered, then, why his grandfather had kept something like that a secret; and the more he wondered, the more he dreamed of going someday to Sicily, to find the remnants of his family and perhaps clear up its now-clouded past. And the opportunity arrived just after he received his M.A. in journalism. Before beginning a job as managing editor of a small upstate newspaper, he gathered up his savings and prepared for a trip to his grandfather's birthplace. Even though his father insisted rather loudly that the Manzaras had no living relatives on the island, Vincent was determined to discover that for himself. After unsuccessfully culling the Immigration Department's records, he enlisted the services of a genealogical society that discovered that the entire Manzara clan had *not* come to America—there was still the sister, Margarita, and a first cousin, Gaetano, who had remained in the place the Greeks had called "the land of Persephone."

Immediately, then, he wrote letters of introduction to Margarita's sister, Theresa Brucculeri, and Gaetano's only surviving son, Tomaso Manzara. Tomaso, a farmer, wrote back a warm, enthusiastic note inviting Vincent to his home; but the letter to Theresa was returned as undeliverable.

There were, then, four relatives scheduled to meet him at the airport and, as he checked through customs, a stewardess touched him lightly on his sleeve and inquired his name. When he told her, she nodded, smiled, and turned to motion to a small group of people standing behind her. There was a short, muscular man with bushy eyebrows and thick, silvering hair. He wore a tan, corduroy sport coat, baggy trousers, and looked very unused to the black tie around his neck. At his side was a portly, middle-aged woman with gray eyes and black hair tied up in a bun. She wore a multicolored crinoline that looked like an out-of-date party dress. Beside them stood a girl in her early teens wearing blue jeans and a peasant blouse, and an older girl—perhaps in her early twenties—who was strikingly beautiful. She was slender, wore a tailored yellow suit, and had enormous almond eyes and long, black hair.

The stewardess said something to them and they instantly erupted into a symphony of smiles. "Vincenzo! Vincenzo!" they all cried at once, and rushed to him. He tried to raise a hand in greeting, but he was immediately engulfed by embraces and kisses. He was stunned for a moment by the sudden display, and allowed himself to be batted about gently. Then they stopped abruptly, stepping back, staring at him; he felt obliged to speak.

"I—I can't speak Italian," he said, embarrassed by the admission.

The short man laughed. "That is no matter. We will all practice our English on you!" He reached out and grabbed his hand. "I am your cousin, Tomaso! Welcome, Vincenzo . . . welcome to Sicily."

Everyone smiled as the old man went through the introductions: Helena, his matronly, round-faced wife; Victoria, the daughter who could have been a fashion model; and Maria, the adolescent who resembled her mother. Vincent smiled and exchanged greetings with them all, but he couldn't keep his eyes from the raven-haired Victoria, doubting if he had ever seen so completely captivating a young woman as this delightfully found new cousin.

Suddenly he was jerked back to the real world as Tomaso scooped up his luggage and guided him through the terminal's sterile, modern architecture to a parking lot where the family's 1949, black, hump-backed Chevrolet awaited them. Though he would have preferred sharing the back seat with Victoria, he settled for the place of honor—between Tomaso and Helena in front.

No sooner had they left the airport than Tomaso began an excited monologue as smooth and complete as any tour-bus driver's; he pointed out landmarks and places of interest, and Vincent was overwhelmed by the sheer power, the utter starkness of the Sicilian countryside leading into Palermo—it was sere and harsh and hot, even in the growing twilight. A suitable place, he thought, to forge strong, resilient people.

Gradually, the expanse of Palermo grew on the horizon ahead while Tomaso continued to ramble on about the splendors of his island. Occasionally, however, Vincent was able to interrupt the flood of information to make a quick comment or ask a short question. This seemed to please the old farmer, and he would continue his delivery with renewed vigor.

When they finally entered the city, Tomaso drove through a maze of narrow, twisting streets, where the long Mediterranean twilight created curious shadows and strange perspectives, giving the back streets and side streets an almost surreal quality. But when he turned onto the Via Ruggero Settimo, Vincent discovered a more cosmopolitan side of Palermo. He saw a wide boulevard lined with brightly lit shops, boutiques, and restaurants; sidewalks thick with olive-skinned crowds, tourist and native alike, all moving with a swiftness and vitality that he could sense even within the musty confines of the family car.

The streets blended and changed, and they came upon the sprawling *Vucciria*—a gigantic outdoor market so brightly spangled with lanterns and candles and electric light that it seemed like midday. He watched the crowds flow and bubble like lava, felt the air crackle with a rush of voices and laughter, smelled the thick, roiling aromas of roasted nuts, baked onions, oregano, and marinades . . . and wished that they could stop and experience the sparkling *life* that flowed in this place.

But the marketplace was soon behind them, and the car threaded again through narrow streets until they reached the outskirts of the city. Tomaso's monologue had finally begun to lose steam, and Vincent used the opportunity to speak to the others, learning that Helena was a true farmer's wife, raising the children, preparing the meals, and keeping the house; that little Maria was just entering high school, but wanted to be a writer someday; that Victoria was single, and worked as a surgical nurse at Palermo's Metropolitan Hospital. He noticed that the entire family spoke English very well, that they were extremely courteous, and never failed to show the utmost respect to old Tomaso. Vincent was impressed with these third cousins, admiring both their healthy appearances and their vivacious attitudes toward life.

With the city behind them, the car followed the contours of rolling shepherd's hills until reaching the vicinity of the Manzara farm. There was an almost-full moon low on the short, rocky horizon, which cast a pale, yellow-blue light over the land. As they approached an unpaved, winding driveway, Vincent studied the scene that stretched before him like a Van Gogh canvas: a stone farmhouse with a tiled roof; a gray, patched barn clutched by a wood-rail barnyard; a white clapboard outbuilding surrounded by fruit trees blistered with ripe blossoms. It was at once a compelling, tranquil picture and a somber, somehow foreboding place.

When the Chevrolet shuddered to a halt by the barn, everyone moved to the farmhouse excitedly, anxious to show Vincent their comfortable, two-story abode. Tomaso carried Vincent's bags through the front door, and the rest of the family gestured for him to enter. Once inside, he noticed that every room was furnished with sturdy, hand-wrought oak pieces. There were embroidered tablecloths, fringed orrises, wall tapestries, candles in brass pots, and wall sconces. And everywhere, Vincent noted, on every available piece of wall space, were icons and prints of Christ and a host of saints. He'd expected an Old World deference to the Church, but Tomaso's display of faith was almost too much to accept. But despite this, the white stucco walls and beamed ceilings seemed to glow with a self-contained warmth. It was a shadowy but pleasant atmosphere.

As the rest of the family went into the large kitchen, Tomaso directed him upstairs and down a narrow hall illuminated by a single electric bulb. The old man showed Vincent to the end room, pointing out a wash basin and pitcher, some towels and bedclothes. After informing him that supper would be ready within the hour, he disappeared down the hall.

Vincent sat down on the edge of the bed, feeling the softness of the mattress. He was extremely impressed with his relatives, who displayed an openness and charm that was lacking in their American counterparts. It seemed to him that their world was more *real,* more natural, and more closely rooted to the earth than his own. Standing up, he faced the mirror over a bureau and studied his reflection. His longish, dark hair, his brown eyes, and his angular jaw were all characteristics found in his newly met relatives, and he felt a sudden rush of pride in sharing these family traits. Coming to Sicily, he thought, had been the best decision of his entire life.

After unpacking and washing up, he joined Tomaso in the front parlor, where the old man was passing the time before the evening meal with *The Observatore,* a newspaper from Rome. As Vincent sat in a delicately carved chair with maroon cushions and brass studs, he listened to the tinkling sounds of supper being prepared in the kitchen, to the liquid flow of Italian instructions and exclamations, and most of all, to the lilting voice of Victoria.

Tomaso looked up at him and smiled, and his old face was instantly a portrait of confident joy. "And so, Vincenzo . . . what do you think of my city? Of my family and this happy house?"

"It's beautiful, sir," said Vincent, breaking into a genuine smile. "We don't have anything like this in America."

"No, of course you don't. There is nothing like Sicily anywhere in the world."

"Do you work the farm all by yourself?"

"It is not that much work, Vincenzo. Not when you have done it all your years. There is no profit here, but we make enough to live, to be satisfied. I was born here. I love this land."

Vincent smiled again. "I can see that you do."

Tomaso waved a large, beefy hand, puffed out his cheeks expressively. "Farming is a proud way to live, Vincenzo. We feed the world. Without us, there would be no time for industry, or for art, or for anything."

Vincent was about to comment when Helena appeared, wearing an embroidered apron, and announced that supper was being served. They all crowded into a small dining room, where the table was immaculately set with a gold service and stoneware plates. Vincent dined on olives cured with garlic, fresh tomatoes, boiled eggs, piping-hot breads, cheeses, sausage, and a tart, red wine. It was a simple fare that suffused him with still more appreciation of Sicily's facile manner. Vincent had never felt more content in his life.

Little was spoken at first, but Tomaso would occasionally interject a remark or statement that did not require a direct response, as if he were mentioning odd thoughts as they occurred to him.

"Life is simple here, Vincenzo," he said, lifting his wine glass. "Each day is always known to us. What we will be doing. In July, we winnow the grain. In November, it is time to harvest the olives. February, and the crops must be weeded."

Near the end of the meal, Maria excused herself to fetch her schoolbooks, and Tomaso nodded, saying, "I don't have it myself, but I know that education is a good thing. Our Maria, she may be the smartest of all of us someday."

Everyone smiled at this, and the girl blushed as she glided out of the room. Vincent noticed, however, that Victoria seemed to be forcing her cheerfulness, as though she had been slighted by her father's boasting. Vincent looked at her until their eyes met, then winked at the brooding, nubile woman, and his pulse seemed to jump as he sensed her smile become instantly genuine.

As the table was cleared and Helena served a light dessert of cantaloupe and ice cream, the conversation drifted toward life in America, and once the subject was broached, Vincent was almost overwhelmed by eager questions. He handled them with as much *savoir faire* as he could muster, and several times he surprised himself in discovering how much he actually knew about his own country.

When they asked him how he had finally located his Sicilian relatives, he described the bureaucratic snags that plagued him at each step, and they were fascinated by the tale.

"I also wrote to my grandfather's sister, Margarita," he added, and told them about the letter he had found. "But no one answered."

Instantly, he sensed that something had gone wrong. His last sentence seemed to echo in the room awkwardly.

Victoria and Helena sat silently, their eyes flashing to Tomaso, as if to take a behavioral cue from him. Their expressions were abruptly solemn, apprehensive.

Tomaso pursed his lips, pushing his mustache up to touch his large nose, his eyebrows knitting tightly. Drawing a breath, he stared for a very long moment into Vincent's eyes.

"No," said the old man finally. "Forget them. She would not write you."

Vincent did not understand, but he knew he had touched an exposed nerve. He wanted to question the sudden mystery, but the man's stormy features did not warrant it.

"Helena," said the patriarch quickly, as if sensing Vincent's awkwardness, "more coffee for our guest. And some brandy."

His wife stood up and scurried into the kitchen. Victoria, as if heeding an unheard signal, gathered up the dessert plates and followed her mother out of the room. Tomaso looked at Vincent again, this time with a softer expression.

"Do not suddenly fear us, Vincenzo," he said. "You have done nothing wrong. Just know that *we* are your only family here. Margarita's family . . . they do not know you. Forget them."

Vincent could only nod. He wanted to speak, and he did not, which was not like him at all. He was normally a forceful, even brash, social type, and he had always prided himself on being able to successfully deal with almost any social situation. But here at this simple table, before a weathered, rustic old man, he felt oddly helpless. He was shocked to see how quickly the mood and atmosphere of the house had changed, and as he sat silently with Tomaso, drinking brandy, the earlier joy of the day seemed distant and unreal.

Finally, Tomaso rose and announced that the hour was late, and that it was time to sleep. Helena guided Vincent up to his room, wished him a pleasant rest, and left him to his thoughts . . .

His first day in Sicily had been fascinating, an almost dramatic blend of emotions and experiences. As he drifted off to sleep, images and memories of the day flickered past his mind's eye, and he thought of some of the things he would like to accomplish during his brief stay. He would see as much of the country as possible; he would become better acquainted with the lovely Victoria; and he would definitely unveil the mystery surrounding Margarita's family.

*

In the morning, Helena woke him and served him a magnificent breakfast of honey and biscuits, eggs, sausage, figs, and walnuts. During idle conversation, he learned that Tomaso was already at work in the fields and Maria had been driven to school by Victoria, who would be then returning home.

"Doesn't she have to work today?" he asked, with more than simple curiosity.

"Oh no, Vincenzo. Did Tomaso not tell you? Victoria asked the doctor bosses for time off . . . so that she could show her American cousin the sweetness of her country."

The gloom of the previous evening seemed to evaporate like mist on a morning pond, and Vincent felt his heart soar. He could not have hoped for a more perfect arrangement.

"How many days will she be home?"

"The entire week, Vincenzo. She will show you much, do not worry."

Vincent smiled, and finished his breakfast in silent apprehension while Helena busied about the kitchen and the other downstairs rooms. Sunlight cascaded through the thick-paned windows, a bird's song thrummed in the distance. Contentment was almost an aroma in the air.

Afterward he retired to his room, washed, and dressed casually for a day of sightseeing with his cousin. His every thought seemed to be about her, and it was an eternity before he saw the Chevrolet rumbling up the bumpy driveway toward the barn. He rushed down the stairs to greet her and was pleased by her simple yet flattering attire— a pair of blue jeans and a knit jersey cinched about her narrow waist. Her long, dark hair was wind-blown, but it still seemed carefully sculpted about her cameo face.

"Are you ready?" she said, standing in the doorway to the parlor. Her eyes were dancing with light and gaiety.

"Of course. Where are we going?"

Victoria smiled. "We shall go everywhere, cousin!"

And they did.

For the next three days, she chauffeured him about the island. They savored its length and breadth from bright morning till late evening. The names of the cities and villages they passed through read like pages from a volume of poetry: Caltanissetta, Pozzo di Gotto, Castelvetrano, Taormina, Messina, Montemaggiore, Agrigento, Syracuse. They stood amid Greek ruins built more than two thousand years before, picnicked on the beach of the Gulf of Castellammare, sampled wines from the vineyards of Trapani, stood in awe of the Norman cathedral at Cefalu, where the world's most detailed mosaics lie hidden like secrets on the coast of the Tyrrhenian Sea. Their days were filled with the sounds of village mandolins and cafe card games, with the smells of citrus groves and olive branches. He had never imagined such a small, mountainous, little island could contain so much richness, so much vitality, so much history.

They traveled extensively, but Vincent felt drawn back to the sprawling capital of Palermo, and on the fourth day, he and Victoria were walking its enchanted streets. His relationship with her had progressed, slowly at first, until they now felt very comfortable with each other. They spoke easily and without affectation. He learned Italian haltingly; she allowed her English to be corrected until it became a small game between them. More than once, as they walked hand in hand, Vincent was tempted to explain his true feelings about her, to feel the firm softness of her waist in his arms. But she was so innocent, it seemed, so unseeing of his emotions, that he could not broach the subject.

So wrapped up in the days of travel and the fascination of Victoria had he been that Vincent almost forgot one of the other objectives of his visit. But a series of odd incidents on the fourth day renewed his interest in the silent part of his Sicilian family—the descendants of Margarita.

Victoria was guiding him down a quiet street toward a museum near the outskirts of the city when they came upon the somber entrance to a very old cemetery. Pausing, he was arrested by the starkness of the gates, as if the gray stone and rusted ironwork led into a colorless, other dimension—as perhaps they did. He saw an inscription above the gate in the form of a short couplet:

Un tempo fummo come voi,
Presto sarete come noi.

"What does it say?" he asked Victoria, who stood silently watching him.

A shudder seemed to pass through her, her eyes lost their sparkle for a moment. "It says: 'Once we were as you, Soon you shall be as we.' "

Vincent was struck by the poetic, chilling thought, and he smiled weakly. "That's very comforting, isn't it?"

"No, but it's not surprising . . . for Sicily," she said, and began to walk away.

'What do you mean?"

"I don't know . . . death seems to be a large part of life in Sicily. You know of the *Giorno dei Morti*, don't you?"

"What's that? The 'Day of Death,' or something like that?" Vincent looked up the street. They were moving toward the center of the city.

"Yes," said Victoria. "That's exactly what it is."

He nodded. "They have something like that in Mexico, I think. There's processions, festivals, the children even get little candy skulls."

"It's very similar here," she said, tossing her long hair off her shoulder. "Only more so. On November 2, everyone exchanges precious gifts, given in the name of dead loved ones."

"No offense, but it seems kind of morbid to me."

"There's other examples, Vincenzo. Whenever someone dies, we advertise it with signs draped in black over front doors. Most of our prayers emphasize the Reaper. It's almost like a . . . what is the word? A cult?"

He nodded slowly. "Yes, that's the word. I suppose it *is* almost like that." He looked at the beautiful girl by his side, admiring her for other attributes now—her objectivity and honesty in the face of a tightly knit culture such as Sicily's.

"But there's more than that," she said, stopping abruptly and staring into his eyes. "Have you ever heard of the Capuchin Convent?"

"No. Should I?"

"Perhaps. They have some catacombs there. Would you like to see them? It's not far, we can walk."

Vincent was not completely positive he wanted to see any catacombs, but it seemed important to Victoria. And he could not deny the evocative mood, the sudden pall, that seemed to have descended upon them since passing the cryptic gates of the old cemetery. It was as though a larger story were waiting to be unfolded, if he would only flow with the situation like a leaf upon a stream.

"All right," he said after a pause. "Yes, I'd like to see them."

"It's this way," she said, indicating an approaching side street on the left.

The Capuchin Convent is one of the older churches and monasteries in Palermo. For the past 350 years, it has also been the location of one of Sicily's most intriguing, yet grotesque, sights—the catacombs. Vincent felt the clinging afternoon heat flee from them like banished demons as they were guided down a flight of winding, stone-cold stairs by an old monk. The padre was dressed in a hooded robe the color of a field mouse's fur. He walked with a sandal-shuffling gait that accentuated the roundness of his shoulders, the stoop of his back, as if he bore the weight of centuries.

Beneath the Convent, the monk told them, were the mummified remains of more than eight thousand Palermitans. He spoke of other statistics, but Vincent paid little attention to the droning, heavily accented voice. His imagination had already carried him ahead, trying to visualize what this place would be like, and he felt a sense of dread drop over him like a cloak.

Reaching the bottom of the stairs, the monk pushed open a thick oak-planked door. As it creaked on its hinges, Vincent caught a faint odor in the air, as if it were waiting for them in the darkness beyond. He stepped through the portal into the dim glow of electric light—an incongruous addition to the old stone passageway. But instead of dispelling the chilling mood of the place, the string of bare bulbs across the arched ceilings emphasized the long, white-washed tunnels, studded with alcoves and naves, *filled* with the dead. His breath seemed to catch in his throat and he involuntarily hesitated for a moment before following the monk into the mortuary.

Grim symbols of Sicily's preoccupation with death, the mummified corpses lined every nook, shoulder to shoulder, along the walls like passengers in a subway car. Despite the embalming efforts, practically all the bodies had lost their flesh, and were little more than brown skeletons. They stood mutely as Vincent passed among them, heads bowed, hands folded like embracing bony spiders. Hundreds of death figures, all dressed in the identifying garments of their professions. Here were row upon row of bishops in musty, color-leeched cassocks and mitered hats. Beyond them, doctors and surgeons in their gowns, lawyers in their *juris* robes, judges, bankers, teachers. It was a gallery of the distinguished, the revered and respected ancestors, all chained to the walls or lying in low, long shelves up the sides of curving walls. The chamber opened into a longer, deeper one, and still the thickly packed skeletal legions stood in silent ranks. At one point, Vincent looked back at Victoria and saw for the first time a hardness in her deep, bottomless eyes, as if she were erecting a barrier against the grisly sights. Turning away from her, he looked up to see the stunted, stooped figures of children mummified and clothed in their Eucharist suits and dresses, in baptismal gowns. There were small shadow-boxes containing infants—their little skeletons not yet completely formed, they now reposed in a grim parody of life. As he passed a small gap among the bodies, he noticed that the air around him was dry and cool, and he imagined that he was suddenly *inhaling* microscopic particles, the dust-mote fragments of decay, of these bodies, taking into his living flesh, as if they were spores, germs that would grow and contaminate him. He fought back a blind urge to flee the place.

As they turned a corner, the monk continued his guide's patter. "It was, in the past, a great honor to be interred here."

Vincent was again aware of his voice. "Not so anymore?" he asked, trying to ease his uneasy thoughts.

The monk sighed. "In 1881, the practice of mummification was officially outlawed. However, that did not stop those who wished, *signore.*"

"You mean it still goes on?"

"On occasion," said the monk.

Vincent was about to ask another question when he saw three people, a tall thin man and two large, old women, standing some distance ahead of them. One of the women appeared to be talking animatedly to one of the corpses against the wall.

Vincent addressed the old monk in a whisper. "Father, those people . . . what are they doing?"

"A family of one of the dead," he said softly. "They come to visit relatives, to change the clothing, and of course they come to discuss important family matters."

The information chilled him, and he instantly imagined himself facing the desiccated remains of his father or mother, coldly peeling dry-rotted suits from their bones.

When he did not reply, the old padre turned and continued the tour, which Vincent, suddenly, fervently hoped would soon be over. Victoria must have sensed his discomfort; she reached out and grabbed his hand, squeezing it. He looked at her and enacted a smile.

The monk took them through another chamber and then to an ascending flight of stairs that led them into the warmer air and light of the day. They thanked their guide, placed a small donation in the poor box, and left hastily.

Once outside, Victoria looked at him. "Well, cousin, what do you think?"

"I don't know . . ." he said, rubbing his eyes as they adjusted to the sunlight. "It's morbid, I guess. Reminds you of things you don't like to think about. But it's a cultural thing, isn't it? All in what you are used to, in what you grow up with."

"*I* don't like the place," said Victoria. "Would you believe this is only the second time I've ever been to Capuchin?"

"Really?"

"My father took me once, when I was still a child . . . but I do not visit the dead."

Vincent paused as they approached the Via della Liberta.

"*Visit?* . . . do you . . . do *we* have relatives back there?"

Victoria tensed ever so slightly as she looked quickly at him. Her dark hair unfurled like a cape over her shoulders, her eyes intense and piercing. "I'm sorry, Vincenzo. Does that bother you?"

It was an odd question, he thought, as if meant to throw him off track, to disarm him. "No, not really," he said as he looked away, pretending to study the path ahead. "It's just that it makes me think of some things. Things that I've been meaning to ask you about."

"Like Margarita?" she asked, her voice almost a whisper.

"Do you think I could forget that first night at your father's table?" he said, wishing instantly he did not sound so sarcastic.

"No, of course not," she said. "As a matter of fact, I've been wondering why it's taken you so long to bring it up." She smiled for the first time, it seemed, in a very long time.

"Well, can you tell me about it? Would Tomaso be mad?"

"Oh it's not my father I'm worried about. It's you. It might be better that you do not know some of the things about the family."

"Why? After you've let it go this far? If you don't tell me now, I'll go to the authorities. There are records. I'll find out for myself."

"I know you would," she said. "Better that you hear it from me. It's a long drive home, and it's a long story. Let's get the car."

Seated behind the wheel of the Chevrolet, Victoria spun out the tale of his grandfather's sister, Margarita, and her family. The woman did not go to America when Francesco had sent for her because she had fallen in love with a young man named Giuseppe Brucculeri, a clerk in Victor Emmanuel's court. She married him two years later and moved to Palermo, where they lived a comfortable life until Margarita gave birth to her only child, Theresa, in 1912. It seemed as if Theresa was doomed to be a child of woe. She was born with a clubfoot and, as she grew older, the affliction colored her life distinctly. She reached adolescence with no friends, a fear of practically everyone—especially doctors—and a brooding, spiteful personality. Giuseppe, husband and father, contracted tuberculosis when Theresa was fourteen, and died the following year. Destitute, Margarita enrolled her daughter in a convent, but the girl remained only six months before running away. It was later discovered that she had fled to the small hill town of Gangi, where she lived with a band of gypsies, who attributed mystic powers to her because of her physical deformity.

Years passed, and Margarita never saw Theresa. The mother grew despondent over the loss of both husband and daughter; Margarita never married again. She wrote infrequently to her brother in America, but was far too proud to ask for passage to the New World. She did, however, have occasional contact with her cousin, Tomaso, who was at that time a young man who had recently inherited a farm from old Gaetano. But the time continued to sweep past her and still there was no word from Theresa. Margarita gradually succumbed to the weight of the years and the cruelty of the Fates, and in the crisp days of spring in 1940, she was stricken with pneumonia. Tomaso took her into his home and cared for her, but it was of little use. On her deathbed, she had Tomaso promise that if he ever found Theresa, he would do his best to take care of her. Secure in this knowledge, the broken woman died peacefully.

Ten years passed without incident, until Theresa returned. At first Tomaso was not sure that it was indeed Margarita's daughter, but he was driven to investigate the tales of an old woman with a deformed foot, dressed in rags, frequenting the shabbier stalls of the *Vucciria*. Theresa would have been around the age of forty at this time, but this woman appeared much older. She wore black, tattered clothes that almost touched the ground in an attempt to conceal her affliction, and her face was creased like old leather. One day, upon spotting her, Tomaso followed the hag from the marketplace to a two-room apartment in Palermo's North End, where the streets were dark and full of gloom, even on the brightest of days, where the docks and warehouses overwhelmed dirty little tenements of the old and the very poor. As he followed the woman, the more he studied her features, the more convinced Tomaso became that it must be Theresa, and he confronted her as she entered a darkened doorway.

At first she denied everything, but under Tomaso's insistent questions she admitted her identity. Tomaso invited himself into her apartment and was appalled by the squalor and abject poverty in which she lived. There was a grayness about the place, an almost colorless vacuum that seemed to suck up all that was alive. Tomaso pressed her for more information, but Theresa was reluctant to give up many details from her past or her present means of subsistence. He did notice, however, that she seemed to derive pleasure, in a singularly morbid kind of way, from her ability to shock and even revolt him. Just as he was about to leave, he became curious about the closed door to the second room of her apartment, and questioned Theresa about it.

When Theresa's mood changed from mild annoyance to complete anger and indignation, Tomaso was convinced that he had touched upon something important. He strode toward the door to open it and Theresa attempted to stop him, cursing violently. But he was not to be stopped, especially after such an emotional display, and he pushed past her and opened the door. He was shocked to see a young man of perhaps twenty lying on his back, eyes closed, hands folded upon his chest, a greasy sheet half covering his otherwise naked body. Tomaso could detect no breathing, no sign of life.

Theresa was shaking as if suffering a seizure, livid with hate and anger. She demanded that Tomaso leave her, but he would not until she explained the young man's presence. Tomaso pressed her, and she must have realized that he was a formidable opponent, because she gave in, revealing that the boy was her son, Antonio, and that he was not dead, as Tomaso had feared. She further revealed that Antonio had been gravely ill and had fallen into a mysterious coma more than a year earlier. But despite protests by Tomaso, she refused to take the boy to any doctors—whom she hated passionately. When Tomaso forced the issue, she became hysterical and he eventually left.

When he reached the street, Tomaso saw a young boy, no older than ten years, staring at him malevolently. Tomaso smiled at him and the boy spat at his feet, saying: "You go to see La Strega!"

Before he could reply, the boy darted into a nearby alley and was lost in the shadows. Tomaso was shaken by the experience, since it underscored his own impressions and the apprehension he had felt in the presence of Theresa. If she was *not* a witch, she did nothing to discourage the impression.

Upset as he was by the encounter, Tomaso still went to the nearest hospital to summon an ambulance to the filthy apartment. Later, however, he was not surprised to learn that when the attendants reached the address, they found it abandoned. For weeks, he searched the area for Theresa and the comatose Antonio, but without success. He considered calling in the police, but the superstitious side of his nature prevented outside involvement in such a personal family affair. All around the *Vucciria*, he listened for rumor of her presence, but she remained hidden to him.

Time passed and the pressing business of farm and family eventually drew his attention away from Theresa. But he never forgot her, or her ashen-skinned son on the bed.

There was little mention of Theresa at the Manzara farm, and it was only through eavesdropping on her parents' conversation that Victoria was able to learn the whole story; it was an incredible tale, and it hardened Vincent's resolve to uncover the rest of the mystery surrounding his great-aunt.

"Where is she now? Anybody know if she's still alive?"

"No one knows, Vincenzo. And to be truthful, we don't think about her much. I believe what my father says about her, that she's an evil woman, that she is a darkness in my family's soul."

"What about Antonio? Whatever happened to him?"

Victoria shook her head. "No one knows, really. He was never seen by anybody but my father . . . and that was long ago."

Vincent looked at her, convinced that Victoria was hesitating, that there was more to the story. He challenged her on this, and the guilt behind her eyes confirmed his suspicions.

"I'm sorry, Vincenzo. It's just that it's so . . . so silly. You would think I was being dumb. Superstitious."

"No I won't. I promise. You can trust me, please, you know that."

She stared straight ahead, watching the road, thinking. Vincent watched her fingers drum nervously upon the steering wheel, watched her bite her lower lip absently. Reaching across the seat, he touched her arm, and she moved to take his hand in hers. It felt strangely cold to him.

"Don't be afraid," he said.

"I'm sorry . . . I'm just being silly. I'm not afraid. It's just that there isn't really much more to tell . . ."

"Go on . . . tell me anyway."

Victoria sighed. "All right . . . about two years ago I was awakened in the middle of the night by the sound of my parents' talking as they lay in bed. My father had just come back from Palermo. He had been late and my mother had been worried about him. I remember that he was very excited, even upset about something."

"About what?" Vincent was anxious, and she seemed to be drawing out her story deliberately.

"He had been haggling over some fruit prices with vendors in the *Vucciria*, and afterward he had stopped at a cafe for a drink. While he was there, he heard an old man who was quite drunk telling stories to a table of listeners. The old one claimed to be a gypsy and one of the stories he told was about a crippled sorceress whose son was caught raping a village girl of thirteen. The gypsies wanted to hang him for the crime on the spot, but the mother saved him by placing a curse on her own son."

"A curse!" said Vincent, not bothering to hide the scorn in his voice. "What kind of curse?"

"She worked a spell on her son. She put him to sleep, vowing that he would sleep until the day the witch mother herself would die. The son would never see her again, and while he slept, his soul would be cleansed in the fires of Purgatory."

"And your father thinks the gypsy was talking about Theresa? And Antonio?"

Victoria nodded. "Of course. Don't you?"

"Maybe. But do you *believe* that?"

She paused for a moment. " I don't know . . . my *father* does. He says that it was just." She would not look at him but continued to watch the road as the car approached the boundaries of the farm.

"And he thinks that Antonio is *still* sleeping after all this time? That's ridiculous . . ."

"Perhaps . . . I don't know."

"But don't any of you *care*? What about Theresa? She sounds like she's mad as a hatter! She probably needs help."

"There's nothing you can do, Vincenzo. Nothing any of us can do."

Vincent felt himself getting upset, and he tried to control his emotions. "Listen, if my grandfather was alive, *he* wouldn't stand around and just let this happen."

"But what can you do?"

"We should find Theresa. She needs help, Victoria. If she actually thought that her son was under the influence of a curse . . . or if she thinks she killed him . . . My God, it's terrible."

Victoria shook her head. "I'm sorry I ever told you any of this."

"No, I'm glad you did. It's just so weird, so hard to believe. It's gruesome."

"To us that is not so. It's cultural, Vincenzo. It's what you grow up with. You said that yourself."

"I just can't believe you'd all let that old woman live like that. Let people believe a crazy, horrible thing like that about her son."

Victoria slowed the car almost to a stop as she drew close to the driveway, turned, and looked at him. Her oval face reflected a calmness, an acceptance of things unknown to him.

"Vincenzo, let me tell you something I read once. Something about us. One of our modern heroes, a very brave, very wise man named Turiddu Giuliano. He was supposed to have said that Sicily is full of sweet, happy music, but that in the end, it's a place where all the songs are sad."

Turning away from him, she started the car slowly up the drive. Vincent looked at her as he repeated Giuliano's words silently to himself. How essentially fatalistic a world view that was, he thought. How grim, and truly *sad* it was. He wondered if Victoria deeply believed in a philosophy like that. He felt suddenly that it was only now that he was beginning to understand how complex these island people actually were.

Once they reached the house, the subject was dropped, and Vincent did not speak to Victoria about it for the rest of the evening. After a supper of antipasto, fresh bread, sardines, and spaghetti with escarole, he passed a few hours playing checkers with Tomaso. The old man was a master of the game and he never ceased delighting in his victories over his American cousin. And so it was that Vincent was still in the parlor when the phone rang for Victoria. He learned that a nurse at the hospital had called in sick for the next day and that Victoria would have to assist in a morning surgery. Her plans with Vincent were forced to be canceled.

The hour grew late and Tomaso finally yawned as he king-jumped over Vincent's section of the board, wrapping up the night's final game. After the old man retired to bed, Vincent remained alone in the parlor, which was illuminated by a single lamp. All around him the white walls reflected its amber glow, illuminating shadowy icons and crucifixes. Old Tomaso, he thought, was not fooling anyone with all that. *Now* he realized why there was such devotion to the saints in this house. The old man was afraid of something—something no one wanted him to discover.

Vincent passed another hour in the dim solitude, not surprised that his thoughts kept coming back to old Theresa. He became convinced that he would not learn the rest of the family's secrets until he found the old woman.

When he went upstairs to bed, he lay for a long time, trying to imagine what he would find. Sleep did not come easily.

He awoke just after sunrise and met Victoria at the breakfast table. Even with her long hair pinned up beneath her nurse's cap, and her figure concealed by the uninspired lines of her uniform, she still looked as fresh and beautiful as a desert flower. He told her of his intentions and, despite mild protests, she agreed to take him into Palermo with her on the way to the hospital. Speaking loudly enough so that Helena could hear him in the kitchen, he announced that he would spend the day sightseeing, and would meet Victoria at the *Il Trionfo* cafe on the Via della Liberta when she finished her shift.

Once outside, in the privacy of the Chevrolet, Victoria looked at him sharply. "I should have never let you talk me into this. I wouldn't have, if my mother had not been there."

"Don't worry about me," he said. "I just want to walk around the *Vucciria* a little bit. Maybe I'll see something. Ask a few questions, that's all."

"Why is this so important to you, Vincenzo? Haven't I told you enough?"

"I don't *know*, Victoria. I don't know if you have or not. I just keep remembering that letter that Margarita sent my grandfather . . . it was one of the things that first made me want to come over here. And now, after I find out how weird things are, you *know* I have to see it for myself."

"But what can you expect to find out that my father doesn't already know? What can you do in a few days that my father couldn't do in twenty years?"

Vincent smiled. "Well, for one, I can't be sure that your father *doesn't* know more than he's telling. Plus, I think your father is afraid."

"*Afraid?*" Victoria's expression became very serious. "Of what?"

"I'm not sure. Maybe he's afraid he'll find out more than he wants to know. Or maybe he knows enough already, enough to put himself in danger . . . I don't know; it could be *anything*."

Victoria did not reply, but Vincent could tell by her eyes that she agreed with him.

"Besides," he said, "I've got something that Tomaso doesn't: Money. American money."

"I don't understand," she said. Her eyes widened slightly, and she looked genuinely concerned, worried.

"Maybe I can buy some information. You see now?"

Victoria pretended to study the road ahead. "Sometimes I think I don't understand you at all, Vincenzo."

He wanted to reply, but the right words would not come, and they passed the remaining kilometers in an awkward silence. His feelings for Victoria ran deep, but her recent behavior and apparent evasiveness bothered him. He wanted her to ask him to stay away from the marketplace, from the surreal Theresa, but she said nothing, even as they entered the outskirts of the city where the rows of stucco houses baked in the morning sun. He would have settled for a half-hearted warning, or simply a wish to be careful, but nothing was forthcoming. Either she was too proud, too scared, or she simply did not care. Whatever the reason, he was troubled by her silence.

Stopping the car on the Via della Fiores, she told him that she would meet him at the same corner at five o'clock. That was all. He smiled thinly, and agreed as he climbed out. The door closed and the old car blended quickly into the snarl of commuter traffic and was lost.

He turned away from the street and headed slowly down the sidewalk, entering a neighborhood of flower stalls where vendors displayed the brightest prizes from their nurseries. As much as he cared about Victoria, he found his thoughts drifting away from her and toward

Theresa. Despite the avenue of color and life in the flower market, he was thinking of some gray place where "La Strega" passed her days and nights. Down narrow streets, he threaded his way, turning corners that were somewhat familiar to him, cutting through an alley where morning laundry was hung to dry in tiny backyards. Within minutes he had arrived at the upper end of the *Vucciria*.

The sidewalk was warm beneath his feet, and the Piazza Caraciollo was filled with a mosaic of sounds and smells and colors. Vincent entered a world of swarthy merchants and barkers, hawking their wares with a studied urgency. He passed gaily painted carts and crepe-papered stands filled with a spectrum of foods: crimson apples, scarlet tomatoes, pale-green zucchini, purple eggplant, golden-yellow lemons, electric limes, oranges like the morning sun. Whole platters of exotic pastries still warm from brick ovens, ices and skewers of *stigghioli* enchanted him. Vincent resisted the urge to pull up a chair at one of the alfresco tables and sample a *canolli* and a cup of dark, thick *demitasse*.

But the purpose of his being in the marketplace kept him from giving in to the temptation. He was positive that someone among all the "regulars" in the *Vucciria* could tell him where to find Theresa. His only job was to locate that person. Walking slowly, he progressed toward the lower end of the vast market, all the time studying the old faces behind piled-up tables of wares. Metalsmiths tapped and fired pieces of tin, leatherworkers cut and tooled ancient designs into straps and pouches, candlemakers poured smoking pots of paraffin into molds. Weavers, spinners, tailors, bakers, they all toiled at their crafts. Vincent looked past their talents, into their eyes where the secrets lived. Which one of them possessed the answer he sought? There was only one way to find out . . .

Hours passed, late into the afternoon, as one by one the pairs of ancient eyes sparked at the mention of Theresa's name, then glazed over when asked of her whereabouts. It was almost time to rendezvous with Victoria, and Vincent had discovered nothing. Practically everyone he had questioned *knew* about the old woman, but no one was willing to share the information with him. He was tired, hot, and growing surly when he approached the hut of a sailmaker, whose doughy face was spiculed with several days of gray whiskers.

"You want La Strega? That *might* be costly, *signore* . . . " said the old man, his eyes as hard and cold as shot.

"How much?" he asked, touching the pocket of his jeans.

The sailmaker laughed. "You are American?"

"Yes," he said, embarrassed but unable to articulate why.

"*Signore*, your money is no doubt heavy in your pockets, but when I spoke of cost, I did not refer to money . . . " His eyes stared up coldly at him.

"Then you won't tell me?"

"I did not say that, *signore*."

Vincent exhaled angrily. "Then what are you talking about?"

"What you want to know is not worth money. I wish that you understand that you may pay . . . in some other way."

"Okay," said Vincent. "I understand that just fine. Now, where can I find her?"

The sailmaker's thin lips twisted into a half grin for a moment, and then evened out. "Very well, *signore*," he said, and spun out a set of fairly simple directions.

"Thank you," said Vincent. "Thank you for everything."

The sailmaker had returned his attention to the seam of a mizzen lying across his lap. He did not look up as he said, "Yes, *signore*, it *is* a very hot day. *Ciao*."

You old bastard, thought Vincent. He was tired of playing games with these people, eager to find his grandfather's niece. He turned away from a row of stalls, ducked away from a low-hanging awning, and moved away from the smells and noisy chatter of the marketplace. The sun was momentarily obscured by clouds, and a somber light briefly enveloped the neighborhood. He worked his way toward the harbor area, passing through small side streets that snaked and twisted through old residential sections.

At one point he was forced to stop a passerby and clarify his directions, but other than that, he encountered no problems. At last he came to La Strada del Cigno, turned left, and faced row after row of very old buildings with crumbling facades, broken windows, battered doors. Most of the entrances were prefaced by shoddy little signs announcing the businesses of the district. Vincent began walking, deciphering the signs slowly. There was a glass-blower's shop, a welding garage, a plumbing supply outlet, scores of warehouses, and several vacant properties. Scattered among this dingy collection were narrow, open doorways that led to the buildings' upper floors, and it was in one of these that Theresa was supposed to live.

Reaching the threshold of a faded brick front, where the address had been slapped on with a careless paint-brush, he peered into the darkness that reached up a flight of partially broken stairs. The interior smelled of rotting garbage, of wet, mangy fur, as if it might be the huddling place of animals during storms. Drawing in breath, Vincent recoiled at the foulness of the place, but entered the foyer and ascended into the shadows. With each step, the impression grew that he was leaving the warm afternoon, and *descending* deeper and deeper into a place that had never known the sun's touch. When he reached the top of the stairs, he felt that the air was somehow *thicker*, that there was a pervasive dampness that penetrated his skin. He stood on a small landing, facing a solitary door: a chill wracked him as he raised his hand and prepared to knock.

He paused for a moment until the sensation passed before rapping his knuckles authoritatively against the old wood. Standing silently in murky light, he awaited the sound of footsteps behind the door. But none came. He knocked again. And again. But no one answered. He considered the possibilities, the most obvious being that the sailmaker had played a very unfunny joke upon him.

The odd chill in the air penetrated his shirt and he wanted to be quickly away from the place. Turning around, inwardly cursing the sailmaker, Vincent prepared to leave the landing when he heard a sound from beyond the door. It was a hoarse, greasy cough, he thought, but was not positive until he heard the sound again ratchet from within the sealed room.

Approaching the door again, he prepared to knock, feeling a rush of adrenalin shock him abruptly. He experienced a moment of vertigo, which increased until he felt great pressure at his temples. What was happening to him? He touched his forehead, surprised to discover perspiration there. He blinked, rubbed his eyes, and gradually the dizziness passed. Again he knocked on the peeling wood.

And this time, straining to hear, he picked up the muffled sound of footsteps. It was the clump-slide of a cripple's gait. Vincent listened as the sounds grew closer, until they stopped on the other side of the door. The doorknob twisted, a crack appeared along the sill, and a single eye peeked out at him.

"*Que essere bisogno?*" said an old woman's voice. It was deep, rough, as if she had something caught in her throat.

"Are you Theresa Brucculeri?" said Vincent in English. Then adding: "*Non parlo Italiano . . . .*"

The old woman wheezed out a short laugh. "Who are you?" she asked in perfect English.

This startled Vincent, but he pressed on. "I'm Vincent Manzara. Your mother and my grandfather, they were sister and brother. I—"

"Francesco? . . ." She opened the door wide enough for Vincent to see her entire face, which was dark and creased with the tracery of years.

"That's right," he said quickly. "I've been looking for you for a long time. I've come all the way from America, and I'd like to talk to you. Can I come in?"

Theresa tilted her head and looked at him with one yellow eye, which seemed to click rapidly in its socket. Then laughed her short, hoarse laugh and nodded her head. "Yes. Yes, you can come in . . . ."

The hinges murmured as she drew open the door, and Vincent stepped across the threshold. Immediately he was assaulted by the vileness of the place. His nostrils were stung by an odor that suggested decaying garbage and excrement, and he involuntarily put his hand to his face. Theresa smiled at this, displaying a set of long teeth that looked like a yellow picket fence in her mouth. Her face was a maze of intersecting lines and folds of sagging flesh. Wisps of gray hair shot out from beneath a red bandanna wrapped tightly about her head. Her eyes bulged like a buzzard's, her mouth a colorless slash beneath a large, shapeless nose.

He noticed that the temperature in the room was unusually cool and there was a dampness in the air. Despite the open window at the end of the room, the room was dim and bleak, and its contents seemed to flicker under the glow of a single candle in a wall sconce. A coal oil stove sat like a dark beast in the far corner; next to it lay a fringe-covered table; a chair draped with a dingy oilcloth rested close to an old chest with leather straps.

Other than these, the room was bleak, barren. The dim light seemed to leech the color from the place, and it was coolly damp. Theresa moved to close the door behind him, and he saw for the first time another door at the opposite end of the room. It could have been a closet, but Vincent was immediately reminded of the bedroom door, which Tomaso had seen many years before. Thinking of Antonio, cold and pallid and still, made Vincent himself feel very cold.

Theresa was staring at him as he looked at the bedroom door. "What do you want here?"

"I came to Sicily to track down my relatives, to meet them. I heard stories about you, and I wanted to see you . . . to see if . . ."

The old woman cocked one eyebrow up. "What *kind* of stories?"

Vincent wanted to fabricate a lie, but the words would not come. Instead, he heard himself blurt out the words, "Your son . . . your son, Antonio. He was . . ."

A fire was now burning behind the woman's yellow eyes. "Yes, he was sick. He is still sick. But that is none of your business." Her voice was even and controlled.

"I'm sorry, I know that. It's just that maybe I could help somehow." Vincent looked around the dreary room. "A different place to stay, perhaps . . ."

Theresa laughed humorlessly. "Why do you plague me so? You are like the rest of them. You cannot leave me alone, can you?"

"But Tomaso said he's tried to find you, to help in some way," said Vincent. He felt vaguely uneasy as he spoke to the old woman. Her voice seemed too controlled, her reactions did not seem to be completely appropriate. He interpreted the signs reluctantly, but could not help but feel that Theresa was mad as a hatter.

Theresa's expression had changed again. She now appeared to be upset, agitated. "Tomaso knows where I am. He pays for this place, generous man that he is." She spat on the floor viciously.

"*Pays* for it? Here? Why?" Nothing made sense now. Why would the old woman lie like this? Why would Tomaso lie? Or Victoria?

"It is too hard to explain. Stay out of it. Stay out before you cannot escape from it."

"From what?" said Vincent. He was thoroughly confused, although the woman's manner had begun to make him uneasy, and he watched her closely.

"You will go now," she said. It was not a question.

"Where is Antonio?" he said quickly. "What happened to him?" He stepped forward one step, and the old woman backed away, nearer to the closed bedroom door. He was about to take another cautious step when he noticed that the light in the room seemed to be dying out, or at least growing perceptibly dimmer. Soft noises seemed to be growing up out of the shadows—scraping sounds, scuttling, clicking sounds from within the walls.

Theresa eyed him as he paused to listen.

"Is he here?" said Vincent, pressing her, trying to ignore the sounds. "Is Antonio here? Can I see him"

"*See* him? You do not *want* to see him."

Her words stopped him as he imagined her reason for saying them.

"But you don't understand," he said, taking another step closer to the door behind Theresa.

"It is *you* who doesn't understand," she said, and the rasping in the walls grew louder.

Vincent imagined the size of the rats that were large enough to sound like that. His arms goosefleshed suddenly, his pulse quickened. He felt a tension building in the air between them, like the charged air in an electrical storm. "You must tell me," he said.

"Tomaso, he took my son once . . . but I got him back. And no one will ever get near him again. Not as long as I live." Her eyes brightened, clicked rapidly at the wall nearest Vincent, and the scuttling sounds grew louder. "Now you must go. Quickly!"

"I can't go," he said and moved toward the door.

"No!" she cried out, as if she could read his thoughts, and stepped in front of him.

He reached out to move her aside and she grabbed his arm. Fingernails bit through his shirt and forearm and he was surprised to feel the strength of her grip. He jerked his arm free and tried to push her out of the way. Suddenly the only thing that mattered was to see what was behind the door, the place she guarded like Cerberus. Theresa was pressing herself against him, and he moved to ease her aside when her hand came up and raked him across his cheek. Long nails burrowed into his face like needles. She was so close now that he could smell her foul breath, her musty clothing. He shoved her away from him and she stumbled back, falling over the old chest.

As she crumpled to the floor, Vincent wheeled about and grabbed the doorknob, twisted it, and shouldered into the door. It swung open and he almost fell into the room. Instantly he was stricken by the stench in the air. It was thick and it clung to the insides of his mouth and nose; a hot column of bile tried to surge up his throat. He fought the sensations as he looked down to see Antonio's outline beneath a yellowed sheet on the bed beside the door.

Theresa stirred in the outer room. He heard her scrambling to her feet, moaning like a wounded animal, just as he reached down and pulled the sheet from the bed.

As if paralyzed, his arm stopped in midmotion; the raised sheet revealed a brown, wizened husk—a thing that had once been a man. It was exactly what Vincent had expected, what he had feared he would find. Old Theresa, old crazy Theresa still thought he was sick. Oh God . . . Vincent felt his stomach convulse as he looked at Antonio's shriveled body. It lay in the bed staring up at the ceiling through dark, eyeless sockets. Pieces of mummified flesh hung from its bones like dry-rotted rags.

Then there was a blur of motion in the doorway. He looked up to see Theresa rushing at him from the shadows, her eyes wide and glazed over. There was a glint of something shiny in her hand.

Instinctively, he raised his arms to his face, and almost immediately felt something cold slide into his wrist as Theresa crashed into him. Pushing her away from him, Vincent saw the blood streaming down his arm. Theresa drew back her hand and he felt metal grind against bone as she raised the blade to slash again. Everything seemed to be happening in slow motion now. He grabbed her knife-wielding arm and squeezed the dry, loose flesh of her wrist, forcing the tip of the knife away from his face. It seemed incredible, like a nightmare, that she was actually trying to kill him. He could hear her grunting and snarling like a rabid animal, thrashing and kicking at him as he struggled against her fury.

His arm was bleeding steadily and pain had started to radiate from the wound and surge up his shoulder and neck. He heard a voice calling out his name as if from a great distance. There was something pounding at the front door. The walls were alive with rustling, scuttling noises. Theresa thrashed violently, trying to free her knife hand. She fell against him heavily, and off-balance, he felt himself go down under her considerable bulk.

As they fell, the knife became tangled in the folds of a ragged mantilla about Theresa's shoulders and, as they struck the floor, Vincent expected to feel the cold, puncturing kiss of its tip. He heard his name called out again, just as he put his hand to Theresa's throat and shoved her away from him. She gagged and shook her head viciously, trying to bite at his hand; he brought up his knee and pushed savagely into her abdomen. Her breath rushed out of her lungs and she fell back away from him, rolling over on her face.

There was a muffled cry as she tried to suck in fresh air, then the old woman tried to struggle up to her elbows, failed, and collapsed. Vincent crawled over to her stilled form and pushed her over, staring at a small trickle of blood at the corner of her mouth. Her yellow eyes were open, but they saw nothing. Her breath bubbled feebly in her breast. Lifting the mantilla, Vincent saw the hilt of her knife marking an entrance just beneath her rib cage. Theresa convulsed once, and was still.

His own breath caught in his chest, and his pulse jackhammered in his ears. Everything blurred momentarily, as if he saw the scene in soft focus. There was sound in the front room, as if very distant. The door swung open and footsteps rattled into the room. He heard Victoria's voice calling out his name. Looking up he saw her, standing in the open doorframe, her eyes riveted upon the scene.

"She's dead," he heard himself say, his voice sounding far away.

"Oh God, no . . . " whimpered Victoria. "What have you done?"

"It was an accident," he said. "She tried to . . . "

"I shouldn't have lied to you, Vincenzo. . . ." Victoria stood rigidly in the doorway; her eyes became vacant, flat.

"Lied? About what?"

"Tomaso *did* take her son. The doctors said he was dead, and Tomaso took him to the catacombs. . . . Oh God, forgive me. . . . I'm sorry, Vincenzo. . . ." Victoria buried her face in her hands, her voice melting into choked sobs, but Vincent was not listening.

He had just looked to the bed, where the thing that had been Antonio was starting to sit up.

R. A. Lafferty looks at the world, not through a glass darkly, but through a glass splintered. Buried beneath a style that no one has yet been able to dissect with any real success without killing it, there is a melancholy and wry grin that is able to twist what is known (or possible) into something as yet unseen by the human mind.

There is humor, to be sure.

But scattered throughout the punchlines, the stories, the asides that seem to smirk at that which has come before, there are implantations of what appears to be cast-off material that, when constructed on the foundation of a last line, contain more shudders than the best Techni-color vampire.

It's an aftereffect.

Like a razor that summons pain after the blood has been spilled.

SPLINTERS

by R. A. Lafferty

The three town-and-country men kept loose hours, so it was just one o'clock in the morning when they began to talk of going fishing at once.

"It would help if we knew what the weather would be for the next few hours," Charles Penstock said. "If it will be fog, we can go and jug for bullhead catfish on Silly Ghost Cove on Keystone Lake. If it will clear to a quick frost, we can drag for walleyes on Tenkiller. Or we can dynamite for pond pickerel on Oolagah."

"If it is heavy dew, we can spear frogs on Euchie," Ed Rivet said. "What did the weatherman give on the evening news?"

"He gave predictions that are now three hours old," Otto Pankration said. "That's too old. We'll just have the weatherman up and see what he says now. He might be intuitive and hit it sharp if we get him out of his sleep."

"What are you going to do, Otto, phone Voiles and wake him up?" Penstock asked.

"More than wake him up, I'll bring him here. Ah yes, I'll bring him here," Otto said calmly. But Otto was shaking in a nervous sort of passion. That meant—well, it meant that he was being excessively Ottoish. Penstock and Rivet looked at each other.

Oh, oh! they thought, almost audibly and almost in concert. Here we go again with a slammer! How can Otto outdo Otto tonight?

Otto Pankration was sometimes an imposing man, and that was his public reputation. But sometimes he was a dubious venture of a fellow. The latter was most often the case when he was with his cronies Penstock and Rivet.

"So bring the weatherman here then, Otto," Penstock said.

"Ah yes, well, you see this high-voltage assembly here—" Otto began.

"The one by which you call spirits from the vasty deeps, as you said the night before last?" Ed Rivet asked. "It is impressive and expensive-looking, yes, and you should be able to use it as a prop for some good illusions. But it looks like an electric furnace to me, and not a high-voltage assembly at all."

"It looks like it, and it isn't," Otto answered. "Well then, to the business at hand." He turned on the mechanism that looked like an electric furnace and wasn't. It didn't spark, it didn't flash. It growled and hummed a little bit. That was all.

And a man was standing there, bare-shanked and angry, and apparently just tumbled out of his sleep. All right, pretend to be unimpressed! Pretend to be blasé about it all. A man had materialized in the room right there! Otto had outdone Otto again tonight. Whether or not the feat should come undone later, it was absolutely top stroke now.

The bare-shanked and angry and confused man was Hector Voiles, the most noteworthy of the local TV weatherpersons. Well, was Hector really there, or was he a projection? Or was he present and yet unsubstantial in some other way?

"How have you brought me here, Pankration?" Hector wheezed. "You could at least have let me put on pants."

"Think 'pants,' Hector, and you will be wearing pants," Otto blared. "Pants are the slightest of illusions at best. Now tell us what the weather will be for the coming hours."

"But I haven't the reports here, or the charts, or even the instruments."

"You are yourself the instrument," Otto said. "Be intuitive! Tell us what the weather will be. Then you can go back to bed."

This wasn't in Otto's big home. That was sort of above them and around the corner. It wasn't in Otto's laboratory either. It was a small room, half underground, fitted out for the comfort of Otto and his cronies, and otherwise filled with a jumble of instruments and equipment that seemed to be out of present use. This was Otto's Little Den. Or it was Little Otto's Den.

"It is overcast and misty now," Hector Voiles said. The light didn't pick him out very well in that room, and indeed the room was poorly lighted. Or else they were all low-resolution persons tonight. "But it will clear within an hour, and then it will quick-frost. Quick-frost, yes, but only at ground level will it freeze. At instrument level it will not fall below thirty-seven degrees. And for a fortnight hence the weather will be good for eidolons. Oh I wonder why I said that? I wonder what I meant?"

"Thank you, Voiles," Otto Pankration said. "Quick-frost you said, and whatever else you said doesn't matter. Leave now."

"I don't know how," said Hector, the bare-shanked weatherman.

"Go the same way you came," Otto said with a mean edge to his voice.

"I can't. I don't know how I came here," said the suddenly shivering Hector.

"Be intuitive. Divine a way," Otto said. "Go from us now and go back to bed."

Hector Voiles the weatherman became unsubstantial and unhinged. He unmaterialized, and he was gone. And Otto Pankration, Charles Penstock, and Ed Rivet loaded into Ed's car to go to Oolagah Lake to dynamite for pond pickerel. The dynamiting goes so much more crisply when there comes a quick frost.

How would Otto outdo Otto on that one? Sluff it off if you can, but it had been a pretty good trick. Otto had materialized a known man against that man's will. He may have used TV data to build the prospectus for a projection, but it was not a TV image that was projected. Hector Voiles did not appear bare-shanked and newly awakened and bumbling on TV. Hector had been caught in the actual moment. He had been jerked out of his sleep and brought to Otto's Little Den, or to Little Otto's Den.

But it was hard in ordinary circumstances to think of Otto Pankration as a little man, for he was quite large.

What would Otto do for an encore now? How would he top the materialization of Hector Voiles?

Well, he didn't really top it. It was already tops. What he did next was materialize two slightly more interesting people. One of these he materialized publicly, the public being those two cronies Charles Penstock and Ed Rivet. But the other he materialized privately, for himself alone. He dipped the dipper for TV persons again.

"I am not restricted to them," Otto explained, "but they are handy objects to sight on and to orient my equipment on. And, of course, I am still experimenting. I will grab and project TV persons, but I will not take them in their TV attitudes."

He next took Barry McNary, that local TV pundit and all-points expert who was so filled with urbanity and scope and interest. He took Barry as he was in the early-morning hours (this was the following early morning), but he didn't take him bare-shanked or bewildered.

Barry was there suddenly, in Little Otto's Den, in a rich crimson dressing gown, smoking an in-style pipe whose genuine aroma filled the cluttered room. You cannot fake an aroma like that. And Barry McNary brought his own setting with him when he came. He was in his own easy chair, reading a book of his own, with his own side table beside him and his own midnight Tokay at hand. And he glanced at the three town-and-country men with absolute boredom. Then he continued his reading, not for effect, but because it was his pleasure. Little Otto might materialize Barry there, but there was no way that he could compel the interest of this pundit.

"Barry McNary, pundit and punko, you will answer questions for us now," Otto said ponderously. "Aye, and you will do tricks as I order you to do them. Do you know any reason I am not able to order you to do tricks?"

"The reason is that I am not here," Barry said, "and I have no knowledge of this romp, nor interest in it. Hound dogs, in some manner you have got hold of the equivalent of an old and discarded undershirt of mine to worry and toss. So worry it then, dogs! But it is long discarded, and I am not in it."

Otto tried again and again to dominate Barry McNary, and he got nowhere. Barry would not answer at all, or he would answer demolishingly. Barry McNary was whipping Little Otto at every turn. A projection should not be able to whip its projector and constructor like that. Barry had a dangerous validity about him even though he said that he wasn't there. It was bad enough to be whipped by a commanded and controlled thing who didn't act as if he were controlled. It was even worse to be whipped by a mere shadow, or by a mere discarded undershirt. Then Barry McNary left him without being dismissed, and he refused to return.

Still and all, Otto had materialized a second known man, one of more moment than the first one, Hector Voiles. Who else in town was doing any authentic materializing at all? And, as Otto said, he was still experimenting with these new techniques.

Then Otto materialized still another TV person, Evangeline Aster, a real sparkler. He materialized Evangeline privately, telling no one about it, not even his two close cronies. Of course, he was proud to be able to materialize and summon and command such a sparkler as Evangeline, but the pleasure he wanted with her was private.

Otto brought Evangeline to him every night for a week. But it started a little slowly.

"The rule is that a person brought here by me must obey my every command," Otto said at an early summons. "I made that rule, just as I made you to come here."

"Oh let's just forget the whole thing," Evangeline said. This was the second night of their encounter and Evangeline was in woolies, though she had been in scanties the first night, not expecting to be transported. "I really don't like it here at all and I want to go back. Let me go."

"You and I are going to have one of the great affairs of the century, Evangeline," Otto said. "Now, to make up for lost time, I will force you to be in rapport with me."

"Forced rapport is no rapport at all," Evangeline said, like one reciting an axiom. "This isn't like you, Mr. Pankration, and it surely isn't like me."

"No. It isn't *like* us. It *is* us," Little Otto said. Wait a minute! Dr. Otto Pankration had the name of being a witty and interesting man. How do you square that with the Otto of these encounters?

But farther than that, Dr. Otto Pankration had the reputation of being absolutely courteous, of being just as absolutely uninvolved, of being a man with no crudity in him at all. Moreover, he was completely faithful to the memory of his dead wife. But Otto-in-the-flesh here was the hot-breathing opposite of that.

And Evangeline Aster, that beautiful sparkler of a woman (she had once coined the name "The TV Sparkler" for herself), she had always been a consummate comic. She was even that still more rare thing on the current scene, a clean comic, a comic with class (she also had coined that phrase for herself). Evangeline had style, she had probity, she had a husband on an important foreign mission at the moment.

(A comic with class? This baggage here?)

She had known Dr. Otto Pankration for five years. But she hadn't at all known this Little Otto who had summoned her to these cluttered quarters here.

"I have a fine old name, one of the most respected of the ancient names of Europe—Pankration," Little Otto said. "But it is really the name of a wrestle named 'Rough and Tumble.' Let us tumble now, Evangeline."

"Oh let's just forget the whole thing," Evangeline said dully. How could this living sparkler seem so dull?

"You and I, Evangeline, we are to have one of the great affairs of the century," Otto said again, "and I believe that we are falling a little behind schedule. Let's pick up the pace and make up for lost time and passion."

So they did. They carried it through. And, for a week there, they had one of the great affairs of the century. Well, maybe it was a bad century. And maybe the great affairs are pretty ordinary when they are stripped down.

After the fifth night, Evangeline stopped watching it. She stopped *watching* it? But she was *in* it, wasn't she?

Evangeline Aster went to see Dr. Sigmund Izzersted. She was about to enter the great marble portals of his famous Coucherie when she heard the doctor call to her in a curious small voice.

"Oh Miss Aster, were you coming to see me?" The voice came from that little side street (it was more a shady lane) that ran along the north boundary of the Izzersted complex. "Just come through this little door in the wall and into my special consulting room and we will have a consultation," the doctor said.

"I never saw that door in the wall before," Evangeline told him. "I don't even believe that I can go through a door that little. Well, I came down sort of to see you, but you're so expensive that I just don't know whether I can afford another session."

"Oh I pay no attention to money," the little doctor said. (Little? No one had ever thought of him as little before), "since money impinges nowhere into the psychology of persons and is of no major interest to them. What have I been charging you?"

"A hundred dollars an hour or part of an hour. It's always at least two hundred dollars a session even if it lasts no more than eight minutes—you know, four minutes in one hour and four minutes in another."

"Oh that's way too much, Miss Aster," Dr. Izzersted said. "I couldn't afford to go myself at that rate. I don't make enough. How about two dollars for as long as the session takes?"

"Are you kidding, doctor?"

"Miss Aster, no! When a psychologist starts kidding, well, that blows him for a psychologist. He might as well break up and be done with it."

They went through the little door in that wall along the shady lane. The consulting room that they came into was quite small, and Evangeline said that the couch looked like a doll couch.

"It will fit you," the doctor said. "Lie down."

Evangeline lay down on the couch and it fit her.

"Your problem, your problem, ah yes," Dr. Izzersted said. "You have been sleeping in woolies for the past few nights, and you never slept in woolies before in your life. You don't understand it, and neither do I."

"How did you know that I had been sleeping in woolies?" Evangeline asked.

"Ah yes," Dr. Izzersted began again. "It is a series of very realistic dreams you have been having, and you are thoroughly ashamed of the role you are playing in them. But you justify yourself by saying that it is not you in the dreams. It is somebody else. You are merely watching while your body cavorts through the episodes. And then you have ceased even to watch them. Is that what you are trying to tell me?"

"I haven't told you anything yet; but yes, that's the case. Why is this consultation room so little, and why does it seem to be in a different place? Yes, I watch myself, or somebody else who is got up to look like me, doing these things, as I might watch them in a drama. But I watch them from the outside. On the other hand, it is myself who does them, for I am bruised and worn from them every morning. Did you know that great affairs of the century are very bruisy? But, on still another hand, there is something secondhand about my bruises, as though they were transferred to my body from another one."

"Bubbly, mighty bubbly, Miss Aster," Dr. Izzersted said. "Do you know that some days are very good for blowing soap bubbles (I blow a lot of soap bubbles in my business), and some days are terrible for it? Yes, on a bad day you can add all the glycerin and gloop that you wish to the mixture and you will still not be able to blow decent bubbles. And some fortnights are good for flying eidolons; but most times are very poor for it. This is an excellent fortnight for flying them. I don't know why this should be."

"What is an eidolon?" Evangeline asked.

"It was an eidolon of yours, Miss Aster, and not yourself, that carried on one of the great affairs of the century with the eidolon of a prominent man. What we are really having this fortnight is an eidolonic epidemic. But I wasn't sure that the primaries were aware of their own eidolons. You seem to be, to some extent, aware of your own."

"Then I'm not responsible for what my eidolon does?"

"Of course you're responsible for it, Miss Aster. There is something wrong going on in you, and that's the way it comes out."

"But I haven't done anything wrong."

"But you are *going* to do something wrong, murder or arson or some such. And eidolons sometimes blow before the wind and arrive at a crux before their primaries."

"And these eidolons have separate bodies?"

"Very infrequently do they have substantial bodies, Miss Aster. Shadow bodies mostly. But this fortnight, as I say, is very bubbly, very good for flying eidolons. I believe there are at least half a dozen solid ones flying in this city of a half million. That is an unusually large component. But it isn't so unusual over a long haul. Every undertaker, after a fortnight such as this, gets bodies that he knows are simply not authentic. Oh they have meat and they have weight, but they are incompletely and sketchily done.

"And there are numerous cases where a body is definitely identified as a person. And then the living person will appear and assert his living identity, and where does that leave the dead and sketchy body? But the first identification will not necessarily have been mistaken. The bodies will (save for the sketchiness of one of them) be bodies of the same person. Even the fingerprints will be identical except that, ah—"

"Except that *what?*"

"Ah change of subject. The way out of your dilemma, Miss Aster, is to junk your eidolon, which is only a splinter of you anyhow. Ah I see a gleam in your eye. Yes, it would be vivid publicity, I suppose. Throw it screaming off a great and prominent height (and you have always had such a terror of heights!), and then you can reappear—"

"Oh yes! I think I recognize it now. It's been done before. And it works."

"You first came into prominence, Miss Aster, as a junior hog-calling champion of Sebastian County, Arkansas, I believe."

"Can we not forget that, doctor?"

"But you are proud of your powerful and blood-curdling scream, with which you won that championship. You believe that, in a more dramatic situation, it might be—"

"Yes, yes, and do I ever have a more dramatic situation in mind for it! It will work, I know that it will."

Evangeline had her genuine sparkle on her now when she saw a shining opportunity. And Dr. Izzersted, who was smaller today than he usually was, had a queer gleam on him like, well, like glycerin in a soap-bubble solution. Yes, he was just a little bit iridescent. He was incompletely and sketchily done. He was not quite as authentic as he might have been. You couldn't exactly see through him, but he did fracture the light a bit.

"Does the real Dr. Izzersted know about you?" Evangeline asked.

"Yes he does," said Little Sigmund," though he came to the knowledge of me with extreme difficulty. He uses me a lot in his studies. I became the analogue for the splinters of many people. What the real Dr. Izzersted doesn't know is that I also use *him* a lot in *my* studies. And yet I *am* the real Dr. Izzersted. All the splinters are of the same authentic wood. If I'm not he, then who am I? Will you time your event for the ten o'clock news?"

"Oh yes, I think so. I believe that it would be the best timing, to do it just a few minutes before the news. Then maybe I will be identified by a bulletin while the program is going on. And then, while they are still staggering from that, I'll appear. I'll electrify everybody, that's what I'll do. Oh thank you, thank you!"

"That will be two dollars, Miss Aster."

"What? You'd actually demand money from a woman on her way to a screaming and plummeting death? Oh you cheese, you cheese!"

Those town-and-country men, Charles Penstock and Ed Rivet, had gone to visit Little Otto Pankration at a loose hour. They knocked at the door of Little Otto's Den, and the door was opened.

They were startled, though, that it was opened by Mr. Pankration himself. But were not Mr. Pankration and Little Otto Pankration the same person? Probably they were. Nevertheless, the two town-and-country men were startled.

"Oh Mr. Pankration," Ed Rivet said, "we were really looking for Little Otto." And then he felt very foolish.

"Oh go away," Pankration growled. "Vagabonds, out-of-season killers of game, dynamiters of fish, spooks of whatever sort, be gone from here. You are only rags and splinters of men who are dead and gone. In any case, I am locking up the storeroom now."

"Mr. Pankration," Ed asked, "What is that thing that looks like an electric furnace, and isn't?"

"It *is* an electric furnace," Mr. Pankration said. He pushed the two town-and-country men out of the doorway, came out the door himself, and closed and locked it behind him. Then he walked around the corner to his main establishment. And Charles Penstock and Ed Rivet stood uncertainly in the road.

Then the door of Little Otto's Den unlocked and opened again, and Little Otto looked out and hissed for them to come in. Still feeling a little foolish, they entered.

"It should be foggy in the next hours," Charles Penstock said. "Let's go to Silly Ghost Cove on Keystone Lake and jug for bullhead catfish."

"I can't go, not anymore, not anywhere," Little Otto said. "He won't let me out of the complex at all."

"Who is *he?*" Ed Rivet asked. "Isn't he really just yourself? How will he keep you from going out? Will he hide your shoes, like the Ozark farmer did to his wife?"

"Not my shoes, my feet," Little Otto said. "He hid my feet."

The other two saw that it was true. Little Otto hadn't any feet. He wouldn't be able to go with them.

"He says that you are spooks," Little Otto said. "He says that your primaries are dead men, and that makes you dirty."

"That's true," Ed Rivet admitted. "You knew that. Ah we're sorry about your feet."

Charles Penstock and Ed Rivet went away from there to Silly Ghost Cove on Keystone Lake to jug for bullhead catfish. It was a favorite spot of theirs.

The pundit Barry McNary gave this account the next morning on his program, "The Morning Sun":

A night of horror rampages on into the glare-eyed dawn. The plummeting, screaming death of the beloved Evangeline Aster was horror enough for any night. But there have been flesh-crawling (yes, and pseudoflesh-crawling) developments since then. And now we are all in stunned and sordid amazement.

Evangeline Aster, that sparkler of the picture tube, that comic with class, had been in unusually high spirits only ten minutes before the tragedy. She had laughed as she told it: "Kids, am I ever going to pull one! I will stand them all on their ears. This stroke is going to put your favorite sparkler into the Big Time. And it will all be good, clean fun. What is more good, clean fun than an absolute horror stroke?"

Then, at nine forty-seven last night, Evangeline climbed the parapet gingerly (she was afraid of heights) and seemed to be talking to someone there, though she was alone. Then she seemed to stumble (it was almost as if she were pushed by invisible hands), and she fell to her screaming death from the veranda of the forty-ninth-floor Penthouse Club.

She was utterly smashed in the street below. But many observers, *including myself,* will swear that her scream was repeated in the high air again and again for several minutes after her horrifying death.

Naturally, considering the close friendship of Miss Aster with the people of this station and her frequent appearances here, her violent death of only thirteen minutes before was the main topic on our ten o'clock news last night. But it was at ten twenty-seven, almost at the end of the news program, that something almost more shocking than Evangeline's death took place.

Evangeline walked into our studio and onto camera, alive and sparkling. Or it seemed as if she did. Something walked into the studio, possibly alive in a gaudy way, and sparkling in a funky manner. And, at first, it looked like Evangeline. I myself had no doubt that it was herself—not for ten seconds or so.

"The reports of my death have been greatly exaggerated," she said. "Oh isn't there any way to update that line? Surely a lot of fuss has been made about an imposter. It is not I who have died, as all of you can see. Here I am, more sparkling and radiant than ever!"

But then something went out of the apparition. It became not Evangeline Aster, but a horrible and revolting caricature of her. What was it? What was it? It was alive. It walked and it talked. And then it staggered and whimpered.

"She tried to push me off," the apparition whined. "That's what scared me. I didn't think she'd do that to me."

We closed the station down then and got the horrible situation off camera.

But the horrible situation has been examined all through the night, from that hour to this, and soon there will be nothing of her left to examine. The horrible situation has been examined by a cosmologist, a meteorologist, a physician, and by a parapsychologist. The walking and talking apparition was, by every basic test, Evangeline Aster. And yet it wasn't Evangeline as solidly as was the dead body that was in police morgue. But the apparition even had the fingerprints of Evangeline, except that, ah—change of subject.

"The weather has been good for eidolons for more than a week now," the meteorologist said. "Rarely is the weather good for them; most of the time it is no good for them at all. We weathermen believe that they (eidolons, fragments, splinters, ghosts, they are sometimes called) are always present. But most of the time they cannot be seen or heard. And in times of very special weather they can be."

"No, it isn't alive," the physician said. "It is apparently an echo or a mirage. It is associated with a certain amount of matter, but it's a loose and perhaps accidental association. No, there's nothing here. It's all illusion."

"Oh it's plain enough," the parapsychologist said. "It's a 'clearly manifest psychic splinter,' presently impaired by the destruction of its primary. Psychic splinters are so ordinary that they are almost the rule. They're personality fragments, no more than that. They are 'partially manifest psychic splinters' when they are poltergeists or other ghosts or presences. But a 'clearly manifest psychic splinter' like this one isn't encountered often. I'd like to study her for a long time, but there's only a couple of minutes left for it.

"There has been something going on around town lately that is almost like a burlesque of my own work, and she's part of it," added the great parapsychologist Dr. Otto Pankration.

"A lot of me went with her when she went," the apparition said. "It was like turning out the light in me. She tried to throw me off the parapet. How damned inconsiderate of her anyhow! She told me one thing; 'Keep screaming, keep screaming.' Oh I'd forgot that she told me that. I kept it up for a while and then I stopped. I'll start again."

"It is pseudo-organic," the cosmologist said. "It is mostly made of glycerin and it is evaporating. Ah glycerin, like we used to put in the soap-bubble mixture. No, there's really nothing to her, gentlemen."

"She tried to throw me off the parapet, but I threw her off instead," the apparition said. "I thought that was kind of a joke on her. But she told me to keep screaming on my way down, and I'm on my way down now. I forgot, and I stopped screaming. But I'll start again now."

The apparition has disappeared. It had become an absolutely horrifying caricature of Evangeline at the moment of its disappearance.

But the screaming continues, continues, continues—

"How long?" we asked.

"No telling," the parapsychologist said. "It's become immaterial now, and there is no way you can make an immaterial entity shut up, particularly if it is obsessed by a single idea or instruction. The Hollbecker phantom in Germany has been screaming for fifty years now, but nobody pays any attention to it anymore. It is just like any other industrial noise."

Oh my God, that scream, that scream, that scream! Will any of us get used to it in even fifty years?

Robert Bloch.

The name itself is an introduction that should need no elaboration.

If the field of fantasy has its surfeits, they must include vampires and werewolves and chain-dangling ghosts. . . and at the top of the list, deals with the devil. The main problem with the latter is that once the trick has been worked, the story is done. The devil either wins or loses, depending upon the wits of the protagonist dumb enough to enter the deal in the first place. The story hangs, then, on how it is done.

Robert Bloch, like all those in the field, has done his share of deals with the devil. Unlike the others, however, this time he has constructed a story that does not end with . . . the end. Once again we have a lingering, an afterimage, an unwritten line that provides more punch than . . .

PICTURE

by Robert Bloch

Farley found the Devil through the Yellow Pages.

Of course, he had to make inquiries first. He haunted the reserved section of the public library until he found an old book containing the right spells. Then he shopped around for chalk and candles and a lot of smelly herbs. By the time he drew a pentagram and set the candles out and burned the herbs Farley was pretty beat.

Next he chanted the spells and conjured up Astaroth—
a rather ugly customer who rode a dragon, carried a viper
in his left hand, and seemed very uptight about being
disturbed.

But Farley kept safely inside the pentagram and told
him what he wanted.

Astaroth shook his head. "Not my department," he
said. "You'll have to talk to the boss."

"And where can I find him?"

"Locally he goes by the name of Dr. Horner. He's in
the book."

"Can I tell him you sent me?"

"Tell him and be damned," said Astaroth. "I'm getting the hell out of here."

And he did.

It took Farley two days just to air out the place
afterward, and he had a rough time squaring things with
the landlady when she complained about the noise. But
finally he picked up the phone book and located Dr.
Horner's name.

Not too surprisingly, he turned out to be a Beverly
Hills psychiatrist.

Getting an appointment was a hassle; the receptionist
did a number about being all booked up until a year from
next Thursday. Then he mentioned Astaroth's name and
it turned out to be the magic word.

"Come in tonight," she said. "Ten o'clock."

So finally Farley found himself in the private office,
face to face with Astaroth's boss.

Dr. Horner turned out to be elderly and a bit on the
short side. The eyes peering from behind heavy glasses
seemed quite normal and there were no unnatural growths
sprouting from his forehead.

"You don't look like the Devil," said Farley.

Dr. Horner blinked. "You don't look like a man suffering from delusions," he said. "But of course when my
receptionist mentioned Astaroth I knew it was my professional duty to see you as quickly as possible. Would you
like to talk about your problem?"

"I'm frustrated," said Leo Farley.

"Aren't we all?" Dr. Horner nodded. "Taxes, inflation, wholesale corruption, retail violence. And on top of everything else, this damned business about malpractice insurance." He broke off abruptly. "Sorry," he said. "Suppose you sit down and tell me."

So Farley told him. About his unhappy childhood— not making top grades in school, not making the team, not making girls. How the war in Nam kept him from college, and how he couldn't enroll when he returned. His parents died in a car crash and he had to go to work in a paint store, even though he was allergic to turpentine.

Then he got into his marriage. Margaret wasn't much for looks and she couldn't cook anything but TV dinners, and though he wanted kids she turned out to be sterile. She was also frigid, a nagger, and a compulsive folk-singer. This latter affliction brought about her death from hepatitis, following the purchase of a secondhand guitar with an infected pick.

So for the past six months Leo Farley had lived alone, a pudgy, middle-aged man whose hair—since he was not a politician—was turning gray. He still worked at the paint store, still ate TV dinners, and it seemed as though all he got out of life was older.

"Ever thought about suicide?" asked Dr. Horner.

"Frequently," said Farley. "Is that your best offer?"

Dr. Horner shook his head. "I'm not suggesting—just wondering. With all the rotten luck you've had through the years, what kept you going?"

"This," said Farley.

He opened his wallet and took out the picture.

Dr. Horner squinted at it through his thick lenses. The three-by-three photo was obviously old and the color was slightly faded, but even so there was no denying the beauty of its subject. The teen-age girl posing full-length in a brief bikini had a voluptuous figure and a sensual, provocative face framed by an aureole of flaming red hair.

The psychiatrist reacted with an unprofessional but highly appreciative whistle. "Who is she?"

"Linda Duvall," said Farley. "That's how she looked when she won the beauty contest back in high school.

Actually, she was even prettier. I cut this picture out of the annual."

"Your girlfriend?"

"I never even met her." Farley sighed. "She only dated jocks. The football team, the basketball team, the track team, guys like that. And, of course, the substitutes."

"Promiscuous, eh?"

"I prefer to think of her as democratic," Farley said. "Though that's just a wild guess. Like I say, I didn't know her."

"But you had a schoolboy crush on her, right?"

"Wrong. A man doesn't carry a picture of a girl in his wallet for twenty years just because of an adolescent hangup. I've looked at it night and day and it still drives me up the wall."

"I see," said Dr. Horner. "So that's why you came to me. You want to get rid of those erotic fantasies."

"No. I want you to make them come true."

Dr. Horner stared at Farley for a long moment. "Then you really did see Astaroth?"

"That's right. And he said you were the boss."

"Astaroth has a leaky mouth." Dr. Horner frowned. "But suppose I could help. Are you prepared to pay the price?"

"Anything you ask. Just get me Linda Duvall."

"What do you intend to do with her?"

Farley explained in detail.

"My, my," said Dr. Horner. "I hope you're up to it! That's a pretty heavy schedule for just one night."

"One night?" Farley scowled. "But I was thinking more along the lines of seven years—"

Dr. Horner shrugged. "Sorry, that's the old contract. We don't use it anymore. In the old days, with only a few clients—people like Faust, you know—we could afford to give them personal attention. But now there's just too many deals to keep track of. I'm afraid one night is all I can offer."

Farley picked up the picture of the red-haired girl and studied it. The sound of heavy breathing filled the room. "I've got to have her," he said. "*Got* to."

Dr. Horner smiled. "I understand."

"Do you?"

"Of course. They don't call me Old Horny for nothing."
He reached into a desk drawer and produced a parchment
covered with crabbed handwriting. "Sign here," he said.

Farley's eyes narrowed as he scanned the document.
"I can't read Latin."

"Too bad. It's really the only civilized language."
Dr. Horner shook his head. "You needn't worry, though—
it's a standard contract. Covers everything except acts of
God. We have the services of some pretty big attorneys."

"That figures," said Farley.

"What's bugging you then? If it's the sight of blood,
don't worry. We can dispense with that formality." Dr.
Horner held out a pen. "Here. All I want is a legal
signature."

Farley took the pen, then hesitated once more.

"Now what?" said Dr. Horner.

"I'll level. You have a reputation for cheating on
your bargains."

"That's a damnable lie!" Dr. Horner said. "I'm not
a crook."

"Seems to me I've heard that before," Farley told him.

Dr. Horner shook his head. "You're getting a fair
deal. One night with the girl in the picture, Linda Duvall.
How could I cheat you?"

"Lots of ways," Farley said. "I tried to locate her
myself, you know, but I came up with zilch. And then I
realized twenty years must have changed Linda as much
as they've changed me. Suppose you find her and I end
up with a fat, middle-aged klutz?"

"She won't be, I promise you."

"For all I know she might even be dead. I don't want
a revived corpse, either."

Dr. Horner chuckled. "Don't worry. She won't be
dead, and she won't be a day older or younger than she is
in the picture. And to anticipate your other objections, I
also guarantee that she won't be mentally or physically
ill, she won't be frigid, and she won't be a lez. Tell you
what I'll do—just to sweeten the deal, I'll make her
a virgin."

"Yeah." Farley licked his lips, then frowned again. "But suppose she hates me?"

"I'll take care of that, too. I give you my word she'll be just as eager as you are."

"You won't make me impotent?"

"What a suspicious mind you have!" Dr. Horner beamed at Farley appreciatively. "I promise you'll be able to perform indefinitely. And definitely, too."

"Then what happens?"

"I'll come for you at dawn."

"But we'll have the night together?"

"Assuredly."

"Just as she is here?" Farley pointed at the picture.

"Exactly."

Farley gripped the pen and signed.

Dr. Horner picked up the parchment and put it back in his desk drawer. "There we are," he said.

"But where is she?"

Dr. Horner smiled. "Linda is waiting for you now—in your apartment."

Leo Farley smiled then too, for the first time. "I hate to eat and run," he said. "Or vice versa. But if you'll excuse me—"

"By all means." Dr. Horner waved Farley to the door. "Drive carefully," he said.

Farley drove very carefully.

One thing he had to say for himself: He was always careful. That's why he'd taken such pains to make sure about the contract—he had no intention of being out-witted. As a matter of fact, he was a little surprised that the Devil didn't have more smarts. The truth was that Farley had cheated *him*.

Now, driving home, it was his turn to chuckle when he thought of how his life story had gone down so easily. Because it hadn't really been such a bummer after all.

His childhood was never unhappy; his parents spoiled him rotten and he was always the biggest bully in the neighborhood. The only reason he didn't do well in school was because he preferred goofing off to studying. He could have been on the football team if he wanted, but he used his time to set up a betting pool instead and made a bundle off his fellow students. His service in Nam was a crock; he'd spent all his time in Saigon as a company clerk by day and a black-market operator by night, which got him an even bigger bundle. And when gambling wiped him out, his parents' death left him a nice chunk of inheritance after he returned. Sure, he'd worked in the paint store, but actually as a silent partner who got 50 per cent of the take. With the chicks through the years he got 100 per cent of the action. And that's what really blew his marriage, when Margaret found out. Slipping her the infected guitar pick was his own idea; it solved all his problems.

Except for Linda Duvall. That part—about the twenty years of frustration—was true. He had the hots for her in school, he had the hots for her all these years, and he had the hots for her now. She was the only thing he wanted that he hadn't been able to get—but he was getting her tonight.

Farley grinned. He'd already damned himself a dozen times over, so there'd been no need for the Devil to make such a bargain. Farley had ripped him off.

Just to make sure, he reviewed the terms of the contract, but he found no loopholes. He was going to get just what he asked for—Linda Duvall, the way she was in her picture, alive, willing, eager. And then—

The mere thought of what was going to happen then set his heart pounding as he parked the car, set his hands trembling as he unlocked the apartment door, set his blood racing as he entered.

But the living room was silent and empty.

For a moment Farley wondered if the Devil had lied to him after all. Then he saw the light in the hall, streaming forth from under the bedroom door.

Of course—that's where she'd be waiting for him. Well, she wouldn't have to wait long.

He ran down the hall, flung the door open, entered.

And there she was.

Farley stared at her. Linda Duvall, in the flesh—a gorgeous redhead, stark naked, sprawled across the bed and smiling up at him in invitation.

The Devil hadn't lied; she was as pretty as a picture. In fact, she was just like her picture.

Leo Farley turned away with a sob and stood waiting for the dawn. There was really nothing else he could do.

Not with a girl who was exactly two inches tall.

Dennis Etchison is a young man who moves extraordinarily quietly through the ranks of fantasy writers, constructing a reputation that will, one of these days, make him an "overnight" success. His stories have been considered by some to be almost stately in their progress toward horror, much like a manservant who moves from room to room in a deserted mansion, seemingly at random until he opens the last door on the last floor. . . .

There is terror in "The Nighthawk," to be sure; but there is also love, an ingredient that does not necessarily dissipate that which has gone before.

THE NIGHTHAWK

by Dennis Etchison

The little girl stood gazing north, toward the rich houses and the pier restaurant that were still faintly outlined through the mist. The high windows captured the white light of the sky in small squares, like a row of mirrors for the gulls; the pilings and struts underneath could have been stiff black legs risen from the sea and frozen in the November wind, never to walk again.

Is Maria coming? she wondered.

She had hurried to the corral first thing, of course, but Pebbles was gone. Maria must have come home early and taken him out, down past the big rocks to the Sea Manor, maybe, or up under the pier to the tidepools by the point at the edge of the Colony. She did not know what time

Maria's school let out, had never asked, but still had always managed to be the first one home; she would be laying out the bridles or patching a break in the fence with driftwood from under the burned-out house by the time Maria came running—always, it seemed. Yes, always. Every time.

She began to wander back along the wet strand, found a stick, and paused to block out a word in the sand—C-O-P-P-E-R—turning round over each letter and humming to herself to keep the chill away. But the fog came settling in now, a thick, tule fog it looked like, and she saw her breath making more fog in front of her face and so hastened the rest of the way with her head down, hearing only the cold breaking of the waves out on the dark, musseled rocks.

She stayed with Copper for as long as she could, leaving extra feed for Pebbles, too, so that Maria would not have to bother when she brought him back. Copper seemed restless, bobbing and pawing the sand, eager to be taken out. She tried to explain that it was too late now for a real ride and instead walked her out and around the cliff-side and back, over the leach line creek that trickled from the cottages to the ocean. The tiny rivulet with its sculptured and terraced bed—she and Maria, trotting the ponies carefully from one crumbling tier to the other, liked to imagine that it was the Grand Canyon. But the truth was that she had no heart for riding, not now. Not with the dark coming on so soon and the fog all around. Not alone.

She was cold and growing colder as she climbed the wooden stairway and let herself in through the side door, the one to the storage room, and then slipped into the house as quietly as she could. She started to close the door on the fog, but decided to leave it ajar for Grandfather, who would probably be coming in soon.

She heard the television voices from the living room, the same ones she always heard when she went into the house after school. They laughed a lot, though there was an edge to the voices whenever they were interrupted by the music or the buzzer, which was almost all the time, it seemed. They were probably pretty nervous, too, about being kept on the program for so long, day after day, week after week; sometimes, of course, one of the voices would say the right things and win enough money to buy its freedom, and then they would have to let it go home and the next afternoon there would be another voice, a new one, to take its place. They always sounded excited and happy when they said a right answer, and then the audience would not laugh and the buzzer would not buzz.

She padded over the jute-covered floor and slipped around the doorway into the kitchen. She stopped with her hands on the refrigerator door. She looked back at the rattan chair and couch, the sandbag ashtrays, the clock and the flying metal geese on the wall, the shiny black panther on the table, the lamp shaped like a Hawaiian dancer, the ivy planter, the kissing Dutch girl and boy, the picture of the crying clown and the ones of the father and mother in the standup frames. She turned away. She opened the refrigerator and poured a glass of Kool-Aid.

"Is that you, Darcy?"

"Ye-es," she called sweetly, *Grandma,* but would not say it.

"Have you seen Maria yet?" She heard the grandmother climbing out of her chair, not waiting for an answer. "I must talk with you, dear. This morning we received a most disturbing telephone call. . . . "

The grandmother was coming, even though the TV was still on. It must be something bad, she thought.

On the other side of the kitchen window the fog was descending heavily, almost like rain. In fact, she heard a tapping begin on the low roof—but no, that would be Grandfather, hammering with his short strokes, scraping his slippers on the rough tarpaper. *Just a minute, I have to talk to Grandfather.* Would that be good enough? She turned from the window to watch the doorway for the black walking shoes, the hem of the flowered dress. Another kind of movement caught her eye, down low by the floor, but she knew that would only be the fog.

There was the hammering on the roof, the plinking of the wind chimes by the geraniums out on the railing of the sun deck, the fog deepening until it, too, could almost be heard settling over the house. There was the slow, unsteady pursuit of the grandmother nearly upon her now.

And something else, something else.

A dull, familiar thumping.

She looked quickly and saw, through the windows, a moving shape approaching along the beach. She knew at once that it was Pebbles. The pony hesitated, breathing steam, and the vapor thinned around him momentarily so that his markings showed clear and unmistakable, like a cluster of moonstones through the white water of a pool at low tide, far out by the broken seawall.

"Got to go," she yelled, *Grandma.* "Maria's got Copper. Ooh, that girl—!"

She darted out and, by the time the refrigerator door had swung shut and before the grandmother could object, had dropped from the deck and was sprinting toward Maria and the pony. It wasn't true, of course; of course not. Maria was riding Pebbles. But it had worked.

"Hey," she called. Then, again, when there was no answer, "He-ey!"

Maria, small and dark atop her pony, reined and turned Pebbles, his hooves slapping the slick, packed sand. She had kept near the water, had not even come close to Darcy's house; but she had had to pass by on the way back, and now she held her body tense and distant, almost as though afraid she might meet something there on the beach— herself, say—with which she knew she would not be able to cope. "Hey, yourself," she said, because she had to say something. But her face did not change.

"Did you stay home today?" tried Darcy. She waited and, trying to make it look like she was not, had not been waiting, leaned forward and watched her feet as they dug down into the sand. She stepped back, and the imprints of her toes began to fill up with water. "Well, were you sick or something?"

"I got to go now," answered Maria.

She was like that. Once, when they were playing and Darcy had said something wrong—it must have been something she had said because nothing had happened, they had only been sitting with their knees up, molding little houses in the sand with a paper cup—Maria had stopped and stared over the water with that smooth, flat face of hers, as if hearing what no one else on the beach or in the world could hear. And then she had said that, the same thing, *I got to go now,* and she had jumped up, brushed off her hands and started running—and not even toward her own house, so that Darcy knew Maria hadn't been called home, even if she couldn't hear it herself. Maria was like that.

The pony started walking.

"You better not ride him anymore today, Maria," yelled Darcy. "Ma-ri-a, he'll get all sweaty and sick for sure, you'll see!"

Maria kept riding.

"Well," said Darcy, staring after, "*I* waited."

At the corral Maria dismounted but did not raise her eyes when her friend finally caught up.

"What do you care about Pebbles," Maria said to her.

Only then did Darcy notice the scratches, fresh and deep, on Pebbles' right flank. Three parallel lines sliced into flesh that was still pink and glistening.

Darcy sucked in her breath. "Maria!" She forgot everything else. "Who did *that?*"

Maria walked away. She trailed her fingers over the makeshift fence, the tarp that covered the hay, and went to sit in the ruins, in the shadows, under the starfish that someone had nailed crucifixion-style to the supports of the big house years ago, before it burned; now the hard, *pointille* arms, singed black at the tips, still clutched tight to the flaking, splintery wood. She put her elbows on her knees and her face in her arms and started to cry.

Copper had sidled over to Pebbles, but the other pony shied away, protecting his flank. Copper snorted and tried to nuzzle. Darcy reached for a blanket to throw over Pebbles, but hesitated because of the wound.

She joined her friend under the house.

After a time Darcy said, "I'll tell Grandfather. He'll get the vet to come over. You'll see."

"No."

Maria was crying deep down inside herself, from a place so protected that there were no sounds and nothing to show, nothing but the tears.

"Well, I'll go get some Zephiran right now from my house. And we'll fix it ourselves. I will if you want me to, Maria."

"No!"

"Maria," she said patiently, "what happened?"

Maria's narrow lips barely moved. "It came. In the night, just like you said."

"What did?"

"You know what. The—the—"

"Oh no." Darcy felt a sinking inside, like an elevator going down too fast; she hadn't felt it for a long, long time. The last had been when she was very small, about the time that the mother and father went away. She couldn't remember the feeling very clearly; in fact, she couldn't even be sure what it was about; surely, she knew, it was about something she did not and could not understand. "Don't you be silly. It wasn't really real." That was right. It wasn't, it wasn't. "Maria, that was only a story. Ma-*ri*-a."

"That was what my Daddy said," the dark girl went on. "But he said you were still evil to make me scared of it." She was beginning to rush the words, almost as though afraid she might hear something and have to go away before she could finish. "You were the one, the one who told me about him, about how he comes at night and sees in your window and if you were bad, then—you know. You know what he does, the Nighthawk."

The Nighthawk. Of course she remembered the story. It had always been just that, a story to scare children into being good, the kind of story thought up by grandmothers to stop too much running in the house and laughing and playing games in bed. But it was also a story you never forgot, and eventually it became a special late kind of story for telling on the beach, huddled close to a campfire, under the stars, seeing who could scare the other the worse, all shivery in sleeping bags, hidden from the unknowable mysteries of a sudden falling star or the sound of wings brushing the dark edge of the moon.

She didn't know what to say.

The two of them sat that way for a while.

"Well, I'll help you take care of him," she offered at last. "You know that."

"It doesn't matter."

"He'll be good as new. You'll see."

"Maybe. But not because of you."

Darcy looked at her friend as though seeing her for the first time.

Maria let out a long sigh that sounded like all the breaths she had ever taken going out at once. "My Daddy's getting a better place. Up in the canyon, by the real stables. He said Pebbles can't stay here till we find out what hurt him. And he says I can't play with you anymore."

"Why?"

"Because."

"But *why?*"

"Because you're the one who scared me of those stories." Her brown eyes were unreadable. "You can't tell me about the Nighthawk, Darcy," she said. "Not anymore, not ever again."

Darcy was stunned. "But I didn't make it happen," she said, her own eyes beginning to sting. "I don't even know what happened to Pebbles. Maybe he—well—" But she was confused, unable to think. She remembered the story from the mouth moving above her in the darkness as she huddled close to her big brother, a long, long time ago, it must have been. "T-there isn't any real Nighthawk, don't you get it? Come on, I thought you were big! You know it, don't you? Don't you?"

"Don't *you?*" said Maria mockingly. "I don't want to have those dreams, like last night. Darcy, I don't want to!"

Darcy's mouth was open and stayed open as she heard a new sound, and it was not the blood pulsing in her ears and it was not the waves smashing out by the seawall and it was not her own heartbeat. She looked over and saw Maria hunch down quickly, struggle to cover her eyes, then jerk herself up—almost wildly, Darcy thought later—

as the sound became loud, louder. Darcy moved her lips, trying to be heard, trying to say that it was only one of those big Army helicopters somewhere above the fog, cruising low over the coastline—they were so much louder than the sheriff's 'copter, their huge blades beating the air like some kind of monster—but Maria was already running. Just like that. In a few seconds she had disappeared completely in the fog.

Grandfather was sorting his tools when Darcy came up. She moved slowly, as though underwater, absently poking at a pile of ten-penny nails, at the chisel, at the claw of the hammer. She had been trying to think of where to begin, but it was no use.

"Well, how goes it today, sweetheart?" he said, when she made no move to go inside.

She knew he would wait to hear her story for today, whatever it might be, before getting around to the next part: the something that might be wrapped clean and special in a handkerchief in his jacket or lying inside on the kitchen table or, if it were another article about horses he had clipped from a magazine, folded and waiting in his shirt pocket. Then and only then would he get onto the serious part. She looked up at him and knew that she loved him.

"Oh—" She wanted to tell. Maybe if she started with a teacher story or a recess story; but she couldn't feel it. "Oh same old stuff, I guess," she said.

He glanced at her, pausing perhaps a beat too long, and said, "The pictures came, the ones we sent away for in the Sunday *Times*. Those prints of the white stallions." He fixed her with his good eye. "Remember?"

She felt a smile beginning in spite of herself. She reached over to help him.

"And I believe your grandmother would like a word with you, Darcy, before you go downstairs."

"I know," she said quickly.

He latched his toolbox, wiped his hands on a rag.

Reluctantly she started inside.

"See you at dinner," he said. "Afterward we can measure them for frames and figure where they should go. All right?"

She turned back.

"Grandpa?"

"Yes?" He waited.

"What—what does it mean when somebody says you're 'evil'?"

He laughed easily.

"Well, Darcy," he said, "I'd have to say it means that somebody doesn't really know you."

She felt her way downstairs. *Now do as you're told.* She made sure to land each foot squarely in the middle of each step. *I'm sure her father knows what's best, leaving it open to the air like that.* That way no part of her would touch the edge. *Remember—but of course you couldn't—* She was aware of a pressure at her heels. *Now why would you ask a thing like that, child? Why can't you leave well enough—* She knew what she would see were she to look back. *You'd better watch yourself, young lady. You're not too old to forget the—* She would see—*I didn't mean anything. I didn't mean anything! Your mama and daddy, rest their souls—* She would see the fog. *Say it.* Curling close. *Say it.* About her ankles. *Say it.* Say it—

"Help me."

She started.

Joel stood there in the semidarkness, one hand extended. The other hand was on the knob to the door next to hers, the door to his room. When her eyes adjusted, she saw that he held something out to her in his stubby fingers.

Without thinking, she took it. A pair of ringed keys, new and shiny. She studied them uncertainly.

Joel picked at a splinter along the doorjamb. As she watched, Darcy made out the bright brass gleam of a new lock.

"It's a dead-bolt," he said, as if that would explain everything. "Can't be forced, not unless you break the frame. The hinges are on the right side, too."

"But—"

"I want you to keep the keys in a safe place. Really safe. Got it?" When she nodded, he added with deceptive casualness. "You want to come in? You hardly ever do anymore, you know."

He opened the door and led her inside, looking like someone who had something terribly valuable to give away but could hardly remember where he had hidden it.

She hadn't seen the inside of her brother's room in weeks, maybe months. Since before she had met Maria. Usually they talked (more correctly, she listened while he talked) in her room, anyway, though, or else she managed to avoid him altogether to lay on her bed, playing her records or writing in her diary or thinking about the horses, the ones in the movie Grandfather had taken her to see, the wild ones leaping through water and fire on a seashore somewhere. It was very much like a dream.

While her own room seemed to be in a perpetual state of redecoration, Joel's remained the same jail-like no color; where she had posters and cutouts to cover her walls, Joel had science and evolution charts and black felt-tip drawings she couldn't understand, marked up and shaded so dark that she couldn't see how he was able to make any sense of them. Still, it all reminded her of something, as it always did; she found herself thinking again about a house with unlocked doors and huge, loving faces bobbing in and out of the darkness over her. And fire, and water, and something else, something else.

The main thing she noticed, of course, was the statue on the shelf over the headboard of Joel's unmade bed. And, as before, it fascinated and frightened her at the same time.

It was a glazed plaster sculpture a couple of feet high, the paint brushed on really fast and sloppily, probably so that it could be sold cheaply in the kind of stores that have pillows and ashtrays with words and pictures of buildings printed on them. Some kind of snake—a cobra, she thought—and it was coiled around what was supposed to be a human skull. Maybe it had come out of the skull, out of one of the eyes; she wasn't sure. But crawling out of the other eye was an animal that looked like a mouse. It was about to attack the snake, to try to bite it on the neck, or maybe to charm it, to hold its attention so that it would do no harm, she didn't know which. The snake was poised, squinting down, his fangs dripping. There was no way of telling which one would win. She had seen another like it once, in the window of a shop in the Palisades where they sold old-looking books and those sticks like Fourth of July punks that smell sweet when you light them. She wondered where Joel had gotten it and why and how much it cost, had even asked him one time, but he had only looked at her funny and changed the subject.

She sat on the edge of the bed.

"Joel," she began, knowing he would jump in about his locks and keys, whatever they were for, if she did not. There were things on her mind now, questions that were as yet only half formed but that needed answers before she would be able to listen and really hear him. "Joel," she said again, trying to find a way to ease into it, "was—was our house always this way? I mean, the way it is now? Or did Grandpa build it over when we were little?"

She glanced around the room, pretending interest in the cluttered walls and cramped ceiling.

"Course it was," he said, casually condescending. "You're thinking about the other place."

"What other place is that, Joel?"

"The first house, the one over by your corral. The place where we lived with Mother and—"

He stopped himself, shot one of his sudden, funny looks at her, as if she had caught him off-guard.

She had an odd feeling then, as if they had begun to talk about something they were not supposed to, and her not even knowing. The feeling attracted her and scared her at the same time.

"You don't go poking around in there, do you?" he asked in a controlled voice. "Not all the way in there, where the house used to be?"

"Anyone can go, Joel. It's right there on the beach. What's left of it."

"You've been in there, underneath there? You've been there before?"

"I've *always* been there before. So what?"

He straightened, his back to her. "You shouldn't, you know. It's not safe."

"What do you mean? Of course it's—"

"There was an explosion once, you know," he said, cutting her off with more information than he had planned to give. "The gas lines are probably still there. Anyway, I don't want you remembering a thing like that. And," he added, as if to cover up, "you ought to stay home more."

"Oh."

She felt a laugh coming on, one of those wild, high ones that she didn't want to stop. She threw herself backward on the bed, her arms over her head. His bed was so bouncy, mounded with all the quilts the grandmother had made for him.

"Safe, not safe," she sang. "Oh Joel, you're just on another one of your *bummers*. I know why you have such bad dreams. You pile on so many blankets, your body heats up at night like a compost heap!"

"Don't you taunt me, Darcy. Don't or I'll—"

There, she had caught him again. *Or you'll what? Send the Nighthawk?*

He turned and stared at her for too long a time, until she stopped laughing and they both grew uneasy. Then he began moving about the room, picking at things, his compass and protractor, the lens cover to his telescope, putting them down again, pacing. It was an unnatural pause; Joel never ran out of crazy things to talk to her about, which was why she always had to be the one to leave.

He faced her again.

"I hear Grandma's pretty mad at you, Darcy." This time he was doing the taunting. The tension was gone from his face now, hidden again just below the surface like one of those sharp, crusted rocks when the tide changes. "What's it about this time?"

"Oh who knows?" It was almost true; the grandmother was pretty nearly always mad at her about something. "I don't know. Why is a mouse when it screams? That probably makes about as much sense." Then, when he didn't laugh, "It was about the ponies, I guess."

"What about the ponies?"

"What do you care?"

"I had a dream about them," he said tightly.

Another one of his dreams. She sighed. She didn't want to hear about it so she went ahead and told about Pebbles. But not the part about Maria. She was not ready to talk about that part yet, least of all to him.

But then she stopped and said, "It was about the corral, your dream, wasn't it? That was where you went. In your dream. *Wasn't* it?"

Sometimes, she did not know why, Joel tried to make himself look like a stone boy; this was one of the times.

"Darcy, I tried to warn you. All of you." And, surprisingly, tears of rage came to his eyes. "I told him, I told *her* to tell him, but she must've thought she could take care of—"

A new thought struck her, cold and fully shaped as a steel bit, and it stayed and would not let go. Perhaps it had been there all along, and only now was she able to feel it fully, its chill, and begin to know what it was.

She said, "What was it that hurt Pebbles?"

There was a ringing silence.

"You know, don't you, Joel? I think you know."

She saw him start to shake. She went on, oddly detached, as if she were watching what was happening through the wrong end of his telescope.

"You know what else I think? I—I think that maybe Mama and Daddy got hurt the same way, a long time ago. I already know they didn't just 'go away,' like everybody says."

She waited.

He did not try to answer. He lost his balance and hunkered close to the floor, by the edge of the bed. His hands clawed into the quilt and pulled it down with him.

Now she did begin to feel afraid. She felt a nervous jolt enter her body, sort of like a charge of static electricity from the air, but she strained to keep breathing, to draw energy from the feeling and not be smothered by it. She had to know.

"Say something!" she said to him.

She saw his face press into the pillow, heard his shallow, rasping sobs. She felt a terrible closeness in her own chest as her breath caught and took hold again. She thought of touching him but could not. Because she never had. Not like that.

"What about—" she began, and this was the hardest part, but it had to be said "—what about the fire? Tell me about the fire, Joel. Tell me about Mother and Father."

I'll help you, I will, she thought, *and never, ever ask again. If only you'll tell me.* And then an answer came, slowly at first and then like something icy melting far away and rushing down to meet the sea. And whether it was his voice or her own she did not know just then, but could only focus on the pictures that appeared in her mind. And the pictures showed the big old house bursting upward into the sky and the boards falling back down again into a new and meaningless configuration on the sand, and she thought of charred pick-up sticks. And before that: within the house a woman, breathing on her knees by the range, the oven open, the burners flickering, and the image rising in a watery, gaseous mirage, and she thought, *Mama.* And before that: a man dying in a hospital bed, his body laced with fresh scars, pink and glistening, and Mama weeping into her closed fists, her hair tumbling forward like brackwater, and a little girl watching, and she thought, *Daddy.* And before that: Daddy's face outside the window the night he brought Copper for her, smiling secretly and then the smile fading, shocked, as something, *something* moved against him beyond the glass, and she turned, turned for her brother who was not there, and she thought *the Nighthawk.* And before that: another face, dream-spinning over them both in the dark when Mama and Daddy were not home, an old face that went on story-telling long after she had fallen asleep, a face she had not let into her room since she had been old enough to lock it out, and again she thought *the Nighthawk.*

She stayed her hand in the air, near his head. Her voice was almost kind; her touch would have been almost cruel.

Outside, the tide was shifting. A single wave, the first of many, rolled and boomed against the retaining wall beneath the house. The bed throbbed once under her, and a pane of dirty glass in the one tiny window shook and rattled.

His head jerked up.

"No!"

"Shh," she said, "she'll hear you."

But of course it didn't matter. The grandmother wouldn't mind. She didn't mind anything Joel did, but only coddled him more. She waited on him, even in the middle of the night sometimes, with soothing cups of soup and those gray-and-red pills that were supposed to be hidden in the back of the top shelf of the medicine cabinet. And if Grandfather heard or cared, he wouldn't do anything about it, either. He left the boy alone, no matter what, to dream his dreams and become what he would. Of course, it was silly to think that Grandfather would be—what? afraid of him? Of course it was. He was only a boy. He was only her brother Joel.

She followed his gaze to the window. The water was rolling in long, slow curls, tipped at the ebb with a pearly-white phosphorescence. But Joel wasn't seeing that.

For the first time she noticed the windowsill.

It was scored with dozens, hundreds of vertical cuts and scratches; the marks shifted and deepened as she watched, as Joel's shadow undulated over the scarred wood. Then she glanced back and saw the burning aureole of the high-intensity lamp behind him, across the room, the one the last tutor, who had stayed the longest, had left on his final visit.

Without warning, Joel lurched up. He stood a moment, turned around, around again, in the manner of an animal who has awakened to find himself trapped in a room with the door shut and the air being sucked from his lungs. Whatever he was looking for he did not see, or even, probably, know how to name it, because just then he did a strange thing, really: He shrank down until he was sitting on the floor, right where he had been standing, without having moved his feet at all. She had seen something like that only once before. It had been the day the grandmother came home from what Darcy knew had been the funeral for the father and the mother; it was as if she now had permission to remember. The grandmother had come in cradling two armloads of groceries. She had stood in the middle of the kitchen, scanning the walls like that, not seeing any of it, least of all the little girl there in the doorway, because Darcy was not what she was looking for, any more than the walls or ceiling or the table and chairs. And she had moved from side to side, turning from the waist, and then the expression had come over her face and she had sunk down onto the linoleum, the bags split and the contents rolling, forgotten, a collapsed doll with its strings cut. She had probably not even known that Darcy was there.

"Use the key," he said to her, "now."

"Why?"

"Do it, Darcy."

She stepped around him carefully and backed to the door.

She saw the way the light played over the sculpture above the bed. The way its eyes shone, forever straining but unable to see the most important thing of all. The way the shadow had grown behind the hood, so that it had come to be larger, darker, more like the monster from a bedtime story than she had ever noticed. She found herself staring into the eyes until she seemed to recognize something; yes, she herself remembered the way it felt, the need to lash out and hurt. What would have happened to her those times if she had not had Grandfather there to help? And there was something else, too, about a snake she had seen in a book, one that had gotten so mad or afraid that it had actually tried to swallow its own tail. . . .

The eyes held her longer than she liked. The sharp eyes that missed nothing, not the other creatures that had come close enough to threaten, not the head that had nurtured it but that was now too old and empty to protect it, not anything but itself, what it had become, the very thing it feared most, the creature of its dreams, the most difficult thing of all to know when the dreams it is given are all nightmares.

She was standing between the door and the lamp. The shadow of Joel's head and body moved and distorted. She drew back involuntarily and, behind her back, her hand brushed the cold doorknob.

She shuddered.

She imagined the fog creeping down the steps from outside, hissing over the floor and pooling by the edges. She pushed the door shut and moved away.

As she moved, her own shadow merged with the other, rendering it somehow less frightening. But the eyes on the headboard shimmered and burned out of the blackness, and she wanted to say, *Does it see, Joel?*

He gestured at her imploringly.

She wished she could say *I got to go now,* the way Maria would have said it, and simply run away as fast as she could. But there was the dark outside, and the fog that followed her down the stairs, waiting to slither under doors and between cracks. There was the grandmother, she knew, waiting at the top of the stars with her words, her stories that would not soothe but only bring more nightmares. She wondered whether the grandmother knew that; probably not, she realized, and that was the most frightening thought of all.

She went to him.

"What do you want me to do, Joel?"

Suddenly she felt her wrist taken in a death grip.

"No, Joel, not me!" she cried, wrenching free. She lunged for the door. "I'm doing it, see, I'm . . ."

She reached up to lock the door, thinking, *Why did he give me both keys?* But it was a good idea to lock it now, yes, she would—

She stared at the door.

Where was the lock? The mechanism was on the outside, as were the hinges. So the keys could not be used to keep anything out.

They could only be used to lock something in.

Very slowly she came back to him, his unblinking eyes following her.

"What do you see, Joel?" she said softly.

There was the room. The window. The luminous waves, aglow now with the pale, dancing green of St. Elmo's fire rippling below the surface. The sky ablaze with a diffused sheen of moonlight above the fog. The glass chill and brittle now, and if she placed her fingers on it they would leave behind five circles imprinted in mist, the record of a touch that would remain to return each time someone sat close and breathed at the night.

Then she was listening to the slapping of the surf, the trembling in the close room, the sound of a sob, and the high, thin weeping on the wind, which might have been the keening of an animal left too long alone.

"Do you hear that, Joel? Is that Copper?"

And she saw the room and that it was only her brother's, and she heard the crying and knew that it came from her own lips, and she reached out her hand to him and felt his moist hair, the bristles at the back of the neck, the fuzz at his temple and the quivering in his cheek and the wetness running to and from his tender mouth and the shaking of his body.

Closing her eyes, she said, "How do you feel?"

He would have told her to go away, just to go away and lock the door and not open it until the morning. But she placed herself between him and the window and said:

"I'm going to stay, Joel. I want to. I'll watch and listen from here and if anyone—if Copper—needs me, I'll know it. Do you understand?"

"No," he said pitifully, after some time had passed.

She kept her eyes shut tight against the fog and the world as she said, "It's all right. I'm only waiting, Joel, for you to go to sleep."

Because, she thought, somebody has to.

And that was the way their first real night together began.

Campbell again.

This time let's note that his wife is named Jenny, he is a native of Liverpool, and from Arkham House has delivered several collections of his stories that, when they are good, are very good indeed.

A single room this time, and a multiple set of characters, and what Ramsey does best: evocation.

DEAD LETTERS

by Ramsey Campbell

The seance was Bob's idea, of course. We'd finished dinner and were lighting more candles to stave off the effects of the power cut when he made the suggestion. "What's the point? The apartment's only three years old," Joan said, though in fact she was disturbed by this threat of a seance in our home. But he'd brought his usual bottle of Pernod to the dinner party, inclining it toward us as if he'd forgotten that nobody else touched the stuff, and now he was drunk enough to believe he could carry us unprotesting with him. He almost did. When opposition came, it surprised me as much as it did Bob.

"I'm not joining in," his wife, Louise, said. "I won't."

I could feel one of his rages building, though usually they didn't need to be provoked. "Is this some more of your stupidity we have to suffer?" he said. "Don't you know what everyone in this room is thinking of you?"

"I'm not sure you do," I told him sharply. I could see Stan and Marge were embarrassed. I'd thought Bob might behave himself when meeting them for the first time.

He peered laboriously at me, his face white and sweating as if from a death battle with the Pernod. "One thing's sure," he said. "If she doesn't know what I think of her, she will for the next fortnight."

I glared at him. He and Louise were bound for France in the morning to visit her relatives; the tickets were poking out of his top pocket. We'd made this dinner date with them weeks ago—as usual, to relieve Louise's burdens of Bob and of the demands of her work as a nurse—and as if to curtail the party Bob had brought their flight date forward. I imagined her having to travel with Bob's hangover. But at least she looked in control for the moment, sitting in a chair near the apartment door, away from the round dining table. "Sit down, everybody," Bob said. "Before someone else cracks up."

From his briefcase where he kept the Pernod he produced a device that he slid into the middle of the table, his unsteady hand slipping and almost flinging his toy to the floor. I wondered what had happened in the weeks since I'd last seen him, so to lessen his ability to hold his drink; he'd been in this state when they arrived. As a rule he contrived to drink for much of the day at work, with little obvious effect except to make him more unpleasant to Louise. Perhaps alcoholism had overtaken him at last.

The device was a large glass inside of which a small electric flashlight sat on top of another glass. Bob switched on the flashlight and pressed in a ring of cork that held the glasses together while Màrge, no doubt hoping the party would quiet down, dealt around the table the alphabet Bob had written on cards. I imagined him harping on the seance to Louise as he prepared the apparatus.

"So you're not so cool as you'd like me to think," he said to her, and blew out all the candles.

I sat opposite him. Joan checked the light switch before taking her place next to me, and I knew she hoped the power would interrupt us. Bob had insinuated himself between Stan and Marge, smacking his lips as he drained his bottle. If I hadn't wanted to save them further unpleasantness I'd have opposed the whole thing.

A thick scroll of candle smoke drifted through the flashlight beam. Our brightening hands converged and rested on the glass. I felt as if our apartment had retreated now that the light was concentrated on the table. I could see only dim ovals of faces floating above the splash of light; I couldn't see Louise at all. Silence settled on us like wax, and we waited.

After what seemed a considerable time I began to feel, absurdly perhaps, that it was my duty as host to start things moving. I'd been involved in a few seances and knew the general principles; since Bob was unusually quiet I would have to lead. "Is anybody there?" I said. "Anyone there? Anybody there?"

"Sounds like you've got a bad line," Stan said.

"Shouldn't you say 'here' rather than 'there'?" Marge said.

"I'll try that," I said. "Is anyone here? Anybody here?"

I was still waiting for Stan to play me for a stooge again when Bob's hand began to tremble convulsively on the glass. "You're just playing the fool," Joan said, but I was no more certain than she really was, because from what I could distinguish of Bob's indistinct face I could see he was staring fixedly ahead, though not at me. "What is it? What's the matter?" I said, afraid both that he sensed something and that he was about to reveal the whole situation as an elaborate joke.

Then the glass began to move.

I'd seen it happen at seances before but never quite like this. The glass was making aimless darting starts in all directions, like an animal that had suddenly found itself caged. It seemed frantic and bewildered, and in a strange way its blind struggling beneath our fingers reminded me of the almost mindless fluttering of hands near to death. "Stop playing the fool," Joan said to Bob, but I was becoming certain that he wasn't, all the more so when he didn't answer.

Then the glass made a rush for the edge of the table, so fast that my fingers would have been left behind if our fingertips hadn't been pressed so closely together that they carried each other along. The light swooped on the letter *I* and held it for what felt like minutes. It returned to the center of the table, drawing our luminous orange fingertips with it, then swept back to the *I*. And again. *I. I. I.*

"Aye aye, Cap'n," Stan said.

"He doesn't know who he is," Marge whispered.

"Who are you?" I said. "Can you tell us your name?"

The glass inched toward the center. Then, as if terrified to find itself out in the darkness, it fled back to the *I*. Thinking of what Marge had said, I had an image of someone awakening in total darkness, woken by us perhaps, trying to remember anything about himself, even his name. I felt unease: Joan's unease, I told myself. "Can you tell us anything about yourself?" I said.

The glass seemed to be struggling again, almost to be forcing itself into the center. Once there it sat shifting restlessly. The light reached towards letters, then flinched away. At last it began to edge out. I felt isolated with the groping light, cut off even from Joan beside me, as if the light were drawing on me for strength. I didn't know if anyone else felt this, nor whether they also had an oppressive sense of terrible effort. The light began to nudge letters, fumbling before it came to rest on each. *MUD*, it spelled.

"His name's mud!" Stan said delightedly.

But the glass hadn't finished. *R*, it added.

"Hello Mudr, hello Fadr," Stan said.

"Murder," Marge said. "He could be trying to say murder."

"If he's dead, he should be old enough to spell."

I had an impression of bursting frustration, of a suffocated, swelling fury. I felt a little like that myself, because Stan was annoying me. I'd ceased to feel Joan's unease; I was engrossed. "Do you mean murder?" I said. "Who's been murdered?"

Again came the frustration, like the leaden shell of a storm. Incongruously, I remembered my own thwarted fury when I was trying to learn to type. The light began to wobble and glide, and the oppression seemed to clench until I had to soothe my forehead as best I could with my free hand.

"Oh my head," Marge said.

"Shall we stop?" Joan said.

"Not yet," Marge said, because the light seemed to have gained confidence and was swinging from one letter to another. *POISN*, it spelled.

"Six out of ten," Stan said. "Could do better."

"Shut up, Stan," Marge said.

"I beg your pardon?" Stan said. "You're not taking this nonsense seriously? Because if that's what we're doing, deal me out."

The glass was shuddering now and clutching letters rapidly with its beam. "Please, Stan," Marge said. "Say it's a game, then. If you sit out now you won't be able to discuss it afterward."

DSLOLY, the glass had been shouting. "Poisoned slowly," Stan translated. "Very clever, Bob. You can stop it now."

"I don't think it is Bob," I said.

"What is it then, a ghost? Don't be absurd. Come on then, ghost. If you're here let's see you!"

I felt Marge stop herself saying "Don't!" I felt Joan tense, and I felt the oppression crushed into a last straining effort. Then I heard a click from the apartment door.

Suddenly the darkness felt more crowded. I began to peer into the apartment beyond the light, slowly in an attempt not to betray to Joan what I was doing, but I was blinded by the glass. I caught sight of Stan and knew by the tilt of his head that he'd realized he might be upsetting Louise. "Sorry, Louise," he called and lifted his face ceilingward as he realized that could only make the situation worse.

Then the glass seemed to gather itself and began to dart among the letters. We all knew that it was answering Stan's challenge, and we held ourselves still, only our exhausted hands swinging about the table like parts of a machine. When the glass halted at last we'd all separated out the words of the answer. *WHEN LIGHT COMS ON*, it said.

"I want to stop now," Joan said.

"All right," I said. "I'll light the candles."

But she'd gripped my hand. "I'll do it," Stan said. "I've got some matches." And he'd left the table, and we were listening to the rhythm he was picking out with his shaken matches as he groped into the enormous surrounding darkness, when the lights came on.

We'd all heard the sound of the door but hadn't admitted it, and we all blinked first in that direction. The door was closed. It took seconds for us to realize there was no sign of Louise.

I think I was the first to look at Bob, sitting grinning opposite me behind his empty bottle of Pernod. My mind must have been thinking faster than consciously, because I knew before I pulled it out that there was only one ticket in his pocket, perhaps folded to look like two by Louise as she laid out his suit. Bob just grinned at me and gazed, until Stan closed his eyes.

Raylyn Moore keeps a low profile in the fantasy field, popping up now and again (mostly in The Magazine of Fantasy and Science Fiction) *to make sure we're all still here while she carefully, almost unobtrusively, tilts what we know to be so into something that we're not quite sure of.*

She is quiet.

She is also deadly.

And, perhaps most importantly, she is unafraid to take what would be a cliché in the hands of a new writer and do with it what she does best. There is possession, you see, and there is possession. There is the screaming, bloody, roof-rattling, door-smashing, furniture-toppling, possession that seems to bank on the fact that we'd rather be shocked into fright than lulled into it.

There is, on the other hand, the lullaby.

A CERTAIN SLANT OF LIGHT

by Raylyn Moore

One of the curious things about that house was that, in past times, things had not been used as they were meant to be used. Locks broken on the kitchen and pantry windows had been replaced not with new locks but with knives and forks. The main goal, sealing the windows against prowlers and freshening breezes, had been accomplished by stuffing the cracks between the sashes with strips of cloth, and then wedging the tableware into the corners. Of course, the windows were then supposed never to be reopened.

Lace, though preoccupied with the thousand other details of the moving-in, couldn't wait to remove those pieces of bent metal, some of them silver-plated, with family monograms. (There was even one piece of sterling, a pickle fork.) Using a screwdriver, she dug out the rags and opened all the windows that would open. Some of the sashes crashed down again because of broken cords.

But this was an interior, rather shortsighted and carping comment on what was really a splendid old dwelling, the basic excellences of which such minor putterings could never mar, and in the long view the house remained to Lace a dream realized. Brought up among the cliff dwellings of Manhattan, then transplanted to the built-yesterday milieu of metropolitan Southern California, she had gone on yearning for the kind of living she had often read about but experienced just once, briefly, when as a child she had been sent for part of a summer to a great-aunt who had an old frame house on a quiet street in Prout's Neck.

Now Lace had her own old frame house, three stories of it rising in dowdy splendor behind a screening growth of elderly maples on a huge, fenced lot that also had an assortment of mossy outbuildings. It was far too large a place and pointlessly extravagant, unless one happened to believe, as Lace did, that a dream never comes too high.

She spent the first few days (and could have spent weeks) just wandering from floor to floor and room to room, surprised anew at what was behind each closed door, at the end of each twisting staircase and narrow tributary corridor. What delighted her especially during these excursions was the curious frisson she experienced when entering some forgotten room on an upper floor where nothing moved but dust motes through angling sunbeams and nothing sounded but her own breathing, and yet she would be convinced beyond argument that Something had just been there and gone. Wishful thinking? At least partly that, Lace admitted. For not only had she always wanted such a house, she had wanted one containing such a hovering Presence, a Thing-in-residence. Wouldn't anyone? And yet it was more than she had dared to hope, for she knew how rare Presences were these days and how valuable. They were being driven into ever-narrower extremities, of course, by all the senseless destruction of old houses in towns everywhere. Soon they would have no remaining asylum. It taxed credulity beyond the breaking point even to try to imagine a Thing inhabiting a home in Stuyvesant Village or Palos Verdes Estates.

The closest neighbors, who at first failed to recognize the name of Lace's husband, Maynard Hummel, wondered why the new family, with just one daughter, needed such a large house, but they considerately did not wonder aloud. And when Lace made it a point to know them immediately, throwing convention to the winds and turning up at their back door to inquire about trash pickup day and mail deliveries, they talked freely with her about the people who had lived in the house before, showing themselves pleased to be able to answer with authority all Lace's excited questions.

These former occupants had been a large family of unmarried brothers and sisters named Wechsmuth, some of whom had lived to advanced age, but all of whom were now gone, each having left—as Lace was shortly to discover—a clear fossil imprint of his or her existence somewhere in the vast primordial dust of that house that the Hummels then bought.

There had been seven of these spinsters and bachelors, Lace's neighbors had told her. Mart, the eldest, the clan chieftain, had been a short, long-armed woman with facial moles growing stiff black bristles. Then came brother Ludy, who since the war (meaning in this case the Spanish-American) had never been quite well, and then Annie, known to the town for some forgotten reason as "the nice one." Arthur and Alice, the twins, were said to have been withdrawn into themselves even from the rest of the family, occupying a castle keep within the greater redoubt, a union within a union.

And there had been Lobithee, a bit dotty in her own way, given to biting off the heads of garden flowers and chewing contemplatively while passersby ogled from the street and God-knew-what thoughts troubled her poor head.

Itsy, the youngest, his Christian name long mislaid, had been a marvelously obese man in a family of thin people and the only one who earned an income. Itsy's was the role of outside monk. He had bought groceries, and answered the doorbell on the rare occasions when it sounded. His job as a casually employed carpenter couldn't have brought in much, but the Wechsmuths required very little. Not only had they never thrown anything away, they also had never permitted anything to wear out, especially not clothing. Prodigious experts at making do, they had cannibalized bits and pieces of rusty garments to mend other, equally rusty garments in much the same fashion as they mended the toolshed roof with strips of linoleum left over from the kitchen floor.

Alone of them all, Lobithee had once been married. In her young womanhood (the story went), a local farmboy had proposed and been accepted. The marriage had lasted a day and enough hours into the night to unnerve Lobithee totally. Shaking in a corner like a rabbit in a snare, she had watched her chance to elude the bumbling farmboy, slipping out at last and racing ahead of him back home to her brothers and sisters across several acres of corn stubble on bleeding bare feet.

The Wechsmuths, except for Ludy, had never traveled. They had made no friends. Every incident (though incidents were kept to a minimum) had enhanced their isolation—Lobithee's marriage, Ludy's military service and ensuing malaria, Itsy's accident. (Itsy had toppled from a silo he was roofing and afterward had a characteristic, swiveling limp.)

It was known too that each sister and brother had kept to his or her own section of the big house, cooking meals separately, mostly on alcohol burners, and tending their austere, individual fires in the many fireplaces, all of which were equipped with coal grates. An exception to this rule of separation was made by the twins, who, it was believed, had a dual household.

Lace returned home satisfied that she now knew everything about her predecessors that was common knowledge in the town. Poking through the house again, she found what she could now identify as one of Itsy's miter boxes being used to block off a mousehole on the second floor, a handmade embroidered corset cover that could have been from Lobithee's trousseau filling one of the window cracks, a prescription bottle with Ludy's name on it, and any number of other things.

And in the garden one day after a summer storm, when the earth was black and loose, a rectangular, flat stone spanning a drainage channel caught Lace's eye. It looked too geometrically regular, too smoothed up for an appearance in that wild, neglected garden. Using a discarded hoe handle, Lace prized it up and discovered its hidden side was inscribed:

SUSAN WECHSMUTH
B. Jan.6, 1890—D. Dec. 24, 1910
Rest in Jesus

Lace's delight was redoubled. She, a newcomer to town, had discovered an eighth Wechsmuth. She fitted various possible explanations to the offhand use of Susan's headstone in the garden. An error had been made at the monumentmaker's in spelling (she had been Susanne?) or in one of the dates? (It *was* too appalling to believe that a girl born on Twelfthnight would die on Christmas Eve.) A corrected version of the stone had been made but since the error had for some reason not been the fault of the stonemason, the Wechsmuths had been obliged to pay for the ruined monument anyway. They had brought it home—this family that wasted nothing—to use when the first occasion arose that a tombstone would come in handy.

Susan had not been enumerated among the Wechsmuths by Lace's neighbors, of course, because she had died so young she'd been long since forgotten by outsiders. She had not lived on and on in that family of grotesques. Had she foreseen, then, what she was escaping? Taken her own life perhaps because of this dismal vision of a future she could not endure? And then the family, at first forgiving of her act, had been persuaded by the dour Lutheran minister to the harsh conclusion that Susan must lie in an unmarked, suicide's grave? Perhaps even removed the marker after it was installed?

That Susan had known *some*thing before her untimely loss of life was the theory that best satisfied Lace in the end. No one really knew what went on in the minds of young girls. Helen, for instance. It was true that Lace's daughter had literally disappeared into her sixteenth year like a mole into a burrow. One of the reasons for their move had been to see what could be done for Helen by the change, and for Maynard. If very few people remembered Maynard Hummel as a prodigy television writer where they had been living before, they might as well come to a place where he was not known as a person either. Not that it was that simple.

The story they had told one another and the friends they'd left was something of a variation on the truth. After investing fifteen of his best years—he'd started at twenty-two—on the kind of television serial that soars to eminence in a day and then for no reason winks out at the height of the arc, when one's back is momentarily turned, Maynard had been freed by fate to write the book he'd been planning for at least that long. Trouble was the telephone rang all the time in California; people came by. He was getting no work done. Have to move to isolation, buy an island, or what these days passes for one, a big old house in a little town in western Pennsylvania, the town selected almost at random. (Because of the fantastic expense, Maynard had warned that they could move this once and no more. Lace, he said, must have no second thoughts. "Oh I *won't*," she promised. "It's what I've always wanted. How could I change my mind, ever?"

Of course, the flaw in the myth about the book was the number of years (ten) that had elapsed since the power shift in the industry, the shift that had dumped Maynard and then kept him out. (One of those things, everyone said. Television was funny that way, a power setup that for some was certain to be a knockdown.) Lace, in her narrower reflections, wondered if the real reason they'd moved wasn't because the excuse of the book, no longer believable in their former community, could now be reused credibly and comfortably—a notion as frugal as any of those of the

Wechsmuths. Never throw away a perfectly good myth just because it gets a little worn. And back of it all was Lace's hope that there really might be a book. Sometime.

There were moments during the renovating when Lace suspected that it would be impossible after all to remove from the premises the powerful impress of the brothers and sisters, that the house would always be theirs and never hers. Yet when everything was over, she was equally sure the Wechsmuths would have found it hard to recognize their former home. Everything had been vigorously scraped, sanded, and refinished. All deficiencies were repaired with more appropriate materials than before. The woodwork was painted white, and some of the more interesting wallpaper had been copied and restored. The architecture and interior were an uneasy agglomeration of periods out of which Lace chose to preserve features she imagined were Colonial. Coming off particularly well, she thought, were the uncovering and repair of the random-width pegged flooring. It showed to best advantage in the third-story room with many dormer windows, a room now occupied by Maynard, his file cases, his tables, his desk.

Two big rooms on the second floor, joined, were done over especially for Helen, who immediately took to remaining in them much of the time. This left Lace the ground floor for herself, though she still prowled the vacant rooms on the higher levels, relieved to discover that the Thing had not been dislodged—she hoped not even discommoded—by all the activity. In fact, she felt it more strongly than ever, and one day she even imagined it delayed its disappearance out of the room she was about to enter and instead stayed to speak with her.

This happened in the attic, where she had gone one day to store a box of winter blankets. Because the third story rose well into the roof, the attic was tiny, just a single, dim lumber room crouching under the steep slope of the main rafters. And as Lace entered that afternoon, there were the ancient silence piled in drifts, the dust-filtered sunlight slanting palely through a round, high window, and the feeling she had learned to recognize.

"You're making a mistake," said a disapproving voice in her mind, "in taking me so lightly, as if I were just another feature of the property, like the summerhouse in the rear garden or the extra pantry behind the breakfast room. You have been far too casual. You outside people don't appreciate the seriousness of this kind of situation. There are some things one absolutely cannot write off as diversion."

Lace did not reply—partly, she realized, because she was uncertain of the protocol. Should she answer the voice aloud? Or simply think the reply and assume it would be conveyed? But while she was trying to make up her mind, the voice went on.

"In your case the mistake was inevitable because you're essentially a frivolous woman. The world could be shattering around you but you wouldn't be likely to see it; no one so preoccupied with trivialities could. Why hasn't it ever occurred to you, however, that I might be evil? You'd better do some research on this kind of phenomenon before something terrible happens. I feel it's only fair to warn you that it could happen cumulatively, over a long period, or suddenly, any day now. But you should prepare yourself. You have certainly asked for it."

Though Lace waited politely, there was nothing more. So she shoved the blanket chest to the rear wall of the lumber room and went back downstairs. The encounter had cleared up one thing, at least. Ever since she'd found the tombstone, she had played with the notion that the Presence might be Susan's restless ghost. Now she knew better. It was certainly not young Susan Wechsmuth's voice that had spoken.

No, the Things that live at the bottoms of old wells and the tops of old houses are old themselves, far older than anybody's ghost. And she knew beyond doubt now that this was one of those. Furthermore, contrary to what the Presence thought, she *had* done some looking into the matter, since it was a subject that naturally went along with her interest in old houses in small towns. It was for this very reason that she *could* take the Thing so casually, of course. Forewarned is forearmed. No doubt the Presence had shaped the lives of the Wechsmuths and those of the people in the house before them. (Had they been grotesques as well?) But it could not shape Lace's life, since she knew what to expect. It was the one thing she must avoid, actually taking the Thing seriously—as seriously, say, as it demanded to be taken. The frisson was enjoyable; real fear would be intolerable. It must not come to that, and there was no reason for it to, so long as they understood each other—she and It—which she believed now that they did.

Along with this determination went Lace's new decision to show the Thing its place by ignoring it for a while. She would stop moping around the house and instead act on the resolution she'd made when she first came to the town. Since she had embraced this way of life, she must live up to it in all ways. One of these ways was to be outgoing, make herself agreeable and acceptable to the townspeople, cause herself (and even more importantly Helen and Maynard) to be invited places.

The difficulty was that the only people she had managed to meet so far were the neighbors who had told her about the Wechsmuths. But they would serve for a beginning. Lace invited them in for coffee and a tour of the house now that the remodeling was accomplished.

These neighbors—a widow and her daughter, an anthropology major home for the summer from graduate school—responded with a show of what seemed to be genuine enthusiasm. The anthropologist daughter added that she looked forward to meeting Helen, whom Lace had mentioned, of course.

So when they arrived, on the appointed morning, Lace set out china cups in the blue-papered breakfast room and said, "Helen's upstairs. If she doesn't come down soon, I'll call her."

"Oh don't do that," Mrs. Bernard said. She was a pursy little woman going a bit stout in her midfifties. "I know how daughters hate being bossed around." And she winked in an exaggerated way at her own daughter, who ignored the signal and remarked:

"How odd it is after all these years to be actually inside this house. I grew up next door, you know, and not only was I never invited in, I never had the guts even to get a close look." Catherine Bernard went on to explain that, going past the house to and from school, she and her friends had titillated one another with dares about going into the Wechsmuth yard, even standing still alone in front of the property. Once they'd been ordered to move on by Mart, who'd made threatening gestures with her long arms from the distant front porch. Catherine, a tall, spectacled, athletic-looking young woman totally different from the mother, laughed at her own reminiscence and accepted her coffee, black, from Lace.

"Hummel, Hummel," Mrs. Bernard burst out suddenly. "Have I told you how familiar your husband's name sounds to me? Not when you first said it. It's only been the past week I've been thinking I'd heard it somewhere before."

So it had come after all, the comment Lace waited for with all new acquaintances, though even so it seemed strangely abrupt in the present context. Yet she was pleased and grateful, even a little relieved. "You remember it from the television shows he used to write," Lace named several of them.

"Oh I used to love those," Mrs. Bernard declared, perhaps just a shade too insistently. "What shows is he writing now?"

"Maynard isn't in television anymore," Lace said. "He can't spare the time from his book."

"How wonderful," Mrs. Bernard said. "I admire anyone who can write a book—so hard to imagine where they get all their ideas. We had a man here in town about six years back, rented the old Whitworth house for a summer. *He* was writing a book."

"Mother, for heaven's sake," Catherine said, and changed the subject. "How does Helen like it here?"

"I don't believe she knows yet. She's hardly been out of the house since we came. She's naturally shy, and a bit overweight. Lacks self-confidence, and in a new situation—" Lace had not meant to go so far, but she felt, suddenly and a bit prematurely, perhaps, with the midmorning sun filling the breakfast room, that the Bernards were her friends.

"I'd be glad to talk with her," Catherine offered. "Tell her about the swimming pool and the tennis. They're the only recreation available here in the summer, but they'd be a start. She could meet people her age at the pool."

"*Would* you?" Lace said gratefully. So one of the results she had secretly hoped for from this meeting had already come. Catherine, a young person, native of this town, knowledgeable, could be no end of help to Helen socially.

Lace examined with calm pleasure the vista into the tangled garden from a window draped crisply in blue linen. She was already proud of the miracles wrought in the house; the garden would be next to receive her attention. She had served hot jam tarts with the coffee, and the odor of sugary pastry clung, a Pennsylvania kind of odor, Lace thought. It went well with the surroundings, anyway. And because she felt comfortable, befriended, Lace began to believe anything was possible. She looked at Catherine and smiled. "How about right now? I'll show you and your mother over the rest of the house, then we can stop by Helen's rooms."

They set off. The Bernards were thoroughly appreciative of the pale paint, the new-old wallpaper, the carved newel post found in the garden toolshed and restored to the terminal of the bannister. The group worked its way through the first floor and prepared to go up. Lace told them about the miter box, the corset cover. Then after a small pause for dramatic emphasis, she sprang the secret of the tombstone.

She could not have hoped for a better response. "Imagine!" said Catherine. "Isn't it just like the crazy Wechsmuths to use a tombstone to walk on? Do you know who Susan was, Mother?"

"Yes," said Mrs. Bernard, equally awed. "I'd almost forgotten. She was the—uh—idiot, poor girl. And in those days they didn't have the proper kind of care for—well, anyway, I don't really *know*, of course. After all, I was very young then, a child, and the girl was already dead by that time, but the rumor was they kept her locked up in the—"

Lace wanted to hear it all, sad and horrifying though it promised to be (her mind had already flown to the small back bedroom on the third floor where she had discovered a triple lock on the *out*side of the door), but they had by now arrived at Helen's door on the second floor. They had not been especially quiet—had been talking animatedly, in fact—and the exposed plank flooring must have echoed their footfalls. So what happened now didn't seem possible under these circumstances.

There was no answer to the first sharp rapping. Lace made the second raps softer, less demanding. Waiting, she had a moment for a thrust of remorse. Helen had been hidden away in these rooms while she, Lace, expended all her care on the house. Of course, that itself was an effort on Helen's behalf. The deficiency, if deficiency it were, lay in its being an indirect effort. Yet perhaps this visit from Catherine would help make up to Helen for any unmotherly remissness.

It was necessary to knock a third time before the answer came. "Go away!"

Lace spoke in tones that were perhaps unwisely dulcet. "Dear, I'd like you to meet someone." Why *couldn't* she have added, "They're here with me now"? Or would it have made a difference. Surely Helen had known?

"I do not *want* to meet anyone. I particularly do not want to meet any of your godawful hicks from this town, and that goes double for the moronic woman and her ugly daughter from next door. Go away, Lace."

Well, there it was, thought Lace.

The trio withdrew numbly from the newly white door, walked down the mile stretch of hall and stairs. The Last Mile, Lace realized, had been well called.

Nor was she at all surprised to see Maynard waiting at the foot of the steps. Her executioner. He would finish the job Helen had begun, almost as if they had worked in collusion.

Maynard, who never came down out of his aerie in the morning or at midday, and sometimes not for several days, now stood leaning against the red-and-white paper of the entrance hall, complexion unwholesomely particolored by the fanlight. He was dressed in dirty, colorless shorts worn without a shirt, and held an iced-tea glass half full of liquid amber. Lace's hope—as if it mattered anyway, with everything else—was that the Bernards were ingenuous enough to believe the glass held iced tea. At the same time she doubted they were.

"How do?" Maynard said maliciously.

Mrs. Bernard recovered herself. "So good to have a famous author for a neighbor, Mr. Hummel. I used to love that series you did, that family series, about the Whatstheirnames—"

Maynard bowed slowly, unbowed equally slowly. "My wife reminded you about it, I suppose. Loyal of her. Did she tell you the big lie about the book too?"

"Well, I understood her to say you're writing a—"

"Ah. Poor Lace. Living in a dream, as always. Romantic. Well, ladies, I can set you straight. What I'm here for. I didn't come to this place to write. I came to rot. A rotter, not a writer. Difference, I think. Though maybe not."

He grew confidential, leaned very close to Mrs. Bernard. Lace thought for a moment he would lay an arm across her neighbor's shoulder. "Want to know who I really am?"

"I'm afraid I—"

"The Tin Woodsman, that's who. Wonderful man, Frank Baum. Some say he was a lush. In one of his more profound utterances, the Tin Woodsman says, 'If I am well oiled, I shall soon be all right again.' What depth, eh? What wit, what a *Weltanschauung!* Now, if Thoreau had ever drunk anything but pond water, *he* could have been the Tin Woodsman."

Maynard laughed all by himself, bowed a second time, fell silent.

Lace led the silent procession around him and down the hall toward the back door. They filed past the breakfast room where an inch of coffee waited, grown cold in the glass pot. A fly droned above two leftover jam tarts.

She saw them out, a ceremonious end to their first and last call. She heard Maynard's unsteady retreat up the front stairs.

Alone now, in full possession of the downstairs, Lace reminded herself that the Bernards would talk; they had talked readily and quite unkindly about the Wechsmuths' fractured lives.

Vividly, she saw how it would be. The Hummels. He on the top floor, their odd daughter whom no one had ever seen on the second. Lace supposed she would become the outside monk.

Bill Pronzini spends most of his time writing mystery and suspense fiction. Once in a while, however, he can be persuaded to take a holiday into a nightmare.

There is a bit of dialogue common to dozens of horror films and stories, a bit not necessarily restricted to those done before the seventies: "There are things that Man is just not meant to know." In a radically different sense, the same can be said of a horror story; while some authors excel and are successful in the descriptive passages that lay out for the reader all the terrors and horrors of monsters and the like, there are others who work on the principle that the less said the better—let the imagination do the heavy work, and nine times out of ten it will come up with a scene no author could ever produce on the printed page. In that sense, then, the last scene of "Deathlove" is missing.

Your move.

DEATHLOVE

by Bill Pronzini

I sit hunched forward in the taxi as it rushes through the dark, empty streets of the city, and I feel exultant. It will not be long now, Judith, my love; a few hours, then a few weeks or a few short months until you and I are one. Forever.

And the truck comes out of nowhere

*

And we come into the quiet residential area six blocks from Lake Industrial Park. I lean forward and tell the driver to stop at the next corner. A moment later I stand alone in the darkness. The night wind is cold, and I turn up the collar on my overcoat as I watch the taxi's taillights fade redly and disappear. Then I begin to walk rapidly toward the park, the fingers of my right hand touching the gun in my coat pocket.

The industrial development is deserted when I arrive; there is no sign of the night security patrols, which I know make periodic checks of the area. I pause and look at my watch: just past nine. Exactly right. I make my way carefully, then, to the squat stone structure that houses McAnally's firm, the unimaginatively named Ajax Plumbing Supply Company. A single light burns in the office, behind blind-covered front windows—the only light in the abandoned park. As always on Friday evenings, McAnally is working late and alone on the company books.

Stealthily I move to the rear of the building, to the shadowed parking area. Only one car is parked there: McAnally's, of course, one I know well. I have seen it every day for four years in the driveway of his house, diagonally across Mayflower Street from my own bachelor dwelling; and I have, in my capacity as insurance broker, written the policy on the vehicle.

I allow myself a small, relaxed smile as I walk some twenty yards distant, to the base of the high cyclone fence that rings the supply yard, and blend into the blackness there. All is progressing just as I have planned; I am supremely confident that there will be no problems of any kind.

This isn't right, the truck

As I wait, I concentrate on the visual image of Judith that lingers perpetually in my mind. Her long auburn hair, her gentle green eyes, her high cheekbones and her tiny ears and the miniature dimple in the center of her chin, the smooth sensuous lines of her body. Judith smiling, Judith laughing, Judith in all her moods from pensive to gay to kittenish. How often do I dream of her? How often do I long to hold her in the warm silent hours of every night from now until eternity. Not often—always. There is no love greater than mine for her, and it is that love and the complete fulfillment of that love that is the very purpose of my existence.

"Soon now, Judith," I whisper in the cold silent hour of this night. "Soon . . . "

I do not have to wait long. Habitually precise as always, McAnally leaves the building at exactly nine-thirty. I tense in anticipation, my fingers firm on the gun, as he crosses the darkened parking area. He reaches the car, but I wait until he begins to unlock it before I step out quickly and approach him.

McAnally hears my footfalls and glances up in a jerky way, startled. I stop in front of him.

"Hello, Fred," I say.

Recognition smooths the nervous frown on his face. "Why—hello, Martin. You gave me a jolt, coming out of the darkness like that. What are you doing *here,* of all places?"

"Waiting for you."

"What on earth for?"

"Because I'm going to kill you."

He stares at me incredulously. "What did you say?"

"I'm going to kill you, Fred."

"Hey listen, that's not funny. Are you drunk?"

I take the gun out. "I'm both sober and deadly serious."

An abrupt mixture of fear and anger begins to shine in his eyes. "Martin, for God's sake, put that thing away. What's the matter with you? Why would you even think of killing *me?*"

"For love," I say.

"For what?"

"Love, pure and simple love. You're in the way, Fred; you stand between Judith and me, between our marriage. Does it all become clear now?"

"You—and Judith?"

I smile faintly.

"No!" McAnally says, and shakes his head in disbelief. "No, it's not true. My wife loves me, she's devoted to me.

She isn't cruel or vindictive; she'd never be a party to cold-blooded murder. . . . "

I am enjoying this; I smile again, enigmatically. "Have you ever wondered about the perfect murder, Fred? Whether or not there is such a thing? Well, I think there is—and in just a little while I'm going to prove it."

"This is . . . insane. You're insane, Martin!"

"Not at all. I'm merely in love. Of course, I do have my practical side as well. There's the fifty-thousand-dollar double-indemnity policy on your life, with my company, and that will take care of Judith's and my needs quite nicely once we're married. After a decent interval of mourning, naturally. We can't have the slightest shadow of suspicion cast on her good name, or on mine."

"You can't do this," McAnally says. "I won't *let* you do it!" And he makes a sudden jump forward, clawing at the gun.

But his fear and his anger destroy all co-ordination, and I move aside with calm ease and bring the barrel down on the side of his head. He falls moaning to the pavement. I hit him again, sharply; then I finish opening the car door, drag him onto the floor in back, and slip in under the wheel.

There is something wrong with all this

As I drive out of Lake Industrial, I am watchful for one of the night-patrol vehicles; but I see none, I see no one at all. Observing the exact speed limit, I follow the route that McAnally always takes to get home—a route that includes a one-mile stretch through Old Mill Canyon. The canyon road is little used since the construction of a by-passing freeway, but McAnally has long considered it a shortcut to the suburban development where we both live, and drives it invariably.

At the very top of the canyon road is a sharp curve, with a bluff wall on the left and a wide shoulder studded with red guardrail reflectors on the right. Beyond the rail is a sheer two-hundred-foot drop into the canyon below. There are no lights behind me as I take McAnally's car to the crest. From there I can see for perhaps a quarter mile past the curve, and that part of the road is also void of headlights.

I stop the car a hundred feet below the shoulder, hold a long breath. And then I press down hard on the accelerator and twist the wheel until the car is headed straight for the guardrail at the shoulder's edge. While the car is still on the road I brake sharply; the tires burn against the asphalt, providing the skid marks that will confirm McAnally's death as a simple if tragic accident.

The truck

I manage to fight the car to a halt a dozen feet from the guardrail. Then I rub sweat from my forehead, and reverse to the road again. When I have set the emergency brake I step out hurriedly to make certain we are still alone. Once assured, I pull the still-unconscious McAnally from the rear floor, prop him behind the wheel and wedge his foot against the accelerator pedal. The engine roars loudly and the car begins to rock. I grasp the release lever for the emergency brake, prepare myself, jerk the brake off, and fling my body out of the way.

The car hurtles forward. An edge of the open driver's door slaps against my hip, knocking me down, but I am not hurt. McAnally's car crashes into the guardrail, splintering it, and goes through; it seems to hang in space for a long moment, amid a shower of wooden fragments, and then plunges downward. The still darkness is filled with the thunderous rending of metal as the car bounces and rolls into the canyon.

I go to the edge and look over. There is no fire, but I am able to see the black outline of the wreckage far below. I say softly, "I'm sorry, Fred. It's not that I hated you, or even disliked you. It's just that you were in the way."

Then I turn, keeping to shadow along the side of the deserted road, and begin the long three-mile walk home.

What is it that's so wrong

*

And late the following morning I stand on the porch of the sprawling ranch-style home that now belongs only to Judith, my Judith. I ring the bell, and my chest is constricted with excitement as I wait for her to answer.

Presently there are steps inside, and the door opens, and my love looks out at me. I stroke her with my eyes, stroke her hair and her sensuous body encased now in black widow's weeds, and the love I possess swells inside me until it is almost like physical pain.

"Hello, Judith," I say, and make my voice grave. "I just heard about Fred, and of course I came right over."

Her grief-swollen mouth trembles. "Thank you," she says. "Thank you, Mr. Martin. It was such a terrible accident, so . . . so *unexpected*. I guess you know how devoted Fred and I were to each other; I feel horribly lost and alone without him."

Inside myself I smile tenderly. Poor Judith. She *is* shocked and sorrowed over McAnally's death—though her pain will not last long—for of course she knows nothing of my plans. Nor of my love, despite what I purposely led McAnally to believe; because of him, I could only worship her from afar. Until now. Until tomorrow and tomorrow and tomorrow.

"You're not alone," I say softly. "I'll always be here, Judith. Always . . . "

The truck!

I know what it is now, I know what is wrong.
None of this has actually happened.

It was planned to happen just this way, a thousand times I envisioned it just this way, it was so brightly vivid in my mind as I rode in the taxi. But something else occurred, something interfered. The truck, the taxi—

There was an accident.

Yes, I remember it now: the taxi rushing through the dark, empty streets, and the truck coming out of nowhere, the truck coming through the red light at the intersection, and the impact, and the spinning, and the pain. And then—nothing.

Where am I?

Utter blackness. No pain, no feeling at all. Vague bodiless sensation of floating, of drifting. Coma? Hospital? No, something else, somewhere else. Thoughts, the sudden remembering, the bodiless drifting

and I am beginning to understand, I am beginning to realize

that I was killed in that accident.

I'm dead.

Fred McAnally is alive and *I'm* dead, Alan Martin is dead. . . .

. . . and the door opens, and my love looks out at me. I stroke her with my eyes, stroke her hair and her sensuous body encased now in black widow's weeds, and the love I possess swells inside me until it is almost like physical pain. . . .

But *am* I dead?

Even though I was killed in that accident, am I truly dead?

Increasing awareness now. If I were dead, I would no longer *be*. There would be no perception, no memories, no emotions, no vague sensation of drifting. I am alive; the essence, the intellect, of Alan Martin survives.

Why?

And the answer comes: It is my love for Judith, the depth and fervor of my love for her. Too strong even for death. Transcending death. My love lives, therefore I live.

But again, where am I? A state of limbo? Or—

The Netherworld?

Yes. Exactly. Drifting—spirit drifting. I *am* spirit.

The blackness is beginning to lighten somewhat, slowly, becoming a soft, swirling gray; and as it does

my awareness continues to increase and I understand with sudden joy that it will not be long before I am capable of vision, of corporeality, of mobility through time and space. I will be able to penetrate the mortal world, re-enter it; even in death I will be able

to go to her, to bring my love to my love.

*

" . . . Judith, I'll always be here. Always . . . "

Oh yes, yes, I will go to her in the night, in the warmth
and silence of a night when she is alone. . . .

And all at once—there is no temporality where I
exist—I find myself standing in her bedroom, that place
where I longed so often and so desperately to be. She is
there, alone, wearing a pale blue dressing gown and sitting
before her vanity mirror while she brushes her hair. Her
face is radiant, smiling, and I know it is Friday night and
she is waiting for McAnally. But I accept this, it does not
disturb me. Nothing can disturb me now that I am in the
presence of my love.

Her voice whispers in the stillness, counting each
brush stroke. "Eighty-nine, ninety, ninety-one . . . " But
she might be counting the minutes until we are together,
and that is how I choose to hear her words. "Ninety-eight,
ninety-nine, one hundred . . . "

Reflected in the vanity mirror, her beauty is so flawless
that it is as if I am looking at a priceless masterwork
painting framed eternally for my eyes alone. I no longer have
a heart, but if I did it would be beating now like the muted
thunder of surf. I no longer have loins, but if I did they
would be aflame with the purity of my desire.

"One hundred and nineteen, one hundred and twenty . . . "

The need to be near her, to touch her, is exquisite. But
how will she react when she sees me? I mustn't frighten her.
And yet I cannot gaze on her any longer from a distance; it
would be unbearable. I *must* go to her, I must.

Slowly and carefully I cross the room, watching her
face in the mirror, preparing gentle words. But as I draw
closer the image of myself that I expect to see behind hers
does not materialize; there is no face in the mirror but
Judith's. Then I am standing close to her, closer than I
have ever been before—and she is alone in the glass.

How is that possible? Is there something I do not
yet understand?

"One hundred and forty-eight, one hundred and . . . "

Abruptly she stops counting, holding the brush against the silkiness of her hair. Her smile fades; small frown lines appear on her forehead.

"Judith," I whisper. "Judith."

She frowns with faint unease at the mirror, puts down the brush.

"I'm here, my love."

And I reach out with trembling fingers and touch the warmth and softness of her shoulder.

She shivers, as though it was not I but a sudden chill draft that caressed her. She turns, looks around the bedroom, and painfully I accept the truth: She can't see me, or hear me, or feel the gentle pressure of my hand. Perhaps it is because I am not strong enough yet. And perhaps . . .

Knowledge comes to me then, sharp and certain. Yes, of course: McAnally. He is still alive, he still stands between us—now like a wall erected between our two worlds, blocking out all perception.

McAnally. Always, always, it has been McAnally.

Judith rises from her chair, crosses to the window, and secures the lock. Then she sheds her dressing gown, and the silhouette of her body beneath the thin nightdress she wears fills me with rapture. I watch her shut off the lights, watch her get into bed and lie with the coverlet pulled up to her chin.

After a time the rhythm of her breathing becomes regular. When I am sure she is asleep I walk to the bed and sit down beside her.

She stirs but does not open her eyes.

With great care, I lift the coverlet. This is the moment I have ached for most, this is the moment that makes even my death inconsequential; I would die a thousand times for such a moment as this.

I take her in my arms.

She moans softly, shivers, tries to turn away in her sleep. But I hold her in a tight though tender embrace. "Judith," I whisper in her ear, "it's all right. I'm growing stronger, and when I'm strong enough I'll find another way to kill Fred. A push as he starts down the basement steps, a falling object from the platform in the garage—I'll find a way. I will, I will."

She continues to make moaning sounds, but I hear them now as murmurs of love. I kiss the warm hollow of her throat, and my hand finds her breast, and in ecstasy I lie there with her, waiting. Waiting.

First, for McAnally.

But most of all for that time when my love will come awake and see and hear and feel me at last and forever, lying beside her in the warm silent hours of the night . . .

Michael Bishop has been a finalist for just about every award ever conceived in the field of science fiction. Yet to classify him solely as a science-fiction writer would be an error of the highest order. He has, on occasion, moved his typewriter over a notch into fantasy and has produced some of the most horrifying stories we have ever read. Not with a splash, however, because that isn't Bishop's style; and because this is so, these same stories vanish under the reputation of his sf.

"A Tapestry of Little Murders," however, is like a burr that will not be shaken. "Darktree, Darktide" is another.

There is, in his not-always-so-gentle stories, the terrifying aspect of the inevitable coupled with the inexplicable. . . when the unknown is here, and we don't know why, and it won't go away . . . and we don't know why.

It simply is.

MORY

by Michael Bishop

Daniel Gholston drives through Colicott Gardens' stucco gateway into a lamppost-studded parking lot surrounded by topiary animal shapes. At fifteen minutes to nine, not many cars are yet in the lot. An unsummery wind is blowing the morning clouds around, and the children waiting with their parents for the park's tractor-drawn "train" to pick them up and deliver them to the ticket booths across the way look like bewildered gnomes, old before their time. The wind snaps at their clothing.

When the customer-pickup train arrives, Gholston gets out of his secondhand Toyota and takes an outward-facing seat on its last car. At sixty-three, he is a grandfather whose entire family—every single member—has died within the past eleven months. He scrupulously ignores the whole families huddled together on the cars in front of his; he wishes them well, but he has no desire to speak to them or to overhear their conversations.

An employee at the front of the train rises to deliver a spiel of welcome and instruction. Gholston listens only because he must—there is a small metal speaker right above his head. He looks forward and sees the girl standing, microphone in hand, on a sort of running board. He starts because she is wearing a uniform with peppermint-green candy stripes very similar to the one his grand-daughter wore when she did volunteer work at the municipal hospital. Soon the train sidles up to a curbing next to a mosaic walkway and everyone begins to disembark.

Gholston waits his turn at a ticket booth made to resemble a huge pumpkin shell. Another young woman wearing candy stripes sits inside this shell dispensing tickets. A single adult ticket is nine dollars, good for every activity in the park.

"What if it rains?" Gholston asks her.

"The indoor amusements remain open, and it has to rain hard to shut down the rides. We don't give rain checks."

"I don't mind if it rains."

"You don't?" She takes Gholston's bill and gives him change.

"No. I've come to have fun." Ignoring the decidedly puzzled look that she turns on him, Gholston accepts his ticket, passes through a stile, and finds himself before a curved wire-mesh wall laden with vines and flowers. A smooth flagstone walk caresses the soles of his feet; the scent of roses and ferns hangs in the air. Already Gholston can hear popcorn popping, and above the wall in front of him he can see the top of the parachute-drop tower at the center of the Gardens. Which way to go? Off to the left, a leaf-covered tunnel leading to an auto show and a whirligig ride. Off to the right, a Wild West Main Street and a number of specialized refreshment stands.

Gholston lifts a pocket lighter to the tip of his cigarette, and a gust of wind blows aside the flame. An eddy of vision-distorting plasma. He tries again and the same thing happens. Nervously, he shakes the lighter and rakes his thumb down its back.

This time, through the brief resulting flame, Gholston catches sight of a small neat black man in ice-cream-vendor whites. The Negro's features ripple inside the flame and shift in a disturbing, almost protean way. Before Gholston can hail him, the man pivots and pushes his ice-cream cart up the tunnel leading to the auto show.

"Why?" Gholston shouts. "Why is that man here?"

A woman who is lowering her child into a stroller gives him a perturbed look. The child, he waywardly notes, has pompons on the toes of its shoes and a touching, spaced-out expression on its face.

"I'm here to have fun," Gholston tells mother and child alike. "But why is *he* here? What does he want with me?"

"I think he just sells ice cream," the mother says. She propels her baby away from him with careful speed.

A year ago Daniel Gholston had been doing a good retail liquor business. Although Michael, the older of his two sons, had acted for him as both manager and counter man, Gholston could not bring himself to retire quite as early as he had promised his wife. Rachel didn't like the late hours he kept or the extent to which the work fatigued him. She couldn't deny, however, that his fatigue was almost a tonic to him or that the store did bring in money. They had a fine house in Clarington Wood, a Mercedes-Benz, a Porsche, and a portfolio of reliable stocks. Dathan's son Hap was going to Harvard in the fall.

"Why don't you quit?" Rachel asked her husband. "All you enjoy is your work. You've never had any fun with the money it's made you."

"I bought the Porsche, didn't I?"

"Hap drives it—you don't."

"Rachel, I don't have the time."

"Exactly."

He tried, not always successfully, to shrug off her concern. His fun was his work. When would Rachel *really* understand that? Even Micheal tried to chase him off to an unproductive retirement. And Dathan, who owned a vacation cottage on the Gulf, was forever after him to take Rachel down there to live within drowsy earshot of the winter ocean. That you may profit from your old age, everyone told him, put on your Banlon and Bermudas and beat it down to Florida. . . .

But the store on Liddon Avenue meant too much to him. His concern was not with the money it made him, nor with the festive and captivating beauty of the bottles on their shelves, nor even with the autocratic little domain that the store might seem to some to represent. What mattered was the pride and purpose that the store's management gave him. After each of his "arguments" with Rachel over his retirement, he returned to the Liddon Avenue store with fresh enthusiasm.

The first catastrophe befell Gholston on a Saturday night late in July. He and Michael were working different registers, his son handling hard-liquor sales and Gholston himself taking care of the beer and wine business. Two or three slick-suited types were browsing in each section of the shop, and nothing whatsoever seemed amiss.

Then, suddenly, an explosion wracked Liddon Avenue and there was a fireball blazing in the street. Gholston saw an unidentifiable make of automobile at the center of the fireball, flames roaring off its contour in ferocious, night-licking waves.

"Jesus," one of Gholston's customers said, "that looks like something you'd see in Belfast. Damn thing's been Molotov'd." With no apparent thought to the possible danger, this man went outside to watch the automobile burn. The other customers in the store crowded outside after him (like sheep, Gholston thought), and even Michael seemed to be moving that way, deserting his register beyond the door connecting the store's two sections. A siren had begun to wail, and shadowy figures were running in the street.

"Stay where you are," Gholston told his son. "Who knows what's going on out there, Michael?"

"Amen," an insouciant voice said, and Gholston saw that Michael was coming into his part of the store with an incredulous look on his face. Behind Michael was the person from whom the "Amen" had issued: a small, leatherjacketed man with a woman's stocking over his head for a mask and a jaunty motoring cap perched atop the stocking. The nylon mesh could not disguise the fact that the man was black.

The intruder gestured at Gholston. "Get out from behind that box, man, and come around here where folks outside can't see."

Gholston did as the man asked. Over his shoulder he could see the automobile blazing in the street. His customers had melded with the rubbernecking shadows in the intersection, and although two or three more sirens were wailing, none sounded very close by.

"Kneel," the man in stocking said.

Michael began to kneel. Gholston, looking at Michael in his unequivocal fear and confusion, realized that his son was truly in his early forties, a middle-aged man with gray in his hair and the paunch of a inveterate beer drinker. My son, Gholston thought. He remembered Michael in shoes with pompons on their toes, and a terrible clairvoyance overwhelmed him.

"Kneel?" Gholston cried. "Sure, kneel! So you can put your pistol to our heads and blow our brains out. That's the one thing I don't do for you hit-and-run artists. We'd rather die on our feet."

"Your brains are safe," the black man replied. "I'm not packin' a gun, anyhow." He showed them his hands, which were empty. "But I *am* sayin' kneel, which if you don't you're both dead men. So kneel." He pointed to the floor in front of the counter.

"I'll knock your head off," Gholston said. He took a step forward and raised his right arm.

"Nah, man. You don't even wanna *try* that." The nylon-hooded man pointed a finger at Gholston—a finger that, for all its ordinariness, seemed infinitely more potent than the barrel of a cheap-jack revolver. Gholston stopped. "That's right. Now you're thinkin'. On your knees."

Father and son knelt at the feet of the weaponless holdup man; and the only good that Gholston could find in their humiliation was that they did not have to face away from their tormentor. . . . But the man has no gun, Gholston reminded himself. Why are we obeying him? Still, somehow, he knew better than to test the intruder, who was now rummaging their cash registers with impunity.

The man returned and dropped an armload of bills onto the floor in front of them. "Neaten up that pile," he commanded, and Gholston saw that the blue strobe of a police car had begun to splinter against and ricochet off a mirror above the black man's head.

Michael picked up several bills that had landed near his knees and added them to the pile.

Abruptly the holdup man dropped a match into it. The money burned with both swiftness and heat.

"You must be new at this," Gholston said. "That ain't the way you do it."

"It's the way I do it. I always like a little fire."

"You don't have to hold up somebody you don't know to watch a fire. Why don't you look at the one in the street? Besides, this way, you won't even get out of here with enough cash to buy your habit an appetizer."

"First, I seen the fire in the street. Second, I don't have no habit. And third, I *know* who you are, Mr. Gholston. I'm not here to enrich myself. I'm here to impoverish you."

"That's a day's receipts. It doesn't make a dent. What difference do you think it's—"

"Papa," Michael put in. "Papa, shut up."

"Oh I know I ain't hit you too hard yet—but I'll be back. And tonight"—he glanced out the window at the strobe-lit and fire-tattered confusion—"I'm takin' No. 1 Son here with me. Get up, Mr. Michael, let's get goin'." The Negro's features smooched around behind his mask as if they were made of a peculiarly runny, coffee-colored Silly Putty.

Michael got clumsily to his feet, and the black man, catching his elbow, swung him toward the rear of the store. He pushed Michael through the stockroom door and turned back to the still-kneeling Gholston.

"Tonight's the last you ever gonna see of him. But I ain't so hard as I may seem. That's why I give you that street bomb and this burned-up money"—he nudged its ashy remains with his toe—"to remember things by. Not that you're really gonna need 'em . . . Evenin', Mr. Gholston." He followed Michael into the stockroom and closed the door.

Gholston got to his feet and lurched across the store to the stockroom. But for the dust-covered crates of various kinds of bottles, the room was empty. He stumbled through the stacked merchandise and opened the door to the alley. The evening's dull, humid air fell on him at once, but not a soul was anywhere in sight. . . .

Michael never came back. Killed offstage, that was how it seemed to Gholston. Taken away and put to sleep out of everyone's range of vision. As dead as if the holdup man had shot him in the forehead while they were kneeling in front of the counter. Or maybe, sometimes, not *that* shockingly dead—just lost, utterly lost, with no hope of recovery . . . It didn't really matter. Rachel couldn't handle Michael's absence in either case, and Gholston felt his own loss to be inestimable. His life had been—and there was no other way to put it—cruelly impoverished.

But why? he asked himself. Why? . . .

Gholston hurries up the tunnel after the ice-cream vendor. It's a fairly steep grade, toward a higher level of the gardens, and his breath comes hard. When two small boys with helium balloons overtake and scamper past him, he is unnerved and chagrined. How could a man pushing a cart get so far beyond him, though? The cart ought to slow him, shouldn't it?

"Ice-cream man!" Gholston shouts. "Ice-cream man!"

At last he comes out of the foliage-hung tunnel and sees the stucco rotunda in front of which the auto show is held. On the lawn are several vintage automobiles, waxed to a day-after-tomorrow shine—the cars look newer than new, despite their running boards and rear-mounted tire cases. The ice-cream vendor is on the walk near a canary-yellow Packard, and Gholston watches him back up and wheel his cart across the flagstones to the whirligig ride called Big Mambo Many Foot. This ice-cream man, he sees, is *not* a man of color.

"Hey!" he shouts in any case. "Hey, ice cream!"

The vendor hears him and stops—a boy, a mere boy with shoulder-length hair and a case of what Hap would have blithely ridiculed as "terminal acne." He waits politely, though, and says, "Yes, sir?" when Gholston finally lumbers up, spent from the chase.

"Where's the other fella? . . . The black ice-cream man? . . . The, uh, one who just came up here?"

"I'm the one who just came up here. But if you mean Mory, you don't have to chase him, sir—he'll chase you. He sells more ice cream than any other three of us put together."

"Mory? Didn't he just come up here, then?"

"No, sir. Today's Wednesday. Mory doesn't work Wednesdays."

"He's here today—I saw him."

"You did? Well, he's off-duty then. He's just here for fun. . . . *I* can sell you ice cream, though. How 'bout it?"

Gholston, looking nervously about, fishes thirty-five cents from his pocket and buys a cone. At ten minutes past nine in the morning. Neither the ice cream's smoothness, nor its sweetness, nor its teeth-tingling cold are comforting to him. There's something sinister about the fact that "Mory" has a job selling ice cream in Colicott Gardens. What's going on here, anyway?

The same thing that's been going on in your life, Gholston answers himself. More of the same.

"Hey, this park's no place to put on a frown," the boy says. "This is a carefree place. Mory'll show up in a while if you really want him to. Relax. Don't worry."

"I'm sure he will."

"Yeah, he will. You don't have to chase Mory." The boy looks at the automobiles on the rotunda's lawn. "Boy," he sighs. "What cars. What really incredible cars."

After Michael's disappearance, Gholston gave the Porsche to Hap. In September Hap and Dathan loaded it down with suitcases, stereo equipment, a disassembled French racer, and God only knew what else; they set off for Massachusetts. After getting the boy settled in at college, Dathan intended to fly home. They left together on a Sunday evening because Hap thought it would be fun to drive the Interstate at night.

Early Monday morning Gholston's telephone rang. He reached for it groggily as Rachel sat up in bed and turned on the lamp over their headboard. A man who identified himself as an out-of-state highway patrolman began speaking in a guarded but strangely crisp way.

"What is it?" Rachel wanted to know.

Gholston waved her to silence.

"Do you think you could get up here?" the patrolman asked. He gave explicit directions to a county hospital over the state line and asked Gholston to inform Mrs. Gholston of what had happened—not Rachel, but Dathan's wife, Susan.

"You haven't called her yet?"

"Before he lost consciousness your son asked us to have *you* call her."

"Is Dathan okay, then?"

"I can't really tell you any more than I have."

Chaotic arrangements were made. Susan and the younger children came to the house in Clarington Wood, and Gholston set out alone in the Mercedes.

He drove north on the cold, photographic-gray ribbon of the expressway, ignoring everything but the blank inevitability of this ribbon. It surprised him when a sign indicated that he had reached the state line. Then, an hour or so before dawn, Gholston saw an array of safety flares set out across both lanes of the north-running half of the Interstate. Behind these smoking ruby-purple flares, the silhouetted bulk of a jackknifed cab and trailer. Thirty miles or more from his destination and he was going to have to stop. If he ran the barricade of flares, he'd collide with the truck sprawled across the highway. But why was he even thinking of running through the flares? He was *supposed* to stop. The flares had been placed to bring motorists up short of an accident, hadn't they? And the wreckage, Gholston told himself, must have something to do with Hap and Dathan.

He braked before the flares and squinted through his windshield at the broken truck and the astounding emptiness of the landscape. Why hadn't traffic backed up here? Where were the police vehicles and county-financed rescue vans? Had these flares been placed just for him? They seemed to be burning out, trailing their plumes of magenta smoke along the concrete like the hems of whorish gowns.

Gholston began quietly to weep. What have I done to warrant this kind of treatment? Why am I being singled out?

"It ain't because you're a liquor man," a familiar voice called from the darkness beyond the flares. "I mean if it wasn't you, it'd be somebody else, right? God's truth, that's exactly how I see it."

Gholston lifted his head. According to the lettering on the trailer, the jackknifed vehicle belonged to a nationally known vodka distillery in Florida. A man was climbing down from the cab. The Mercedes' headlamps picked him out through the smoke of the dying flares.

Gholston wiped his eyes. He got out of his car to meet the truck driver at the line the flares made. He was not surprised to discover that this man was a small, neat Negro wearing a leather jacket and a logger's knitted cap. His face, however, the man kept carefully in shadow, well out of the dimming illumination of the flares and the naked brightness of the Mercedes' headlamps. His whole form had a quicksilver insubstantiality.

"What did you just say?" Gholston asked him belligerently.

"I was talkin' bout me—how it ain't fair that I should wreck like this just 'cause I'm drivin' a vodka rig. A man's gotta make a livin'."

"That's not what you were talking about. And you goddamn well know it wasn't." In the no-man's-land above the flares Gholston shook his fist at the black man, then drew it back to himself, frighteningly chilled.

"Yes, sir, I 'magine I do know that. You're right."

"What's happened to my son? What's happened to Hap?"

"The boy's dead, just like that patrolman told you long-distance. He was an unthinkin' boy, sometimes. Didn't have no business in a sporty job like that Porsche. Totaled it against a bridge abutment a little ways up the road. Broke his neck for him."

Gholston rubbed his hand against his chest. "Dathan?"

"He's gonna live—"

"Thank God."

"—until next February. In intensive care. On all sorts of special apparatus. Lung machines and suchlike. Company that's got his medical insurance ain't gonna pay for it, either. You're gonna pay for it, Mr. Gholston. A good part of your savin's is gonna go right down the tubes."

"Who are you?"

"A fella who's gotta get out of here 'fore the fuzz arrive, Mr. Gholston. I ain't even got a driver's license, you see, and my company don't know that."

"Then what are you doing out here? Why the hell did you arrange this . . . this . . . this *mess?* Why are you plaguing me?"

"It seemed to me," the driver of the vodka rig said calmly, "that I ought to be the one to tell you." He pointed a finger at Daniel Gholston and stepped through a swirl of gaudy smoke toward the Mercedes. "I'm assumin' you left the keys in the ignition. Somebody'll be along shortly. Enjoy the scenery. The mornin's gonna be beautiful."

He ducked into the car; and when Gholston, who was weeping openly now, turned to get a good look at his face, the Negro activated the windshield spray under the Mercedes' hood and set its wipers in motion.

"Look over that way, Mr. Gholston," he said. "Some farmer's up early burnin' off the stubble of his summer crop. Sure is purdy."

Daniel Gholston faced to the west and saw a line of fire marching down a gentle hill beyond the south-running lanes of the Interstate. The dawn, when it came, would be mirrored by the ruddiness in the west. Then Gholston saw his Mercedes backing rapidly away from him, its driver wheeling it expertly down the middle of the Interstate, out of his life forever. Soon its headlamps cut off, and the car was absorbed into the threadbare blackness of what remained of the night. A dream and a loss . . .

It was almost an hour before Gholston was rescued. First Michael, he thought as he waited, then Hap, and Dathan slowly dying . . .

I've come here to have fun, Gholston reminds himself. Why am I trying to find the man who, either through his own agency or his delight in my misfortune, has brought me such grief? He finishes his cone and walks down one of Colicott Gardens' amusement-lined flagstone paths to the parachute drop at the center of the park.

Only three of the eight parachutes are in operation this morning, he sees, because it's a weekday and the morning crowd is still sparse. He won't have to stand in line for fifteen or twenty minutes before an attendant gestures him into one of the swinging seats and brusquely straps him in. In fact, it looks as if he can have his pick of the three working 'chutes and ride as often as he likes. The collapsed 'chutes halfway up the tower, he notes, look like weird, wilted orchids.

"Do you have a weak heart?" a boy in a candy-striped blazer asks him.

Startled, Gholston replies, "If I did, I'd be dead by now."

"Sorry. We're supposed to advise folks that very small children, pregnant women, and people with heart conditions probably shouldn't ride the Crying Fall."

"The 'Crying Fall'?"

"That's what we call the parachute drop."

"Well, that's quite a nice name, if it has to have one. At least you didn't mistake me for a very small child or a pregnant woman."

"No, sir—I didn't."

Gholston pats the boy on the shoulder and goes through one of the switch-backing sets of rails to the central 'chute now in operation. Looking up, he sees that for a good portion of the tower's height the lines on the parachutes permit a kind of free fall—before they take sudden, gasp-provoking hold and then release the passengers again from this lesser height. Gholston notices that the clouds above the tower have imparted to it a slow but sense-befuddling motion.

"Looks like fun," he says loudly.

Each parachute has its own controls, a plastic and metal box mounted on a pole, and the attendants sending the 'chutes up and releasing the locks on the passengers' safety belts are dressed more like ice-cream vendors than turn-of-the-century music-hall emcees. The white-jacketed attendant beside Gholston is a slender, pretty black girl with a lovely but inconstant smile. When it is his turn to be hoisted aloft, she straps him in without even looking at him.

Back at her control box she says, "Up you go," and up he goes.

Off to his right another parachute is coming down, and the people sitting below it look pleasantly terrified. He waves at them, but they're too busy holding on to return his wave. His own feet dangle free beneath him, and he finds that his principal worry is not whether he will survive the sudden descent, once it begins, but that his shoes will fall off and kill the pretty black girl who has sent him up. He curls his toes in an effort to prevent such an accident.

Then he is at the top of the tower—from which he can see, he believes, all of Colicott Gardens. He can also see the skyline of the city where he has lived and worked for more than six decades. For no reason he can properly understand, the sight terrifies him. He doesn't want to go down. He wants to hang above this clean and friendly park until the wind has scoured away his flesh, and his bones have begun to whiten in the sun.

"I don't want to go down!" he shouts at the people rising toward him under the partially collapsed parachute to his left. They smile and wave.

The Crying Fall drops him heartlessly, but he represses a scream and even leans forward a bit to see how fast the ground is coming up. Below him, on the flagstone margin of the ride, one of the Gardens' strolling clowns is juggling three firebrands. Appearing from out of nowhere, a man in a white jacket catches one of these brands away from the clown and juggles with him for no more than a second or two.

Gholston watches in amazement as this interloper then jumps over several of the ride's access rails and positions himself next to the control box under his 'chute. The girl there makes way for the newcomer. Meanwhile, the strolling clown continues to juggle his firebrands, and the ground inexorably rises. The white-jacketed 'chute attendants look like interns awaiting a festival of death . . . .

Gholston shouts, "There's nothing more you can do to me!" He doesn't even feel the snap of the cables when the parachute is caught and released a second time. He strains to see the man who has commandeered the control box, but once his feet touch down, the oily smoke of the clown's flaming Indian clubs is drifting—predictably, all too predictably—across the line of his vision.

"Not much more," the man agrees. "Just wanted to settle your mind, Mr. Gholston, and let you know I was really here."

"Unstrap me! Let me out of this contraption!"

"Not this time. Up you go again. Might as well enjoy it up there all you can; it never seems to last too long. I'll be seein' you later."

"Let me out!"

But the man has pushed the ascent button on the box, and the 'chute is lifting Gholston to the top of the tower again. It's a temptation to dislodge one of his shoes and let it fall, but there are too many other people down there, a holiday contingent of what look like medical personnel. . . .

Dathan, of course, died in a hospital; and Rita, Michael's daughter, was assaulted by an unidentified man in the basement vending-machine facility of the hospital where she was doing volunteer work. In attempting to escape, her assailant tore away a piece of wallboard and ripped out a handful of electrical wiring. A fire started. After the current to that part of the building had been shut off and a battery-powered lighting system taken downstairs, the fire was contained by conventional methods. But the man responsible escaped somehow, and the girl's body was discovered in the ruins of the vending-machine room.

Gholston got the news over his Toyota's radio while driving home from the Liddon Avenue store. The announcer gave information that was not ordinarily released to the general public before next of kin were notified—but this didn't surprise Gholston, because the announcer's voice clearly belonged to the same man who had abducted his son and stolen the Mercedes after Hap and Dathan's accident. Besides, he felt sure that no one else had heard the broadcast.

Upon learning of Rita's death, Rachel suffered a stroke. She succumbed to it on the second morning after the hospital fire.

To Daniel Gholston's remaining family there occurred a series of calamities that were almost banal in their predictable unexpectedness. Numbingly banal. A kind of rage asserted itself behind the hurt as the series progressed. Arson, accident, illness, and each time the evil messenger was a small, neat black man whose face Gholston never saw.

He was informed of the torching of Dathan's house in the steam-filled sauna room of his golf club, where Negroes, although not officially excluded, were seldom seen. On another occasion he was made to brace against the wall in the second-floor corridor of his own home while the mocking voice told him that Michael's wife was dying of a rare variety of influenza she had been exposed to at the international trade center where she worked. Gholston, weeping, pounded a fist against the wall as the man spoke—but Gholston was powerless to turn around.

When the man left, Gholston hurried down the stairs and threw his front door open on a chill winter landscape. At the foot of his lawn he saw an old black man in a filthy topcoat burning cement sacks—a neighbor had had a new driveway laid before the snowfall—to keep warm.

Gholston kicked the sacks apart and took the reluctant black man into his kitchen for coffee and toast. He emptied his heart out to the man and then sent him on his way with two hundred dollars in cash, a pair of shoes, and one of his least-worn winter coats. Alone again, he cursed heaven.

Inevitably, one of the local television stations picked up on "The Gholston Story." He was interviewed.

"I haven't deserved what's happened to me," he told the cameras and the conspicuously proffered microphone. "I haven't been an evil man. And if I *had* deserved the things that have happened to me, *I* should've been the one who was stricken down. Not Rachel. Not my sons. Not Hap. Not . . . " His voice broke, and the cameras continued remorselessly to grind.

Although members of the news staff privately conceded that Gholston would have garnered more sympathy if they had not taken a camera crew to his store, viewer reaction was positive. Perversely, Gholston refused all offers of help. He argued that he had seen many instances of *human* goodness in his life; what he wanted now was a direct manifestation of *God's* mercy. He was quoted to this effect on an eleven o'clock news broadcast, and the offers of help abruptly dwindled. Several people called in to say that Gholston had got no more than what was coming to him. At home the calls came so frequently that he finally began leaving his telephones off the hook. Their muted buzzing, when he walked through the empty house, reminded him of how fearfully alone he was. He kept three television sets on for company.

One afternoon in midsummer he stopped in front of one of them long enough to watch an advertisement for Colicott Gardens.

Down from the top of the tower again, Gholston sees only the girl who first sent him aloft. She comes forward to free him from his seat.

"Where's Mory?" he asks her. "I assume that was Mory."

"That was him. Don't know where he's off to now. He likes to see people havin' a good time. He didn't mean any harm sendin' you up again."

Looking down one of the Gardens' paths, Gholston sees the juggling clown sauntering along with his three fire-brands extinguished. The clown salutes passersby with one of the Indian clubs, lets the other two dangle from a polka-dot belt dipping just below his polka-dot derrière. The sight of him is amusing. I've come here to be amused, Gholston tells himself; I'm not going to worry about this phantom whom the employees of Colicott Gardens know as Mory. I'm going to enjoy myself . . . . He nods a good-bye to the girl, negotiates the turns in the exit stall, and plods off toward a psuedo-Swiss village featuring a cable-lift platform to the west side of the park.

He is happy in his anonymity.

The day passes for Gholston with a great deal of activity, but without incident. He rides rides, devours hot dogs, ogles girls, sees a puppet show, watches a Bengal tiger ride a motorcycle, dips his nose in beer foam, smells flowers, tours the spook house, sits on benches, skewers with wasted wit a pinched-face little man who is upbraiding a tired child, gets a crick in his neck looking at the sky, reads the graffiti in a restroom, eavesdrops on an ardent young man who is telling his sweetheart that it's sad, it's sad, but too many obstacles stand in their way, catches the porpoise show, laughs at his inability to advance a mechanical greyhound to the top of a baize track by levering a ball into a target, notices that the day is slipping away—but doesn't see Mory again at all.

At ten o'clock, Colicott Gardens lit from side to side and bottom to top with haloed lanterns, the chill of the morning subtly reasserting itself, Gholston trudges wearily up a winding flagstone path to the beautiful old carousel on a hill near the west side of the park. It begins to sprinkle. The flagstones grow slick and slatelike; a giggling flock of people come scampering past him on their way to low-lying shelters.

But Gholston continues to the top of the hill, and lifts himself astride a dapple-gray carousel horse, and watches himself fragment and reappear in the mirrors encircling the machine house at the center of the merry-go-round. Only two or three other people are riding with him, and the muted chiming of the carousel's recorded calliope meshes perfectly with the dreamlike motion of the ride and the surreal panorama of the rain-transfigured gardens below. There is nothing to do but acquiesce in the moment and weep. Gholston does so. At last the gentle calliope music breaks off and the carousel slows.

"Are you all right?" a girl asks him as he dismounts and tries to reorient himself.

"Fine. I'm sixty-three years old, and I've done everything it's possible to do here." Carefully, without shame, he wipes his eyes with a handkerchief and notes how perky and vital the carousel girl seems to be.

"That's wonderful," she says. "Even the roller coaster?"

"No," he answers, surprised. "I didn't even know you had one."

"Yes, sir. The Himalayan Heartstopper. It's one of the largest in the country. You have to ride it if you come to Colicott Gardens. Everyone'll ask you if you have, you know." Solicitously, she leads him around one of the carousel's walks to a small knoll from which the roller coaster, a monster of many lights, its hills and hairpins bridging a number of tiny black pools, is visible but ghostly-looking in the intensifying rain. "Just take this path here," the girl tells him. "You can probably get down there for one of its last trips of the day. If you've ridden everything else, you *have* to ride the Himalayan Heartstopper."

"I guess I do," Gholston replies seriously. "I guess I do."

Unmindful of the rain, he descends the path thinking on the girl's spontaneous kindness and her concern that he made his day at the Gardens a total success. I *am* having fun, he says to himself wonderingly; I really am.

A covered waiting area of parallel queue lanes stands next to the passenger-loading ramp of the Himalayan Heartstopper, but the lanes are empty and Gholston goes through one of these stalls feeling both excited and intimidated. The roller-coaster skeleton beyond the ramp is prodigious, brontosaurian. It seems to sprawl over half the county and three quarters of the night, and yet he has been in the Gardens all day without stumbling upon it or (now that he thinks of it) even hearing the distinctive ratcheting of coaster cars being winched to the top of an ascent, the screams of the train's riders, and the cars' careening rumble along the slopes and straightaways. He is a little consoled by the fact that when he rode the Crying Fall his seat did not permit him to look over this way without craning his neck, but still he wonders. Alone in the waiting area, he realizes that no one at all stands across the tracks from him at the operator's lever. The roller-coaster cars await him, but how is he going to be able to ride?

"I got you covered there," a familiar voice says. "Just don't turn around to thank me yet."

"Are you Mory?" Gholston asks, staring straight ahead. "The abductor, the rapist, the arsonist, the murderer, the bearer of bad tidings, the . . . ?"

"Mory'll do for a name," the man says. "I do a lot of patrollin', Mr. Gholston, all kinds of places. But I want you to know one thing: I do *all* my own dirty work. I don't sublease responsibility. The power's all one, anyhow. Not too many folks understand that or believe it . . . But you know, don't you, Mr. Gholston?"

"Know what?"

"That it's my face on both sides of the coin."

"I've never seen your face."

"Well, the one I'm wearin' now ain't important anyway. I took it 'cause it's safe for my purposes."

"No one would suspect a black man of being . . ."

"No one but another black person, Mr. Gholston. Have a cold, sweet one on me." A dark hand clutching an ice-cream cone shoots under Gholston's arm, and Gholston sees his fingers closing around the cone.

He hears himself protesting, "I don't want this."

"Get on the coaster, Mr. Gholston. Front seat in the last car. I'm gonna be right behind you."

Gholston walks down the open platform, onto which the wind is lobbing fusillades of rain, and squeezes under the safety bar in the final coaster car's front seat. The bar falls automatically across his lap. Although he is unable to turn his head, he knows that Mory is in the seat behind him—he hears that bar click into place, too. He wonders what to do with the ice cream in his hand.

He asks, "Why was I singled out? I still don't understand that. Try as I might, I can't fathom it."

"It isn't for you to fathom, Mr. Gholston."

The train lurches forward. In a moment it is sliding out into the undifferentiated dark where the wind is brisker and the rain more chillingly cold. Gholston clutches the safety bar with one hand, holds onto the ridiculous ice-cream cone with the other. The coaster picks up speed.

"You better eat that before we get goin' good."

Gholston tosses the cone into the night and grips the bar across his lap with both hands. Mory laughs mirthlessly, and Gholston shouts, "I've never tormented my children with mysteries beyond their understanding! Never! If I was ever cruel, it wasn't in a premeditated way!"

"You're just *full* of pride, Mr. Gholston. Listen to you."

The coaster cars, after sweeping to the base of the Himalayan Heartstopper's most Himalayan ascent, have slowed again. They are beginning their noisy, chain-assisted climb to the summit. Gholston glances back toward the Gardens and notes the beauty of the lights, the liquid harmony of trees and cupolas and towers. He wishes he could see the carousel, but he cannot. The rain galvanizes his every nerve, beads on his face and forearms.

"I don't think so," he says quietly. "I really don't think I am."

The man behind him says nothing. The clicking of the upward-crawling cars sends tremors through Gholston's bones. Even though he is at the mercy of the train and the man in the back seat, he feels alive and powerful. His senses leap as they have not done in years.

"I would like to see your face!" he shouts as the train's first car inches toward the top. "Couldn't I see your face?"

At that moment, off to the right, across one of the pools below the frame of the roller coaster, an explosion occurs. Another explosion follows. Roman candles and fragmenting bombs of color are shooting into the air, blazing skyward against the iridescent relentlessness of the rain. This is the fireworks exhibition, Gholston realizes, that nightly signals the closing of Colicott Gardens. The noise, the color, and the wet all seem separate manifestations of the same slippery phenomenon, and he turns his head up to watch the lambent streamers exfoliate like scales or leaves or flower petals. The night has bloomed in fire. Caught between stasis and fall, his coaster car is poised on the summit. . . .

"There it is, Mr. Gholston. Go ahead and look. . . . I just wish you hadn't tossed that cone away . . . ."

Gholston looks. His tormentor's face has formed in the pyrotechnic display overhead, in the many-colored burstings and streamings, and the inhuman brilliance of this face is uncompromising. Is there any way to communicate with this brilliance? Gholston wonders. Even praise seems inadequate to the task. Inhuman, inhuman. He feels gravity displacing his stomach forcibly to his mouth, and for a moment he fears that he has been struck blind.

The roller coaster is plunging. Gholston brings his eyes away from the face in the fireworks and looks downward. He sees that the formerly empty cars ahead of him now contain the members of his family—Michael, Hap, Dathan, Rachel, Rita, Susan, everyone who had been taken from him over the course of the past year! They sit mutely in their places, unaware of him, buffeted by a wind they should not even be able to feel. He wants to call out to them, but the wind roaring up from the pit beneath their train sucks his breath away and stops his mouth. His terror beats inside him almost as loudly as his heart, and the sudden click of disengagement of the safety bar behind him savages his soul.

He is alone, Gholston understands, with his most cherished dead, none of whom will ever acknowledge him. For reasons that he cannot articulate, that he has no time to consider, he is happy in his overmastering fear. Humbly and defiantly happy . . .

Both The Deep *and* Beasts, *by John Crowley, have heralded the arrival of a major new talent in the field of sf/fantasy. Unlike so many other "heralded" arrivals, however, Crowley is doing something to maintain the respect he has already accumulated among his peers and his readers. If he is not the most prolific writer in the world, he is certainly one of the most careful and, like Avram Davidson, one of the most demanding.*

There are layers and there are layers, of course, and to enjoy one does not diminish the pleasure of the other; there are also gods and demons, angels and devils, and a prayer for one does not always promote the banishment of the other.

WHERE SPIRITS GAT THEM HOME

by John Crowley

When Phillippa Derwent at last got through the various switchboards and operators, and a young voice said "Hello?" in a remote, uncertain way, it was as though she had tracked some shy beast to its secret lair, and for a moment she wished she hadn't embarked on this; she hated to be thought a busybody, and knew that sometimes she could act like one.

"This is Phillippa Derwent," she said, and paused a moment. When there was no response: she said, "Are you John Knowe? Amy Knowe was my . . . "

"Yes. Yes, of course. Aunt Phil. I'm sorry. It's been so long. . . ."

It had indeed been long—over twenty years—years which, Phillippa knew, would have passed far more slowly for her nephew, aged eleven when she had last seen him, than for herself. A certain amount of constrained catching up was thus the next duty. Her nephew's life, she had always supposed, had been filled with incident and probably not happy; her own, which seemed to her happy, hadn't been eventful. Her sister Amy had married a man she hadn't loved, for her son John's sake, she said: they had left New England—the last Phillippa had seen of them—and begun a series of removes farther and farther West. Amy's letters, not pleasant to read, had grown more and more infrequent, now reduced to a Christmas card with a distracted note written on the back. The stepfather had vanished; at any rate, he ceased to be mentioned. When their mother—with whom Phillippa had lived alone for many years—died, Amy hadn't come to the funeral.

Somewhere down the years Amy had written that John had entered a seminary, and when Phillippa saw mentioned in her local paper that a John Knowe had been appointed to the faculty of a Catholic girl's school in Westchester, the possibility that this might be her nephew, revolved eastward, grew slowly (for it was hard for her to think of him as other than a shy, large-eyed, and undergrown boy) to a certainty. For many reasons (mostly not the reasons she chose to give herself) she didn't call him; but when the lawyer's letter came informing her that Cousin Anne's will had at last been straightened out, she took it on herself to inform John of it. Foolish, she told herself, living so near and not reopening relations; if he wouldn't begin, she would.

"She had some property in Vermont," she told him. "Nothing very grand; but she's left some of it to you, or rather you've come into it by default or something. . . ."

"Not the old farm," he said, his voice far away.

"Oh no. No, Mother and I sold the farm years ago. No, a parcel of land—not too far north of the farm—and I thought perhaps you might like to see it. I was planning a trip up there in any case—the leaves ought to be just at their peak—and I thought . . . "

"I don't drive."

"Well, I do." She was growing faintly impatient. "There are apparently some papers to sign at her lawyer's up there. It could all be taken care of."

"Well," he said, "it's very kind of you." There was a pause, and then he said: "I'm sorry about the farm."

Slight, darkly bearded, not in clerical dress, he stood on the steps of the college with an abstracted yet attentive air that struck her as familiar. Who was she reminded of? Of him, no doubt; him as a boy. For a while she studied him without getting out of the car or hailing him, feeling unaccountably swept into the past.

"John."

"Aunt Phil." He was as astonished as she was not. She felt embarrassed; she must appear a ghastly crone in comparison to his mental image. Yet he took her hand warmly, and after a moment's hesitation, kissed her cheek, tenderly almost. His large eyes were as she remembered them. For a moment a hard thickness started in her throat, and she looked at the sky as an excuse to turn away.

"I should warn you," she said, "I'm a weather jinx. I can go anywhere and a blue sky will turn black." And in fact, in the west, hard, white clouds were moving over, preceded by wind-twisted pale mare's-tails—stormbringers, her mother always called them.

Parkways north: Already along these most civilized of turnpikes the ivy had turned, burdening the still-green trees with garments of many colors. Since the twenties, when her father had bought the farm for their summers, she had made this journey many times, at first on dirt roads through then-rural Connecticut, later on traveling under these arching bridges each one different; and now skating along superhighways that reached—it had once seemed impossible to her that they ever would—deeply into Vermont itself. At this season, she and Amy and her parents would have been traveling the other way, not toward but away from the farm, where they lived from May to October; going home, they always said, but to

Phillippa at least it had always seemed the reverse: leaving the true home for the other, the workaday place, the exile.

"We sold it in 1953," she said in answer to his question. "The summer after you left this part of the world. It had become just a burden. Dad was dead, and you children weren't coming up anymore; Mother and I needed money to buy the house in Rye. We got a sudden offer at the end of the summer—a pretty good one—and sold. We were grateful. I guess."

"What was a pretty good offer then?"

"Five thousand. And another hundred or so for the furnishings; the buyer took most of those too."

"Five thousand." He shook his head.

"We paid two, in the twenties. And much of the acreage was gone by then."

"Nineteen fifty-three," he said softly, as though the date were something precious and fragile; and then nothing more, looking out the window, absorbed.

She had rather feared this, his remoteness, a probably inevitable constraint. She passed a remark about the weather—the trees were turning up their silvery undersides, as though raising hands in dismay, and the sky was growing increasingly fierce—and then asked about his work. It seemed to be the right question; talking about theology, about the politics of the soul, he became animated and amusing, almost chatty.

Phillippa's religion, or lack of it, was that of the woman in the Stevens poem, sitting on Sunday morning with her coffee and her cockatoo. "Why should she give her bounty to the dead" And that about April . . .

> There is not any haunt of prophecy
> Nor any old chimera of the grave,
> Neither the golden underground, nor isle
> Melodious, where spirits gat them home,
> Nor visionary South, nor cloudy palm
> Remote on heaven's hill, that has endured
> As April's green endures. . . .

*

"Yes," he said, putting the tips of his fingers together, "heaven is a difficulty. It seems hardly worth all the effort, to end up in a white robe singing praises; like an infinity of choir practice. Of course, there's to be an ineffable, indescribable bliss; but it's damn hard to imagine, isn't it?"

"I suppose really religious people sense it," Phillippa said, feeling odd to be defending heaven.

"I don't know. I think people who really believe it invest the ordinary things they love with the idea of heaven; so that when they say 'This is heavenly,' they really mean it." Phillippa noticed his shapely hands, mobile now where they had been meekly folded before. They too reminded her of someone; yet how could so changeful a thing as hands, so markable by time, retain a reminder of him as a boy?

"Mother—Amy—always said," he went on, "that she didn't care about heaven if she couldn't have around her all the people and places and times she loved most, in their characters—I mean not abstracted; not in white robes; not on clouds. I think I believe that. Heaven is where you are—or will be, or have been, there being no time in heaven—most happy."

Where for her, Phillippa wondered; and knew, without assenting to the possibility: the farm, in high summer, years ago. If that were so . . . But it wasn't. If there was one thing Phillippa knew, it was that happiness is something you lose, fast or slow. "I wouldn't think," she said, "your Church would go along with those ideas."

He laughed, pleased. "No, well. All that is up in the air, now, you know. I'm something of a heresiarch anyway, really. In fact, I've recently worked up a new heresy, or refurbished an old one. Would you like to hear it?"

"If you can promise we won't be punished for it," Phillippa said. To the north, a vast, curdled darkness was advancing across their path. "I mean look at that sky."

"It goes like this," he said, crossing one sharp-kneed leg over the other. "I've decided that not all men have immortal souls. Immortality is what Adam and Eve forfeited in the garden. From then on it was dust to dust. What Jesus promised to those who believed in him was eternal life—the possibility of not dying eternally. So that the believer, if his faith and hope and charity are strong, *creates* his own immortality through Jesus—the first immortal man since Adam: the new Adam."

"What about the outer darkness, and the weeping and wailing and gnashing of teeth?"

"A metaphor for death. I think it's easier to explain those few references to fires and so on as metaphors for death than to explain all the many references to death as metaphors for eternal punishment. Jesus said, He who believes in me *shall not die;* that seems clearly to mean that everybody else will."

"No hell?"

"No. A great problem solved there. Those who don't care about salvation merely go under the ground, utterly extinguished, having failed to accomplish their immortality."

"Comforting."

"Isn't it. Also clears up the problems of infant damnation and the Good Pagan. More than that, though: It makes the choice harder. The choice for Jesus. When the alternative doesn't seem so terrible."

"In fact—I'm sorry—preferable. Eternal life doesn't appeal to me."

"Well, there you are. Perhaps it isn't an unalloyed good. Perhaps it's quite difficult—as difficult as any kind of life."

"Dear me."

"Maybe some have no choice. The God-possessed, the saintly." He had grown more still, more inward. She wondered if he were still joking. "In fact, I would think the population of heaven would be small."

Phillippa thought of medieval pictures of the court of heaven, the winged saints in rows intended to suggest great numbers but really absurdly few. But that wasn't the heaven he envisioned, was it? Where ripe fruit never falls. If it were to be a heaven composed of the things one loved most, it would have to include (as far as Phillippa was concerned) change of season, fall of leaves, days like this one, raddled with dark, flying clouds; the flame of swamp maples, going out; April's green. And yes, for there to be enough of it to go around, perhaps there would need to be only a few to divide it among; the rest of us, mortal, resigning it to them. She thought, suddenly, of an old convertible turning in at the stone gateposts of the long weedy drive leading up to the farm.

Who could that be? her mother said. *No one we know.*

The car, with orange leaves stuck beneath its windshield wipers, nosed into the drive tentatively, uncertainly.

Just turning around, perhaps, lost, Phillippa said. They sat together on the porch, for it was quite warm in the sun. It was so utterly still and blue that the leaves fell seemingly for no reason, skating with slow agility to the ground. Their clicking fall among the rest was sometimes audible: It was that still.

The car stopped halfway up the drive and a young man got out. He wore a wide fedora—every man did then—and smoked a long, straight pipe. He stood with his hands in the pockets of his pleated slacks, looking at the house, though not, it seemed, at them. When at last he began to walk toward them, he did so not purposefully, nor did he hail them; he might have been arriving at a deserted house, or a house of his own. When at last he did greet them, it was with a kind of lazy familiarity. He wasn't a Vermonter, by his voice.

He had been told, he said, in the village, that the ladies were thinking of selling. He was in the market for just such a place; a writer, he needed someplace quiet to work. Were they in fact selling? Might he see the place?

It had been that very week that Phillippa and her mother had come to see that another summer in this house wasn't possible. The people in the village had, apparently, come to the same conclusion; not surprising, really, but a little forward of them to put it up for sale without asking. Well, her look asked her mother, here he was; why not show him around?

It's kind of a rambling old place, she said as they went in through the straining screen door. He stood in the parlor, seeming less to see the place than to inhale its fragrance, of wood stoves and old furniture and cidery autumn air. *Wouldn't it be too big for you?*

Room to spread out, he said, smiling as though he didn't really care. She showed him the kitchen, deprecatingly; there was no inside plumbing but a pump; no toilets; no stove but this iron monster. It would need a lot of improvement.

I think I'll leave it as it is, he said complacently. *It suits me.*

But the winter, Mother said. *What will you do then?*

He shrugged happily. *Hibernate, maybe.* He touched the huge old sinks fondly. *Soapstone,* he said. *When I was a kid I thought these sinks were called soapstone because you washed in them.*

It was difficult to move him through the house. Whatever room he entered he seemed to want to stay in forever, looking around dreamily. Phillippa found she couldn't be impatient with him, because he was so obviously taken with what she so much loved. By the end of the tour she found herself rather wanting this stranger to have her house.

And in the end he did have it, over her mother's objections—she wanted to give it to the local real-estate broker, an old friend—and most of the furniture too, Victorian junk they had collected through twenty summers of auctions.

"Junk," John Knowe said. "It wouldn't be that now, would it?"

"No. Antiques. But of course we didn't know that then."

"The fat horsehair sofa. Grandpa's big desk in the den, with the brass paperweight, very heavy, and the letter opener like a sword. The old clock, with weights like pine cones . . ."

"You remember that?"

"Yes. Of course. All of it."

He said it simply, as though it were no feat; and so he would, Phillippa thought: Not having seen it since he was eleven, his memories of it all must be very sharp, as though preserved in a clear amber unclouded by grown-up perceptions of use, worth, price, burdensomeness. The farm had not altered for him, grown problematic, in the end insupportable. She felt unwanted, a pang of loss; for herself more than for him. A few fat raindrops exploded against the windshield, then no more.

Through Massachusetts the storm that they seemed to be driving fast toward, as toward a destination, had grown, changed shape continually; as though hung for a pageant, moving on wires, two and sometimes three ranks of clouds crossed the sky at different speeds, and spotlights of sun picked out now this, now another bit of golden hillside. When they crossed into Vermont, the wind began to press hard on the car, and great flights of leaves blew across the highway like the flights of starlings in the brown fields. Northwest the clouds were not distinct, they were a solid cloak of the deepest gray, fuzzy with unseen rain. "That's where we go," Phillippa said. "But at least here's Vermont." She knew it was foolish, but couldn't help saying, "Whenever I cross the border, I always think of the lines about *Breathes there a man with soul so dead, Who never to himself has said . . .*"

"*This is my own, my native land.*" He said it without irony, as though just discovering it to be true. "The land of heart's desire."

She remembered a photograph Amy had sent once. John, perhaps thirteen, stood before a shabby stand of alders and nameless undergrowth. Through the thin growth a midwestern landscape could be seen, featureless. Caught in the twiggy undergrowth were bits of paper, trash, human residue. Amy had written on the back "John's 'woods,' " as though that were what John called them. Exile. Maybe hell was where you had been most unhappy. No: No hell in his heresy. "We'll see Ascutney soon," she said. "Or maybe not, in this weather."

"Outside the kitchen door," he said—and it took her a moment to realize he was still thinking of the farm—"there were raspberry bushes."

"Yes."

"Very thick; so thick it was hard to open the door. And a little stone porch."

"Just a flagstone step. It was large to you, maybe."

"Bees. And the smell of those bushes . . ."

You can pick quarts of them in the summer, she said. *The smell of them in the sun is terrific.*

Yes, he said, looking not at the brown November garden but at her. Inside, her mother and the movers walked back and forth, their footsteps hollow. *I'm sorry, really, to be taking it all from you.*

Don't be silly. His eyes, large, liquid, remote, were— were whatever is the opposite of silly. She felt no anger at him, and not envy; she did want him to have her house; only—for a wild moment—wanted desperately not to lose it either. She wanted to share it, share it all; she wanted . . . He went on looking at her, fixedly and unashamedly as a cat; and there came a flaw in time, a doubling of this moment, a shadow scene behind this scene in which he asked her to come now, come to stay, stay now, stay always, yield it all to him and yet have it all. . . . As instantly as she perceived it, the flaw healed as though her eyes uncrossed; and *No, no,* she said, blinking, turning back to the kitchen door, shaken, as though unaware that she had found herself walking out on ice.

She remembered that moment now, a cold wave rising beneath her heart. Mount Ascutney rose up very suddenly, blackish and with storm clouds disturbed by its head as though it wore wild hair. The pale gash of the road seemed to plunge into it.

"You never went back," John Knowe said.

"No. Never. It would be very changed, I'm sure."

"Yes. No doubt."

Wind shoved them suddenly, violently. The road had become shiny as a ballroom floor, the day dark as night. No doubt, no doubt. John Knowe drew a long, straight pipe from his pocket and put it unlit in his mouth. "It looks like this is it," he said.

Rain coursed down the windshield as they rose up and shot down a rise with heartsickening speed, blind. She fumbled for the wiper button, peering into the silver nothing. Hail fell clattering, roaring; the wipers stuck. She braked, panicking, and they seemed to rise up smoothly off the road, accelerating, gliding toward the cloudy head of Ascutney—she could see it fast approaching. The brake, pressed down, had no effect in air—that was the thought she had—and a piece of mountain, a tall black rectangle of it, detached itself and flew out of the nothing to meet them, changing size swiftly.

You can come too, John Knowe said, and it was already not his voice. *You can come now.*

NO, and she twisted the wheel violently away from the black rectangle that would have engulfed them

and when she was helped from the car, rain washing the sticky blood from her hands and face, in the deep fearful calm of shock she saw not this car half crushed beneath, against the black stalled truck, but an old convertible, with autumn leaves caught beneath its wipers, turning carefully, lost yet found, into an old weed-spined drive between stone gateposts; and heard, not the shriek of sirens and the shouts *He's dead, he's dead,* but the faint yet audible click of a falling leaf joining the others on the littered ground.

Stephen King is the highly respected author of Carrie, Salem's Lot, *and* The Shining. *He is an ex-high school teacher from Maine who has vowed to sooner work hauling crates in a Pepsi plant than return to the classroom again. He is not very visible to the community of fantasy authors, but I can vouch for the fact that he is like most of us . . . unassuming, unmonsterlike, and determined to make his readers feel at least once the ice grip of fear.*

There is a deception in his work, too, as there is in "Nona"; a characteristic accumulation of detail that weaves a false fortress of security around the reader while, at the same time, propelling him toward a climax that arrives much like a bat laid across the back of one's skull.

A stillness in the air. Thunder.
Wind.

NONA

by Stephen King

I don't know how to explain it, even now. I can't tell you why I did those things. I couldn't do it at the trial, either. And there are a lot of people here who ask me about it. There's a psychiatrist who does. But I am silent. My lips are sealed. Except here in my cell. Here I am not silent. I wake up screaming.

In the dream I see her walking toward me. She is wearing a white gown, almost transparent, and her expression is one of mingled desire and triumph. She comes to me across a dark room with a stone floor and I smell dry October roses. Her arms are held open and I go to her with mine out to enfold her.

I feel dread, revulsion . . . and unutterable longing. Dread and revulsion because I know what this place is, and longing because I love her. I will always love her. There are times when I wish there were still a death penalty. A short walk down a dim corridor, a straight-backed chair fitted with a steel skullcap, clamps . . . then one quick jolt and I would be with her.

As we come together in the dream my fear grows, but it is impossible for me to draw back from her. My hands press against the smooth plane of her back, her skin near under silk. She smiles with those deep, black eyes. Her head tilts up to mine and her lips part, ready to be kissed.

That's when she changes, shrivels. Her hair grows coarse and matted, melting from black to an ugly brown that spills down over the creamy whiteness of her cheeks. The eyes shrink and go beady. The whites disappear and she is glaring at me with tiny eyes like two polished pieces of jet. The mouth becomes a maw through which crooked yellow teeth protrude.

I try to scream, I try to wake up.

I can't. I'm caught again. I'll always be caught.

I am in the grip of a huge, noisome graveyard rat. Lights sway in front of my eyes. October roses. Somewhere a dead bell is chanting.

"Mine," this thing whispers. "Mine, mine, mine." The smell of roses is its breath as it swoops toward me, dead flowers in a charnel house.

Then I do scream, and I am awake.

They think what we did together has driven me crazy. But my mind is still working in some way or other, and I've never stopped looking for the answers. I still want to know how it was . . . and what it was. . . .

They've let me have paper and a pen with a felt tip. And I'm going to write everything down. I'll answer all their questions and maybe while I'm doing that I can answer some of my own. And when I'm done, there's something else. Something they didn't let me have. Something I took. It's here, under my mattress. A knife from the prison dining hall.

I'll have to start by telling you about Augusta.

As I write this it is night, a fine August night poked through with blazing stars. I can see them through the mesh of my window, which overlooks the exercise yard and a slice of sky I can block out with two fingers. It's hot, and I'm naked except for my shorts. I can hear the soft summer sound of frogs and crickets. But I can bring back winter just by closing my eyes. The bitter cold of that night, the bleakness, the hard, unfriendly lights of a city that was not my city. It was the fourteenth of February. See, I remember everything.

Look at my arms—covered with sweat, they've pulled into gooseflesh.

Augusta . . .

When I got to Augusta I was more dead than alive, it was that cold. I had picked a fine day to say good-bye to the college scene and hitchhike West; it looked like I might freeze to death before I got out of the state.

A cop had kicked me off the interstate ramp and threatened to bust me if he caught me thumbing there again. I was almost tempted to wisemouth him and let him do it. The flat, four-lane stretch of highway had been like an airport landing strip, the wind whooping and pushing membranes of powdery snow skirling along the concrete. And to the anonymous Them behind their Saf-T-Glas windshields, everyone standing in the breakdown lane on a dark night is either a rapist or a murderer, and if he's got long hair you can throw in child molester and faggot on top.

I tried it awhile on the access road, but it was no good. And along about a quarter of eight I realized that if I didn't get someplace warm quick, I was going to pass out.

I walked a mile and a half before I found a combination diner and diesel stop on 202 just inside the city limits. JOE'S GOOD EATS, the neon said. There were three big rigs parked in the crushed-stone parking lot, and one new sedan. There was a wilted Christmas wreath on the door that nobody had bothered to take down, and next to it a thermometer showing just five degrees of mercury above the zero mark. I had nothing to cover my ears but my hair, and my rawhide gloves were falling apart. The tips of my fingers felt like pieces of furniture.

I opened the door and went in.

The heat was the first thing that struck me, warm and good. Next a hillbilly song on the juke, the unmistakable voice of Merle Haggard: *"We don't let our hair grow long and shaggy, like the hippies out in San Francisco do."*

The third thing that struck me was The Eye. You know about The Eye once you let your hair get down below the lobes of your ears. Right then people know you don't belong to the Lions, Elks, or the VFW. You know about The Eye, but you never get used to it.

Right now the people giving me The Eye were four truckers in one booth, two more at the counter, a pair of old ladies wearing cheap fur coats and blue rinses, the short-order cook, and a gawky kid with soapsuds on his hands. There was a girl sitting at the far end of the counter, but all she was looking at was the bottom of her coffee cup.

She was the fourth thing that struck me.

We're both old enough to know there's no such thing as love at first sight. It's just something Rogers and Hammerstein thought up one day to rhyme with moon and June. It's for kids holding hands at the Junior Prom, right?

But looking at her made me feel something. You can laugh, but you wouldn't have if you'd seen her. She was almost unbearably beautiful. I knew without a doubt that everybody else in Joe's knew that the same as me. Just like I knew she had been getting The Eye before I came in. She had coal-colored hair, so black that it seemed nearly blue under the fluorescents. It fell freely over the shoulders of her scuffed tan coat. Her skin was cream-white, with just the faintest blooded touch lingering beneath the skin—the cold she had brought in with her. Dark, sooty lashes. Solemn eyes that slanted up the tiniest bit at the corners. A full and mobile mouth below a straight, patrician nose. I couldn't tell what her body looked like. I didn't care. You wouldn't have, either. All she needed was that face, that hair, that *look*. She was exquisite. That's the only word we have for her in English.

Nona.

I sat two stools down from her, and the short-order cook came over and looked at me. "What?"

"Black coffee, please."

He went to get it. From behind me someone said: "Looks just like Jesus Christ, don't he?"

The gawky dishwasher laughed, a quick yuk-yuk sound. The truckers at the counter joined in.

The short-order cook brought me my coffee back, jarred it down on the counter and spilled some on the thawing meat of my hand. I jerked it back.

"Sorry," he said indifferently.

"He's gonna heal it himself," one of the truckers in the booth called over.

The blue-rinse twins paid their checks and hurried out. One of the knights of the road sauntered over to the juke and put another dime in. Johnny Cash began to sing "A Boy Named Sue." I blew on my coffee.

Someone tugged on my sleeve. I turned my head and there she was—she'd moved over to the empty stool. Looking at that face close up was almost blinding. I spilled some more of my coffee.

"I'm sorry." Her voice was low, almost atonal.

"My fault. I can't feel what I'm doing yet."

"I—"

She stopped, seemingly at a loss. I suddenly realized that she was scared. I felt my first reaction to her swim over me again—to protect her and take care of her, make her not afraid. "I need a ride," she finished in a rush. "I didn't dare ask any of them." She made a barely perceptible gesture toward the truckers in the booth.

How can I make you understand that I would have given anything—*anything*—to be able to tell her, *Sure, finish your coffee, I'm parked right outside*. It sounds crazy to say I felt that way after half a dozen words out of her mouth, and the same number out of mine, but I did. I did.

Looking at her was like looking at the Mona Lisa or the Venus de Milo come to breathing life. And there was another feeling: It was as if a sudden, powerful light had been turned on in the confused darkness of my mind. It would make it easier if I could say she was a pickup and I was a fast man with the ladies, quick with a funny line and lots of patter, but she wasn't and I wasn't. All I knew was I didn't have what she needed and it tore me up.

"I'm thumbing," I told her. "A cop kicked me off the interstate and I only came in here to get out of the cold. I'm sorry."

"Are you from the university?"

"Not anymore. I quit before they could fire me."

"Are you going home?"

"No home to go to. I was a state ward. I got to school on a scholarship. I blew it. Now I don't know where I'm going." My life story in five sentences. It made me feel depressed.

She laughed—the sound made me run hot and cold— and sipped her own coffee. "We're cats out of the same bag, I guess."

I was about to make my best conversational shot— something witty like "Is that so?"—when a hand came down on my shoulder.

I turned around. It was one of the truckers from the booth. He had blond stubble on his chin and there was a wooden kitchen match poking out of his mouth. He smelled of engine oil.

"I think you're done with that coffee," he said. His lips parted around the match in a grin. He had a lot of very white teeth.

"What?"

"You're stinking the place up, fella. You are a fella, aren't you? Kind of hard to tell."

"You aren't any rose yourself," I said. "You smell like a crankcase."

He gave me a hard palm across the side of my face. I saw little black dots.

"Don't fight in here," the short-order cook said. "If you're going to scramble him, do it outside.

"Come on, you goddamned Commie," the trucker said.

This is the spot where the girl is supposed to say something like "Unhand him" or "You brute." She wasn't saying anything. She was watching both of us with feverish intensity. It was scary. I think it was the first time I'd noticed how huge her eyes really were.

"Do I have to sock you again, fag?"

"No. Come on, shitheels."

I don't know how that jumped out of me. I don't like to fight. I'm not a good fighter. I'm an even worse name-caller. But I was angry, just then. It came up all at once and I wanted to hurt him, kill him.

Maybe he got a mental whiff of it. For just a second a shade of uncertainty flicked over his face, an unconscious wondering if maybe he hadn't picked the wrong hippie. Then it was gone. He wasn't going to back off from some long-haired elitist effeminite snob who used the flag to wipe his ass with—at least not in front of his buddies. Not a big truck-driving son-of-a-gun like him.

The anger pounded over me again. *Faggot? Faggot?* I felt out of control, and it was good to feel that way. My tongue was thick in my mouth. My stomach was a slab.

We walked across to the door, and my buddy's buddies almost broke their backs getting up to watch the fun.

Nona? I thought of her, but only in an absent, back-of-my-mind way. I knew Nona would be there, Nona would take care of me. I knew it the same way I knew it would be cold outside. It was strange to know that about a girl I had only met five minutes before. Strange, but I didn't think about that until later. My mind was taken up—no, almost blotted out—by the heavy cloud of rage. I felt homicidal.

The cold was so clear and so clean that it felt as if we were cutting it with our bodies like knives. The frosted gravel of the parking lot gritted harshly under his heavy boots and under my shoes. The moon, full and bloated, looked down on us with a vapid eye, faintly rheumed with a rime of high atmospheric moisture, from a sky as black as a night in hell. We left tiny dwarfed shadows behind our feet in the monochrome glare of a single

sodium light set high on a pole beyond the parked rigs.
Our breath plumed the air in short bursts. The trucker
turned to me, his gloved fists balled.

"Okay, you son-of-a-bitch," he said.

I seemed to be swelling—my whole body seemed to be
swelling. Somehow, numbly, I knew that my intellect was
about to be eclipsed by some huge, invisible something
that I had never suspected might be in me. It was terrifying—
but at the same time I welcomed it, desired it, lusted for it.
In that last instant of coherent thought it seemed that my
body had become a stone pyramid of violence incarnate,
or a rushing, murderous cyclone that could sweep everything in front of it like so many colored pick-up sticks. The
trucker seemed small, puny, insignificant. I laughed at
him. I laughed, and the sound was as black and as bleak as
that moonstruck sky overhead.

He came at me swinging his fists. I batted down his
right, took his left on the side of my face, and then kicked
him in the guts. The air whoofed out of him in a white,
steaming rush. He tried to back away, holding himself
and coughing.

I ran around in back of him, still laughing like some
farmer's dog barking at the moon, and I had pounded him
three times before he could make even a quarter turn—
the neck, the shoulder, and one red ear.

He made a yowling noise, and one of his flailing hands
brushed my nose. The fury that had taken me over mush-
roomed—*me! he tried to strike at me!*—and I kicked him
again, bringing my foot up high and hard, like a punter.
He screamed into the night and I heard a rib snap. He
folded up and I jumped on him.

At the trial one of the other truck drivers testified I
was like a wild animal. And I was. I can't remember much
of it, but I can remember that, snarling and growling at
him like a wild dog.

I straddled him, grabbed double handfuls of his
greasy hair, and began to rub his face into the gravel. In
the flat glare of the sodium light his blood seemed black,
like beetle's blood.

"Jesus, stop it!" somebody yelled.

Hands grabbed my shoulders and pulled me off. I saw whirling faces and I struck at them.

The trucker was trying to creep away. His face was a staring mask of blood, and dazed eyes. I began to kick him, dodging away from the others, grunting with satisfaction each time I connected on him.

He was beyond fighting back. All he knew was to try to get away. Each time I kicked him his eyes would squeeze closed, like the eyes of a tortoise, and he would halt. Then he would start to crawl again. He looked stupid. I decided I was going to kill him. I was going to kick him to death. Then I would kill the rest of them, all but Nona.

I kicked him again and he flopped over on his back and looked up at me dazedly.

"Uncle," he croaked. "I cry uncle. Please. Please—"

I knelt down beside him, feeling the gravel bite into my knees through my thin jeans.

"Here you are, bastard," I whispered. "Here's uncle for you."

I hooked my hands onto his throat.

Three of them jumped me all at once and knocked me off him. I got up, still grinning, and started toward them. They backed away, three big men, all of them scared green.

And it clicked off.

Just like that it clicked off and it was just me, standing in the parking lot of Joe's Good Eats, breathing hard and feeling sick and horrified.

I turned and looked back toward the diner. The girl was there, her beautiful features were lit with triumph. She raised one fist to shoulder height in salute.

I turned back to the man on the ground. He was still trying to crawl away, and when I approached him his eyeballs rolled fearfully.

"Don't you touch him!" one of his friends cried.

I looked at them, confused. "I'm sorry . . . I didn't mean to . . . to hurt him so bad. Let me help—"

"You get out of here, that's what you do," the short-order cook said. He was standing in front of Nona at the foot of the steps, clutching a greasy spatula in one hand. "I'm calling the cops."

"Aren't you forgetting he was the guy who started it? He—"

"Don't give me any of your lip, you lousy queer," he said, backing up. "All I know is you started trouble and then just about killed that guy. I'm calling the cops!" He dashed and went back inside.

"Okay," I said to nobody in particular. "Okay, okay."

I had left my rawhide gloves inside, but it didn't seem like a good idea to go back in and get them. I put my hands in my pockets and started to walk back to the interstate access road. I figured my chances against hitching a ride before the cops picked me up were about ten to one. My ears were freezing and I felt sick to my stomach. Some night.

"Wait! Hey, wait!"

I turned around. It was her, running to catch up with me, her hair flying out behind her.

"You were wonderful!" she said. "Wonderful!"

"I hurt him bad," I said dully. "I never did anything like that before."

"I wish you'd killed him!"

I blinked at her in the frosty light.

"I heard the things they were saying about me before you came in. Laughing in that big, brave, dirty way—haw, haw, lookit the little girl out so long after dark. Where you going, honey? Need a lift? I'll give you a ride if you'll give me a ride. *Damn!*"

She glared back over her shoulder as if she could strike them dead with a sudden bolt from her dark eyes. Then she turned them on me, and again it seemed like that searchlight had been turned on in my mind. "I'm coming with you."

"Where? To jail?" I tugged at my hair with both hands. "With this, the first guy that gave us a ride would be a state cop. That cook meant what he said about calling them."

"*I'll* hitch. You stand behind me. They'll stop for me."

I couldn't argue with her about that and didn't want to. Love at first sight? I doubt it. But it was something.

"Here," she said, "you forgot these." She held out my gloves.

She hadn't gone back inside, and that meant she'd had them all along. She'd known she was coming with me. It gave me an eerie feeling. I put on my gloves and we walked up the access road to the turnpike ramp.

She was right about the ride. We got one with the first car that swung onto the ramp. Before that happened I asked, "What's your name?"

"Nona," she said simply. She didn't offer any more, but that was all right. I was satisfied.

We didn't say anything else while we waited, but it seemed as if we did. I won't give you a load of bull about ESP and that stuff; there was none of that. But we didn't need it. You've felt it yourself if you've ever been with someone you were really close to, or if you've taken one of those drugs with initials for a name. You don't *have* to talk. Communication seems to shift over to some high-frequency emotional band. A twist of the hand does it all. You don't need the social amenities. But we were strangers. I only knew her first name and now that I think back, I don't believe I ever told her mine at all. But we were doing it. It wasn't love. I hate to keep repeating that, but I feel I have to. I wouldn't dirty that word with whatever we had—not after what we did, not after Blainesville, not after the dreams.

A high, wailing shriek filled the cold silence of the night, rising and falling.

"That's an ambulance, I think," I said.

"Yes."

Silence again. The moon's light was fading behind a thickening membrane of cloud. I thought we would have snow before the night was over.

Lights poked over the hill.

I stood behind her without having to be told. She brushed her hair back and raised that beautiful face. As I watched the car signal for the entrance ramp I was swept with a feeling of unreality—it was unreal that this beautiful girl had elected to come with me, it was unreal that I had beaten a man to the point where an ambulance had to be called for him, it was unreal to think I might be in jail by morning. Unreal. I felt caught in a spiderweb. But who was the spider?

Nona put out her thumb. The car, a Chevrolet sedan, went by us and I thought it was going to keep right on going. Then the taillights flashed and Nona grabbed my hand. "Come on, we got a ride!" She grinned at me with childish delight and I grinned back at her.

The guy was reaching enthusiastically across the seat to open the door for her. When the dome light flashed on I could see him—a fairly big man in an expensive camel's hair coat, graying around the edges of his hat, prosperous features softened by years of good meals. A businessman or a salesman. Alone. When he saw me he did a double take, but it was a second or two too late to put the car back in gear and haul out of there. And it was easier for him this way. Later he could fib himself into believing he had seen both of us, that he was a truly good-hearted soul giving a young couple a break.

"Cold night," he said as Nona slid in beside him and I got in beside her.

"It certainly is," Nona said sweetly. "Thank you!"

"Yeah," I said. "Thanks."

"Don't mention it." And we were off, leaving sirens, busted-up truckers, and Joe's Good Eats behind us.

I had gotten kicked off the interstate at seven-thirty. It was only eight-thirty now. It's amazing how much you can do in a short time, or how much can be done to you.

We were approaching the yellow flashing lights that signal the Augusta toll station.

"How far you going?" the driver asked.

That was a stumper. I had been hoping to make it as far as Kittery and crash with an acquaintance who was teaching school there. It still seemed as good an answer as any and I was opening my mouth to give it when Nona said:

"We're going to Blainesville. It's a small town just south of Lewiston-Auburn."

Blainesville. That made me feel strange. Once upon a time I had been on pretty good terms with Blainesville. But that was before Ace Carmody messed me up.

He brought his car to a stop, took a toll ticket, and then we were on our way again.

"I'm only going as far as Gardner, myself," he said, lying smoothly. "One exit up. But that's a start for you."

"It certainly is," Nona said, just as sweetly as before. "It was nice of you to stop on such a cold night." And while she was saying it I was getting her anger on that high emotional wavelength, naked and full of venom. It scared me, the way ticking from a wrapped package might scare me.

"My name's Blanchette," he said. "Norman Blanchette." He waved his hand in our direction to be shaken.

"Cheryl Craig," Nona said, taking it daintily.

I took her cue and gave him a false name. "Pleasure," I mumbled. His hand was soft and flabby. It felt like a hot-water bottle in the shape of a hand; the thought sickened me. It sickened me that we had been forced to beg a ride with this patronizing man who thought he had seen a chance to pick up a pretty girl hitching all by herself, a girl who might or might not agree to an hour spent in a motel room in return for enough cash to buy a bus ticket. It sickened me to know that if I had been alone this man who had just offered me his flabby, hot hand would have zipped by without a second look. It sickened me to know he would drop us at the Gardner exit and then dart right back on down the southbound ramp, congratulating himself on how smoothly he had solved an annoying situation. Everything about him sickened me. The porky droop of his jowls, the slicked-back wings of his hair, the smell of his cologne.

And what right did he have? What right?

The sickness curdled, and the flowers of rage began to bloom again. The headlights of his prosperous Impala sedan cut the night with smooth ease, and my rage wanted to reach out and strangle everything that he was set in among—the kind of music I knew he would listen to as he lay back in his La-Z-Boy recliner with the evening paper in his hot-water-bottle hands, the blue rinse his wife would use in her hair, the kids always sent off to the movies or off to school or off to camp—as long as they were off somewhere—his snobbish friends and the drunken parties they would attend with them.

But maybe his cologne was the worst. It seemed to fill the car with the sweet, sickish stench of his hypocrisy. It smelled like the perfumed disinfectant they use in a slaughterhouse at the end of each shift.

The car ripped through the night with Norman Blanchette holding the wheels in his bloated hands. His manicured nails gleamed softly in the lights from the instrument panel. I wanted to crack a wing window and get away from that cloying smell. No, more—I wanted to crank the whole window down and stick my head out into the cold, purifying air of the night, wallow in its chilled freshness—but I was frozen, frozen in the dumb maw of my wordless, inexpressible hate.

That was when Nona put the nail file into my hand.

When I was three I got a bad case of the flu and had to go to the hospital. While I was there, my dad fell asleep smoking in bed and the house burned down with them and my older brother Drake in it. I have their pictures. They look like actors in an old 1958 American-International horror movie, faces you don't know like those of the big stars, more like Elisha Cook, Jr., and Mara Corday and some child actor you can't quite remember . . . Brandon DeWilde, maybe.

I had no relatives to go to and so I was sent to a home in Portland for five years. Then I became a state ward. That means a family takes you in and the state pays them thirty dollars a month for your keep. I don't think there was ever a state ward who acquired a taste for lobster. Usually a couple will take two or three wards as a hard-headed business investment. If a kid is fed up he can earn his keep doing chores around the place and that hard thirty turns into gravy.

My folks were named Hollis and they lived in Falmouth. Not the fancy part near the country club or the yacht club but farther out toward the Blainesville town line. They had a three-story farmhouse with fourteen rooms. There was coal heat in the kitchen that got upstairs anyway it could, and in January you went to bed with three quilts on you and still weren't sure if your feet were there when you woke up in the morning until you put them out on the floor where you could look at them. Mrs. Hollis was fat. Mr. Hollis was dour, rarely spoke, and wore a red-and-black checked hunting cap all year round. The house was a helter-skelter mess of white-elephant furniture, rummage-sale stuff, moldy mattresses, dogs, cats, and automotive parts laid on newspaper. I had three "brothers," all of them wards. We had a nodding acquaintance, like co-travelers on a three-day bus trip.

I made good grades in school and went out for spring baseball when I was a high school sophomore. Hollis was yapping after me to quit, but I stuck with it until the thing with Ace Carmody happened. Then I didn't want to go anymore, not with my face all puffed and cut, not with the stories Betsy Dirisko was telling around. So I quit the team, and Hollis got me a job in the local drugstore.

In February of my junior year I took the College Boards, paying for them with twelve bucks I had socked away in my mattress. I got accepted at the university with a small scholarship and a good work-study job in the library. The expression on the Hollises' faces when I showed them the financial-aid papers is the best memory of my life.

One of my "brothers," Curt, ran away. I couldn't have done that. I was too passive to take a step like that. I would have been back after two hours on the road. School was the only way out for me, and I took it.

The last thing Mrs. Hollis said when I left was, "You write, hear me? And send us something when you can." I never saw either of them again. I made good grades my freshman year and got a job that summer working full-time in the library. I sent them a Christmas card that first year, but that was the only one.

In the first semester of my sophomore year I fell in love. It was the biggest thing that had ever happened to me. Pretty? She would have knocked you back two steps. To this day I have no idea what she saw in me. I don't even know if she loved me or not. I think she did at first. After that I was just a habit that's hard to break, like smoking or driving with your elbow poked out the window. She held me for a while, maybe not wanting to break the habit.

Maybe she held me for wonder, or maybe it was just her vanity. Good boy, roll over, sit up, fetch the paper. Here's a kiss good night. It doesn't matter. For a while it was love, then it was like love, then it was over.

I slept with her twice, both times after other things had taken over for love. That fed the habit for a little while. Then she came back from the Thanksgiving break and said she was in love with a guy from Delta Tau Delta, a guy who also came from her hometown. I tried to get her back and almost made it once, but she had something she hadn't had before—perspective. It didn't work and when the Christmas vacation was over they were pinned.

Whatever I had been building up, all those years since the fire wiped out the B-movie actors who had once been my family, that broke it down. That pin on her blouse.

And after that, I was on again-off again with the three or four girls who were willing. I could blame it on my childhood, say I never had good sexual models, but that wasn't it. I'd never had any trouble with the girl. Only now the girl was gone.

I started being afraid of girls, a little. And it wasn't so much the ones I was impotent with as the ones I wasn't, the ones I could make it with. They made me uneasy. I kept asking myself where they were hiding whatever axes they liked to grind and when they were going to let me have it. I'm not so strange at that. You show me a married man or a man with a steady woman, and I'll show you someone who is asking himself (maybe only in the early hours of the morning or on Friday afternoon when she's off buying groceries), *What is she doing when I'm not around? What does she really think of me?* And maybe most of all, *How much of me has she got? How much is left?* Once I started thinking about those things, I thought about them all the time.

I started to drink and my grades took a nose dive. During semester break I got a letter saying that if they didn't improve in six weeks, my second-semester scholarship check would be withheld. I and some guys I hung around with got drunk and stayed drunk for the whole holiday. On the last day we went to a whorehouse and I operated just fine. It was too dark to see faces.

My grades stayed about the same. I called the girl once and cried over the telephone. She cried too, and in a way I think that pleased her. I didn't hate her then and I don't now. But she scared me. She scared me plenty.

On February 9 I got a letter from the dean of Arts and Sciences saying I was flunking two of three courses in my major field. On February 13 I got a hesitant sort of letter from the girl. She wanted everything to be all right between us. She was planning to marry the guy from Delta Tau Delta in July or August, and I could be invited if I wanted to be. That was almost funny. What could I give her for a wedding gift? My penis with a red ribbon tied around the foreskin?

On the fourteenth, Valentine's Day, I decided it was time for a change of scene. Nona came next, but you know about that.

You have to understand how she was to me if this is to do any good at all. She was more beautiful than the girl, but that wasn't it. Good looks are cheap in a wealthy country. It was the her inside. There was sex, but the sex that came from her was like that of a vine—blind sex, a kind of clinging, not-to-be-denied sex that is not so important because it is as instinctual as photosynthesis. Not like an animal—that implies lust—but like a plant. I knew we would make love, that we would make it as men and women do, but that our joining would be as blunt and remote and meaningless as ivy clutching its way up a trellis in the August sun.

The sex was important only because it was unimportant.

I think—no, I'm sure—that violence was the real motive force. The violence was real and not just a dream. The violence of Joe's Good Eats, the violence of Norman Blanchette. And there was even something blind and vegetative about that. Maybe she was only a clinging vine after all, because the Venus flytrap is a species of vine, but that plant is carnivorous and will make animal motion when a fly or a bit of raw meat is placed in its jaws. And it was all *real.* The sporulating vine may only dream that it fornicates, but I am sure the Venus flytrap tastes that fly, relishes its diminishing struggles as its jaws close around it.

The last part was my own passivity. I could not fill up the hole in my life. Not the hole left by the girl when she said good-bye—I don't want to lay this at her door—but the hole that had always been there, the dark, confused swirling that never stopped down in the middle of me. Nona filled that hole. She made me her arm. She made me move and act.

She made me noble.

Now maybe you understand a little of it. Why I dream of her. Why the fascination remains in spite of the remorse and the revulsion. Why I hate her. Why I fear her. And why even now I still love her.

It was eight miles from the Augusta ramp to Gardner and we did it in a few short minutes. I grasped the nail file woodenly at my side and watched the green reflectorized sign—KEEP RIGHT FOR EXIT 14—twinkle up out of the night. The moon was gone and it had begun to spit snow.

"Wish I were going farther," Blanchette said.

"That's all right," Nona said warmly, and I could feel her fury buzzing and burrowing into the meat under my skull like a drill bit. "Just drop us at the top of the ramp."

He drove up, observing the ramp speed of thirty miles an hour. I knew what I was going to do. It felt as if my legs had turned to warm lead.

The top of the ramp was lit by one overhead light. To the left I could see the lights of Gardener against the thickening cloud cover. To the right, nothing but blackness. There was no traffic coming either way along the access road.

I got out. Nona slid across the seat, giving Norman Blanchette a final smile. I wasn't worried. She was quarter-backing the play.

Blanchette was smiling an infuriating porky smile, relieved at being almost rid of us. "Well, good ni—"

"Oh my purse! Don't drive off with my purse!"

"I'll get it," I told her. I leaned back into the car. Blanchette saw what I had in my hand, and the porky smile on his face froze solid.

Now lights showed on the hill, but it was too late to stop. Nothing could have stopped me. I picked up Nona's purse with my left hand. With my right I plunged the steel nail file into Blanchette's throat. He bleated once.

I got out of the car. Nona was waving the oncoming vehicle down. I couldn't see what it was in the dark and snow; all I could make out were the two bright circles of its headlamps. I crouched behind Blanchette's car, peeking through the back windows.

The voices were almost lost in the filling throat of the wind.

" . . . trouble, lady?"

" . . . father . . . " wind " . . . had a heart attack! Will you . . ."

I scurried around the trunk of Norman Blanchette's Impala, bent over. I could see them now, Nona's slender silhouette and a taller form. They appeared to be standing by a pickup truck. They turned and approached the driver's-side window of the Chevy, where Norman Blanchette was slumped over the wheel with Nona's file in his throat. The driver of the pickup was a young kid in what looked like an Air Force parka. He leaned inside. I came up behind him.

"Jesus, lady!" he said. "There's blood on this guy! What—"

I hooked my right elbow around his throat and grabbed my right wrist with my left hand. I pulled him up hard. His head connected with the top of the door and made a hollow *thock*! He went limp in my arms.

I could have stopped then. He hadn't gotten a good look at Nona, hadn't seen me at all. I could have stopped. But he was a busybody, a meddler, somebody else in our way, trying to hurt us. I was tired of being hurt. I strangled him.

When it was done I looked up and saw Nona spotlighted in the conflicting lights of the car and truck, her face a grotesque rictus of hate, love, triumph, and joy. She held her arms out to me and I went into them. We kissed. Her mouth was cold but her tongue was warm. I plunged both hands into the secret hollows of her hair, and the wind screamed around us.

"Now fix it," she said. "Before someone else comes."

I fixed it. It was a slipshod job, but I knew that was all we needed. A little more time. After that it wouldn't matter. We would be safe.

The kid's body was light. I picked him up in both arms, carried him across the road, and threw him into the gully beyond the guardrails. His body tumbled loosely all the way to the bottom, head over heels, like the ragbag man Mr. Hollis had me put out in the cornfield every July. I went back to get Blanchette.

He was heavier, and bleeding like a stuck pig to boot. I tried to pick him up, staggered three steps backward, and then he slipped out of my arms and fell onto the road. I turned him over. The new snow had stuck to his face, turning it into a hideous skier's mask.

I bent over, grabbed him under the arms, and dragged him to the gully. His feet left trailing grooves behind him. I threw him over and watched him slide down the embankment on his back, his arms up over his head. His eyes were wide open, staring raptly at the snowflakes falling into them. If the snow kept coming, they would both be just two vague humps by the time the plows came by.

I went back across the road. Nona had already climbed into the pickup truck without having to be told. I could see the pallid smear of her face, the dark holes of her eyes, but that was all. I got into Blanchette's car, sitting in the streaks of his blood that had gathered on the nubby vinyl seat cover, and drove it onto the shoulder. I turned off the headlights, put on the four-way flashers, and got out. To anyone passing by, it would look like a motorist who had engine trouble and then walked into town to find a garage. Simple but workable. I was very pleased with my improvisation. It was as if I had been murdering people all my life. I trotted back to the idling truck, got in behind the wheel, and pointed it toward the turnpike entrance ramp.

She sat next to me, not touching but close. When she moved I could sometimes feel a strand of her hair on my neck. It was like being touched with a tiny electrode. Once I had to put my hand out and feel her leg, to make sure she was real. She laughed quietly. It was all real. The wind howled around the windows, driving snow in great, flapping gusts.

We ran South.

Just across the bridge from Gretna, as you go up 126 toward Freeport, you come up on a huge renovated farm that goes under the laughable title of the Blainesville Youth League. They have twelve lanes of candlepin bowling with cranky automatic pinsetters that usually take the last three days of the week off, a few ancient pinball machines, a juke featuring the greatest hits of 1957, three Brunswick pool tables, and a Coke-and-chips counter where you also rent bowling shoes that look like they might have just come off the feet of dead winos. The name of the place is laughable because most of the Blainesville youth head up to the drive-in at Gretna Hill at night or go to the stock-car races at Oxford Plains. The people who do hang out there are mostly toughies from Gretna, Falmouth, Freeport, Yarmouth. The average is one fight per evening in the parking lot.

I started hanging out there when I was a high school sophomore. One of my friends, Chris Kennedy, was working there three nights a week and if there was nobody waiting for a table he'd let me shoot some pool for free. It wasn't much, but it was better than going back to the Hollises' house.

That's where I met Ace Carmody. He was from Gretna, and nobody much doubted that he was the toughest guy in three towns. He drove a chopped and channeled '51 Ford, and it was rumored that he could push it all the way to 130 if he had to. He'd come in like a king, his hair greased back and glistening in a perfect duck's-ass pompadour, shoot a few games of double-bank for a dime a ball (Was he good? You guess.), buy Shelley a Coke when she came in, and then they'd leave. You could almost hear a reluctant sigh of relief from those present when the scarred front door wheezed shut. Nobody ever went out in the parking lot with Ace Carmody.

Nobody, that is, but me.

Shelley Roberson was his girl, the prettiest girl in Blainesville, I guess. I don't think she was terrifically bright, but that didn't matter when you got a look at her. She had the most flawless complexion I had ever seen, and it didn't come out of a cosmetics bottle, either. Hair as black as coal, dark eyes, generous mouth, a body that just wouldn't quit—and she didn't mind showing it off. Who was going to drag her out back and try to stoke her locomotive while Ace was around? Nobody sane, that's who.

I fell hard for her. Not like the girl and not like Nona, even though Shelley did look like a younger version of her, but it was just as desperate and just as serious in its way. If you've ever had the worst case of puppy love going around, you know how I felt. She was seventeen, two years older than I.

I started going down there more and more often, even nights when Chris wasn't on, just to catch a glimpse of her. I felt like a bird watcher, except it was a desperate kind of game for me. I'd go gack home, lie to the Hollises about where I'd been, and climb up to my room. I'd write long, passionate letters to her, telling her everything I'd like to do to her, and then tear them up. Study halls at school I'd dream about asking her to marry me so we could run away to Mexico together.

She must have tumbled to what was happening, and it must have flattered her a little, because she was nice to me when Ace wasn't around. She'd come over and talk to me, let me buy her a Coke, sit on a stool, and kind of rub her leg against mine. It drove me crazy.

One night in early November I was just mooning around, shooting a little pool with Chris, waiting for her to come in. The place was deserted because it wasn't even eight o'clock yet, and a lonesome wind was snuffling around outside, threatening winter.

"You better lay off," Chris said, shooting the nine straight into the corner.

"Lay off what?"

"You know."

"No I don't." I scratched and Chris added a ball to the table. He ran six and while he was running them I went over and put a dime in the juke.

"Shelley Roberson." He lined up the one carefully and sent it walking up the rail. "Jimmy Donner was telling

Ace about the way you been sniffing around her. Jimmy thought it was really funny, her being older and all, but Ace wasn't laughing."

"She's nothing to me," I said through paper lips.

"She better not be," Chris said, and then a couple of guys came in and he went over to the counter and gave them a cue ball.

Ace came in around nine and he was alone. He'd never taken any notice of me before, and I'd just about forgotten what Chris said. When you're invisible you get to thinking you're invulnerable. I was playing pinball and I was pretty involved. I didn't even notice the place get quiet as people stopped bowling or shooting pool. The next thing I knew, somebody had thrown me right across the pinball machine. I landed on the floor in a heap. I got up feeling scared and sick. He had tilted the machine, wiping out my three replays. He was standing there and looking at me with not a strand of hair out of place, his garrison jacket half unzipped.

"You stop messing around," he said softly, "or I'm going to change your face."

He went out. Everybody was looking at me and I wanted to sink right down through the floor until I saw there was a kind of grudging admiration on most of their faces. So I brushed myself off, unconcerned, and put another dime in the pinball machine. The TILT light went out. A couple of guys came over and clapped me on the back before they went out, not saying anything.

At eleven, when the place closed, Chris offered me a ride home.

"You're going to take a fall if you don't watch out."

"Don't worry about me," I said.

He didn't answer.

Two or three nights later Shelley came in by herself around seven. There was one other guy there, a porky kid named John Dano, but I hardly noticed him. He was even more invisible than I was.

She came right over to where I was shooting, close enough so I could smell the clean-soap smell on her skin. It made me feel dizzy.

"I heard about what Ace did to you," she said. "I'm not supposed to talk to you anymore and I'm not going to, but I've got something to make it all better." She kissed me. Then she went out, before I could even get my tongue down from the roof of my mouth. I went back to my game in a daze. I didn't even see John Dano when he went out to spread the word. I couldn't see anything but her dark, dark eyes.

So that night I ended up in the parking lot with Ace Carmody, and he beat the living Jesus out of me. It was cold, bitterly cold, and at the end I began to sob, not caring who was watching or listening, which was everybody. The single sodium arc lamp looked down on all of it mercilessly. I hadn't even landed a punch on him.

"Okay," he said, squatting down next to me. He wasn't even breathing hard. He took a switchblade out of his pocket and pressed the chrome button. Seven inches of moon-drenched silver sprang into the world. "This is what you get next time. I'll carve my name on your balls." Then he got up, gave me one last kick, and left. I just lay there for maybe ten minutes, shivering on the hard-packed dirt. No one came to help me up or pat me on the back, not even Chris. Shelley didn't show up to make it all better.

Finally I got up by myself and hitchhiked home. I told Mrs. Hollis I'd hitched a ride with a drunk and he drove off the road. I never went back to the bowling alley again.

Ace got killed two years later when he drove his fancy '51 Ford into a road-repair dumptruck while passing on a hill. I understand that he had dropped Shelley by then and that she had really gone downhill, picking up a case of the clap on the way. Chris said he saw her one night in the Manoir up in Lewiston, hustling guys for drinks. She had lost most of her teeth, and her nose had been broken somewhere along the line, he said. He said I would never recognize her. By then I didn't much care one way or the other.

The pickup had no snow tires, and before we got to the Lewiston exit I had begun to skid around in the new powder. It took us over forty-five minutes to make the twenty-two miles.

The man at the Lewiston exit point took my toll card and my sixty cents. "Slippery traveling?"

Neither of us answered him. We were getting close to where we wanted to go now. If I hadn't had that odd kind of wordless contact with her, I would have been able to tell just by the way she sat on the dusty seat of the pickup, her hands folded tightly in her lap, those eyes fixed straight ahead on the road with fierce intensity. I felt a shudder work through me.

We took Route 136. There weren't many cars on the road; the wind was freshening and the snow was coming down harder than ever. On the other side of Gretna Village we passed a big Buick Riviera that had slued around sideways and climbed the curb. Its four-way flashers were going and I had a ghostly double image of Norman Blanchette's Impala. It would be drifted in with snow now, nothing but a ghostly hump in the darkness.

The Buick's driver tried to flag me down but I went by him without slowing, spraying him with slush. My wipers were clogging with snow and I reached out and snapped at the one on my side. Some of the snow loosened and I could see a little better.

Gretna was a ghost town, everything dark and closed. I signaled right to go over the bridge into Blainesville. The rear wheels wanted to slide out from under me, but I handled the skid. Up ahead and across the river I could see the dark shadow that was the Blainesville Youth League building. It looked shut up and lonely. I felt suddenly sorry, sorry that there had been so much pain. And death. That was when Nona spoke for the first time since the Gardener exit.

"There's a policeman behind you."

"Is he—?"

"No. His flasher is off."

But it made me nervous and maybe that's why it happened. Route 136 makes a ninety-degree turn on the Gretna side of the river and then it's straight across the bridge and into Blainesville. I made the first turn, but there was ice on the Blainesville side.

"*Damn—*"

The rear end of the truck flirted around and before I could steer clear, it had smashed into one of the heavy steel bridge stanchions. We went sliding all the way around like kids on a Flexible Flyer, and the next thing I saw was the bright headlights of the police car that was behind us. He put on his brakes—I could see the red reflections in the falling snow—but the ice got him, too. He plowed right into us. There was a grinding, jarring shock as we went into the supporting girders again. I was jolted into Nona's lap, and even in that confused split second I had time to relish the smooth firmness of her thigh. Then everything stopped. Now the cop had his flasher on. It sent blue, revolving shadows chasing across the hood of the truck and the snowy steel crosswork of the Gretna-Blainesville bridge. The dome light inside the cruiser came on as the cop got out.

If he hadn't been behind us it wouldn't have happened. That thought was playing over and over in my mind, like a phonograph needle stuck in a single flawed groove. I was grinning a strained, frozen grin into the dark as I groped on the floor of the truck's cab for something to hit him with.

There was an open toolbox. I came up with a socket wrench and laid it on the seat between Nona and me. The cop leaned in the window, his face changing like a devil's in the light from his flasher.

"Traveling a little fast for the conditions, weren't you, guy?"

"Following a little close, weren't you?" I asked. "For the conditions?"

He might have flushed. It was hard to tell in the flickering light.

"Are you lipping me, son?"

"I am if you're trying to pin the dents in your cruiser on me."

"Let's see your driver's license and your registration."

I got out my wallet and handed him my license.

"Registration?"

"It's my brother's truck. The registration is in his wallet."

"That right?" He looked at me hard, trying to stare me down. When he saw it would take a while, he looked past me at Nona. I could have ripped his eyes out for what I saw in them. "What's your name?"

"Cheryl Craig, sir."

"What are you doing riding around in his brother's pickup in the middle of a snowstorm, Cheryl?"

"We're going to see my uncle."

"In Blainesville?"

"Yes."

"I don't know any Craigs in Blainesville."

"His name is Barlow. On Bowen Hill."

"That right?" He walked around to the back of the truck to look at the plate. I opened the door and leaned out. He was writing it down.

He came back while I was still leaning out, spotlighted from the waist up in the glare of his headlights. "I'm going to . . . What's that all over you, boy?"

I didn't have to look down to know what was all over me. It was all over Nona, too. I had smeared it on her tan coat when I kissed her. I used to think that leaning out like that was just absent-mindedness, but writing all of this has changed my mind. I don't think it was absent-minded at all. I think I wanted him to see it. I held onto the socket wrench.

"What do you mean?"

He came two steps closer. "You're hurt—cut your-self, looks like. Better—"

I swung at him. His hat had been knocked off in the crash and his head was bare. I hit him dead on, just above the forehead. I've never forgotten the sound that made, like a pound of butter falling onto a hard floor.

"Hurry," Nona said. She put a calm hand on my neck. It was very cool, like air in a root cellar. My foster mother, Mrs. Hollis . . . she had a root cellar. . . .

Funny I should remember that. She sent me down there for vegetables in the winter. She canned them herself. Not in real cans, of course, but in thick Mason jars with those rubber sealers that go under the lid.

I went down there one day to get a jar of waxed beans for our supper. The preserves were all in boxes, neatly marked in Mrs. Hollis's hand. I remember that she always misspelled raspberry, and that used to fill me with a secret superiority.

On this day I went past the boxes marked "razberrys" and into the corner where she kept the beans. It was cool and dark. The walls were plain dark earth and in wet weather they exuded moisture in trickling, crooked streams. The smell was a secret, dark effluvium composed of living things and earth and stored vegetables, a smell remarkably like that of a woman's private parts. There was an old, shattered printing press in one corner that had been there ever since I came, and sometimes I used to play with it and pretend I could get it going again. I loved the root cellar. In those days—I was nine or ten—the root cellar was my favorite place. Mrs. Hollis refused to set foot in it, and it was against her husband's dignity to go down and fetch up vegetables. So I went there and smelled that peculiar secret earthy smell and enjoyed the privacy of its womblike confinement. It was lit by one cobwebby bulb that Mr. Hollis had strung, probably before the Boer War. Sometimes I wiggled my hands and made huge, elongated rabbits on the wall.

I got the beans and was about to go back when I heard a rustling movement under one of the old boxes. I went over and lifted it up.

There was a brown rat beneath it, lying on its side. It rolled its head up at me and stared. Its sides were heaving violently and it bared its teeth. It was the biggest rat I had ever seen, and I leaned closer. It was in the act of giving birth. Two of its young, hairless and blind, were already nursing at its belly. Another was halfway into the world.

The mother glared at me helplessly, ready to bite. I wanted to kill it, kill all of them, squash them, but I couldn't. It was the most horrible thing I'd ever seen. As I watched, a small brown spider—a daddy longlegs, I think—crawled rapidly across the floor. The mother snatched it up and ate it.

I fled. Halfway up the stairs I fell and broke the jar of beans. Mrs. Hollis thrashed me, and I never went into the root cellar again unless I had to.

I stood looking down at the cop, remembering.

"Hurry," Nona said again.

He was much lighter than Norman Blanchette had been, or perhaps my adrenalin was just flowing more freely. I gathered him up in both arms and carried him over to the edge of the bridge. I could barely make out the Gretna Falls downstream, and upstream the GS&WM railroad trestle was only a gaunt shadow, like a scaffold. The night wind whooped and screamed, and the snow beat against my face. For a moment I held the cop against my chest like a sleeping newborn child, and then I remembered what he really was and threw him over the side and down into darkness.

We went back to the truck and got in, but it wouldn't start. I cranked the engine until I could smell the sweetish aroma of gas from the flooded carb, and then stopped.

"Come on," I said.

We went to the cruiser. The front seat was littered with violation tags, forms, two clipboards. The short-wave under the dash crackled and spluttered.

"Unit Four, come in, Four. Do you copy?"

I reached under and turned it off, banging my knuckles on something as I searched for the right toggle switch. It was a shotgun, pump action. Probably the cop's personal property. I unclipped it and handed it to Nona. She put it on her lap. I backed the cruiser up. It was dented but otherwise not hurt. It had snow tires and they bit nicely once we got over the ice that had done the damage.

Then we were in Blainesville. The houses, except for an occasional shanty trailer set back from the road, had disappeared. The road itself hadn't been plowed yet and there were no tracks except the ones we were leaving behind us. Monolithic fir trees, weighted with snow, towered all around us, and they made me feel tiny and insignificant, just some tiny morsel caught in the giant throat of this night. It was now after ten o'clock.

*

I didn't see much of college social life during my freshman year at the university. I studied hard and worked in the library shelving books and repairing bindings and learning how to catalogue. In the spring there was jayvee baseball.

Near the end of the academic year, just before finals, there was a dance at the gym. I was at loose ends, studied up for my first two tests, and I wandered down. I had the buck admission, so I went in.

It was dark and crowded and sweaty and frantic as only a college social before the ax of finals can be. There was sex in the air. You didn't have to smell it; you could almost reach out and grab it in both hands, like a wet piece of heavy cloth. You knew that love was going to be made later on, or what passes for love. People were going to make it under bleachers and in the steam plant parking lot and in apartments and dormitory rooms. It was going to be made by desperate man/boys with the draft one step behind them and by pretty coeds who were going to drop out this year and go home and start a family. It would be made with tears and laughter, drunk and sober, stiffly and with no inhibition. But mostly it would be made quickly.

There were a few stags, but not many. It wasn't a night you needed to go anyplace stag. I drifted down by the raised bandstand. As I got closer to the sound, the beat, the music got to be a palpable thing. The group had a half circle of five-foot amplifiers behind them, and you could feel your eardrums flapping in and out with the bass signature.

I leaned up against the wall and watched. The dancers moved in prescribed patterns (as if they were trios instead of couples, the third invisible but between, being humped from the front and back), feet moving through the sawdust that had been sprinkled over the varnished floor. I didn't see anybody I knew and I began to feel lonely, but pleasantly so. I was at that stage of the evening where you fantasize that everyone is looking at you, the romantic stranger, out of the corners of their eyes.

About a half hour later I went out and got a Coke in the lobby. When I went back in somebody had started a circle dance and I was pulled in, my arms around the shoulders of two girls I had never seen before. We went around and around. There were maybe two hundred people in the circle and it covered half the gym floor. Then part of it collapsed and twenty or thirty people formed another circle in the middle of the first and started to go around the other way. It made me feel dizzy. I saw a girl who looked like Shelley Roberson, but I knew that was a fantasy. When I looked for her again I couldn't see her or anyone who looked like her.

When the thing finally broke up I felt weak and not well. I went back over by the bleachers and sat down. The music was too loud, the air too greasy. I could hear my heartbeat in my head, the way you do after you threw the biggest drunk of your life.

I used to think what happened next happened because I was tired and a little nauseated from going around and around, but as I said before, all this writing has brought everything into sharper focus. I can't believe that anymore.

I looked up at them again, all the beautiful, hurrying people in the semidarkness. It seemed to me that all the men looked terrified, their faces elongating into grotesque, slow-motion masks. It was understandable. The women— coeds in their sweaters, short skirts, their bellbottoms— were all turning into rats. At first it didn't frighten me. I even chuckled. I knew what I was seeing was some kind of hallucination, and for a while I could watch it almost clinically.

Then some girl stood on tiptoe to kiss her fellow, and that was too much. Hairy, twisted face with its black buckshot eyes reaching up, mouth spreading to reveal teeth . . .

I left.

I stood in the lobby for a moment, half distracted. There was a bathroom down the hall, but I went past it and up the stairs.

The locker room was on the third floor and I had to run the last flight. I pulled the door open and ran for one of the bathroom stalls. I threw up amid the mixed smells of liniment, sweaty uniforms, oiled leather. The music was far away down there, the silence up here virginal. I felt comforted.

*

We had come to a stop sign at Southwest Bend. The memory of the dance had left me excited for a reason I didn't understand. I began to shake.

She looked at me, smiling with her dark eyes. "Now?"

I couldn't answer her. I was shaking too badly for that. She nodded slowly.

I drove onto a spur of Route 7 that must have been a logging road in the summertime. I didn't drive in too deeply because I was afraid of getting stuck. I popped off the headlights and flecks of snow began to gather silently on the windshield. Some kind of sound was escaping me, being dragged out of me. I think it must have been a close oral counterpart to the thoughts of a rabbit caught in a snare.

"Here," she said. "Right here."

It was ecstasy.

We almost didn't get back onto the main road. The snowplow had gone by, orange lights winking and flashing in the night, throwing up a huge wall of snow in our way.

There was a shovel in the trunk of the police car. It took me half an hour to dig out, and by then it was almost midnight. She turned on the police radio while I was doing it, and it told us what we had to know. The bodies of Blanchette and the kid from the pickup truck had been found. They suspected that we had taken the cruiser. The cop's name had been Essegian, and that's a funny name. There used to be a major-league ballplayer named Essegian— I think he played for the Dodgers. Maybe I had killed one of his relatives. It didn't bother me to know the cop's name. He had been following too close and he had gotten in our way.

We drove back onto the main road.

I could feel her excitement, high and hot and burning. I stopped long enough to clear the windshield with my arm and then we were going again.

We went through West Blainesville and I knew without having to be told where to turn. A snow-crusted sign said it was Stackpole Road.

The plow had not been here, but one vehicle had been through before us. The tracks of its tires were still freshly cut in the blowing, restless snow.

A mile, then less than a mile. Her fierce eagerness, her need, came to me and I began to feel jumpy again. We came around a curve and there was the power truck, bright orange body and warning flashers pulsing the color of blood. It was blocking the road.

You can't imagine her rage—our rage, really—because now, after what happened, we were really one. You can't imagine the sweeping feeling of intense paranoia, the conviction that every hand was out to cut us down.

There were two of them. One was a bending shadow in the darkness ahead. The other was holding a flashlight. He came toward us, his light bobbing like a lurid eye. And there was more than hate. There was fear—fear that it was all going to be snatched away from us at the last moment.

He was yelling, and I cranked down my window.

"You can't get through here! Go on back by the Bowen Road! We got a live line down here! You can't—"

I got out of the car, lifted the shotgun, and gave him both barrels. He was flung forcibly back against the orange truck and I staggered back against the cruiser. He slipped down an inch at a time, staring at me incredulously, and then he fell into the snow.

"Are there more shells?" I asked Nona.

"Yes." She gave them to me. I broke the shotgun, ejected the spent cartridges, and put in new ones.

The guy's buddy had straightened up and was watching incredulously. He shouted something at me that was lost in the wind. It sounded like a question but it didn't matter. I was going to kill him. I walked toward him and he just stood there, looking at me. He didn't move, even when I raised the shotgun. I don't think he had any conception of what was happening. I think he thought it was a dream.

I fired one barrel and was low. A great flurry of snow exploded up, coating him. Then he bellowed a great terrified scream and ran, taking one gigantic bound over the fallen power cable in the road. I fired the other barrel and missed again. Then he was gone into the dark and I could forget him. He wasn't in our way anymore. I went back to the cruiser.

"We'll have to walk," I said.

We walked past the fallen body, stepped over the spitting power line, and walked up the road, following the widely spaced tracks of the fleeing man. Some of the drifts were almost up to her knees, but she was always a little ahead of me. We were both panting.

We came over a hill and descended into a narrow dip. On one side was a leaning, deserted shed with glassless windows. She stopped and gripped my arm.

"There," she said, and pointed across to the other side. Her grip was strong and painful even through my coat. Her face was set in a glaring, triumphant rictus. "There. There."

It was a graveyard.

We slipped and stumbled up the banking and clambered over a snow-covered stone wall. I had been here too, of course. My real mother had come from Blainesville, and although she and my father had never lived there, this was where the family plot had been. It was a gift to my mother from her parents, who had lived and died in Blainesville. During the thing with Shelley Roberson I had come here often to read the poems of John Keats and Percy Shelley. I suppose you think that was a damned weird thing to do, but I don't. Not even now. I felt close to them, comforted. After Ace Carmody beat me up I never went there again. Not until Nona led me there.

I slipped and fell in the loose powder, twisting my ankle. I got up and walked on it, using the shotgun as a crutch. The silence was infinite and unbelievable. The snow fell in soft, straight lines, mounding atop the leaning stones and crosses, burying all but the tips of the corroded flagholders that would only hold flags on Memorial Day and Veterans Day. The silence was unholy in its immensity, and for the first time I felt terror.

She led me toward a stone building set into the whitened rise of the hill at the back of the cemetery. A vault. She had a key. I knew she would have a key, and she did.

She blew the snow away from the door's flange and found the keyhole. The sound the turning tumblers made seemed to scratch across the darkness. She leaned on the door and it swung inward.

The odor that came out at us was as cool as autumn, as cool as the air in the Hollis root cellar. I could see in only a little way. There were dead leaves on the stone floor. She entered, paused, looked back over her shoulder at me.

"No," I said.

She laughed at me.

I stood in the darkness, feeling everything begin to run together—past, present, future. I wanted to run, run screaming, run fast enough to take back everything I had done.

Nona stood there looking at me, the most beautiful girl in the world, the only thing that had ever been mine. She made a gesture with her hands on her body. I'm not going to tell you what it was. You would know it if you saw it.

I went in. She closed the door.

It was dark but I could see perfectly well. The place was alight with a slowly running green fire. It ran over the walls and snaked across the leaf-littered floor in writhing tongues. There was a bier in the center of the vault, but it was empty. The petals of withered roses were scattered across it. She beckoned to me, then pointed to the small door at the rear. Small, unmarked door. I dreaded it. I think I knew then. She had used me and laughed at me. Now she would destroy me.

But I couldn't stop. I went to that door because I had to. That mental telegraph was still working at what I felt was glee—a terrible, insane glee—and triumph. My hand trembled toward the door. It was coated with green fire.

I opened the door and saw what was there.

It was the girl, my girl. Dead. Her eyes stared vacantly into that October vault, into my own eyes. She smelled of stolen kisses. She was naked and she had been ripped open from throat to crotch, her whole body turned into a sterile womb. And yet something lived in there. The rats. I could not see them but I could hear them, rustling around in there, inside her. I knew that in a moment her dry mouth would open and she would speak to me of love. I backed away, my whole body numb, my brain floating on a dark cloud of fear.

I turned to Nona. She was laughing, holding her arms out to me. And with a sudden blaze of understanding I knew, I knew, I knew. The last test had been passed. *I was free!*

I turned back to the doorway and of course it was nothing but an empty stone closet with dead leaves on the floor.

I went to Nona. I went to my life.

Her arms reached around my neck and I pulled her against me. That was when she began to change, to ripple and run like wax. The great dark eyes became small and beady. The hair coarsened, went brown. The nose shortened, the nostrils dilated. Her body lumped and hunched against me.

I was being embraced by a rat.

Her lipless mouth stretched upward for mine.

I didn't scream. There were no screams left. I doubt if I will ever scream again.

It's so hot in here.

I don't mind the heat, not really. I like to sweat if I can shower, I've always thought of sweat as a good, masculine thing, but sometimes there are bugs that bite—spiders, for instance. Did you know that female spiders sting and eat their mates? They do, right after copulation. Also, I've heard scurryings in the walls. I don't like that.

I've given myself writer's cramp, and the felt tip of the pen is all soft and mushy. But I'm done now. And things look different. It doesn't seem the same anymore at all.

Do you realize that for a while they almost had me believing that I did all those horrible things myself? Those men from the truck stop, the guy from the power truck who got away. They said I was alone. I was alone when they found me, almost frozen to death in that graveyard by the stones that mark my father, my mother, my brother Drake. But that only means she left, you can see that. Any fool could. But I'm glad she got away. Truly I am. But you must realize she was with me all the time, every step of the way.

I'm going to kill myself now. It will be much better. I'm tired of all the guilt and agony and bad dreams, and also I don't like the noises in the walls. Anybody could be in there. Or anything.

I'm not crazy. I know that and trust that you do, too. If you say you aren't, that's supposed to mean you are, but I am beyond all those little games. She was with me, she was real. I love her. True love will never die. That's how I signed all my letters to Shelley, the ones I tore up.

I didn't hurt any ladies, did I?

I never hurt any ladies.

She was the only one I ever really loved.

It's so hot in here. And I don't like the sounds in the walls.

True love will never die.

PLAYBOY NOVELS OF HORROR AND THE OCCULT

ABSOLUTELY CHILLING